Death of a High Maintenance Blonde

By
Debra Gaskill

*To Sheri
Best Wishes
D Gaskill*

Chapter 1: Addison

I sat up in bed, gasping for air.

Sweat glistened on my body, and my heart pounded. After forty years, I could still hear the roar of the tornado as it ripped through my hometown of Jubilant Falls, Ohio, that April day in 1974.

I was back cowering in the root cellar of my grandmother's Victorian home as winds of more than two hundred fifty miles an hour roared around the big, white house like freight trains at high speed. The smell of the cellar's moldy dirt walls was as fresh in my nostrils tonight as it was the afternoon my grandmother, Ida Addison, in her home-sewn cotton apron and orthopedic shoes, covered me while the windows upstairs exploded from the unequal pressures inside and outside the house.

I saw his body again, too. Lying beneath a tree on his grandfather's farm, Jimmy Lyle was one of the tornado's victims, pinned to the earth with the posthole digger he'd been using when the storm struck.

At least that's what everyone said happened to him. What other proof did they have? Even forty years later, something told me 'they' were wrong.

I didn't have the dream very often, but when I did, the terror was still very real. I reached across the bed and touched my husband Duncan's shoulder. Tonight, my dream hadn't disturbed him and his breath came rhythmically as he slept. It was three forty-five. In just about an hour or so, he'd be up and we'd start milking our herd of Holsteins, then I'd head off to my job as managing editor of the *Jubilant Falls Journal-Gazette*. No sense disturbing him now. I tossed the summer quilt off my legs and tiptoed down the stairs.

I flipped the kitchen light on and began to make the morning pot of coffee as crickets chirped outside in the morning dark.

It was early June, bringing with it all the promise of a hot, dry summer, so we'd left the windows open overnight. The cricket singing outside reminded me of life's continuity, despite what that April day permanently encoded in my psyche.

The old chipped pot filled quickly. I poured myself a cup, found my lighter and pulled a cigarette from the pack on the counter, then went outside to the front porch.

The quarter moon was beginning to descend into the far western horizon as I took a seat on one of the old McIntyre rocking chairs. Separated from our farmhouse by a field of fledgling soybeans, a single Ford Explorer drove down the road, its headlights brightening the road a few feet in front of it as it hurtled toward its destination. To my right, I heard the Holsteins begin to wake from their pasture beds, mooing as they, ever creatures of habit, began to amble toward the milking parlor.

This farm had been my home for more than twenty-five years and it had always been a safe haven, as well as for Duncan and our daughter, Isabella.

Except on nights like tonight, when my nightmare came back. Why, then, since putting out a fortieth anniversary commemorative edition on the tornado, did I wake bathed in sweat and fear at least once a week? I wanted to believe it was just putting those horrible memories on paper one more time, but something down deep told me that wasn't it.

I took a sip of coffee and leaned back into the old rocking chair. I knew from experience, the best way to get through my terror was to work through it, piece by piece. Over the years, I learned it was the only way to guarantee the next night's peaceful sleep.

*****

After the roaring stopped, Grandma and I came up out of the storm cellar. She climbed the stairs in front of me, opening the heavy, slanted double doors that led to the back yard.

Grandma gasped as we walked into the strange, silent sunlight.

The house behind us was a smoking pile of sticks and brick. Down deep in the rubble, someone cried for help. Our lawn was littered with white wooden gingerbread and shingles from our own roof; pieces of rain-spattered glass shone among the leaves and branches from my grandmother's magnificent backyard maples and elms. The white picket fence that separated Grandma's ornate rose garden from our neighbor's backyard lay fractured across the yard and into the driveway.

Like Grandma Addison's home, the other houses on our street were stone and brick relics from another era. Because of this, most stood wounded but upright, despite whatever just blasted through our neighborhood. The frame houses on the block behind us, however, were destroyed, leaving nothing but piles of splinters and shingles. A wall of one house was completely gone, exposing an upstairs bedroom with the dresser and bed hanging precipitously over the floor's exposed edge, a story above the ground. Smoke was beginning to show from beneath some of the piles of rubble that moments ago had been homes. Geysers shot from broken front yard water mains.

The brick coach house beside Grandma's was the only undamaged building across our block. Grandma had converted the upper story years ago to the apartment where my father, Walter Addison, and I lived. Below Grandma parked her massive Chevy Impala, and, when he was off duty, Daddy parked his Ohio State Highway Patrol cruiser.

The cries from the rubble of the house behind ours grew louder.

"Oh, sweet Jesus," Grandma whispered. She began to run toward the cries beneath the shattered house, then stopped and turned to me. "Penny, run to the firehouse as fast as you can and tell them someone's trapped in Mr. Johnson's house!"

"Why don't you just call?" Terrified of moving, I pointed toward our house.

"We've had a tornado, Penny! Only the Lord knows how much damage has been done! The phones won't be working and if they are, the lines will be so jammed, you can't get through! Run, girl! Run, like I told you!" Grandma turned and darted toward the destroyed house.

I turned and fled, as fast as my sixteen-year-old legs would carry me.

It was two blocks to the firehouse, blocks that I'd walked thousands of times with my best friend, Suzanne, to spend my allowance downtown.

Even in this early morning's easing darkness, I could remember the buildings as they had been before that day: the post office, the firehouse, a furniture store with an expansive parking lot, then Washington Street, followed by a solid block of merchants: a women's clothing store, a book store, Sven Olin's drug store with the soda fountain across the store's dark back wall, a barber shop, a diner and at the corner with its rounded stone face, the First National Bank and Trust.

It wasn't like that now.

As I ran, the familiar street looked like a war zone: a semi lay upended in the furniture store window, the store's roof and two walls caved in. A Pontiac, crushed by bricks, sat in its parking spot in front of where the barbershop formerly stood. Windows were shattered; the glass crunched under my feet as I ran along the sidewalk, dodging fallen bricks. Someone's pick-up truck was on its side in the window of the diner.

People were staggering out of damaged buildings, bloodied by the collapsing roofs and glass shrapnel. Women screamed for their children and men worked frantically to pull the wounded out of buildings. Moments ago, they'd been leaning on the counters or were waiting for a haircut, staring out the window at young men in low-slung bellbottoms and loud paisley shirts sauntering down the sidewalk.

Across the street, the old stone courthouse stood, circled in red-slate shingles from its roof, the walls largely undamaged.

Next to it, the sheriff's brick office stood untouched, along with the jail. The art deco city building, sitting behind the courthouse on Detroit Street was also untouched.

Within minutes, I was at the firehouse. Josh Whitacre, a fireman friend of my dad's, was in his turnout gear, ready to jump on the only fire truck left in the bay. I grabbed the sleeve of his heavy protective coat as he swung into the passenger seat.

"Please, Josh! You gotta help me! The house behind us collapsed and somebody's trapped inside! Please! Please!"

"You're Walt Addison's girl, ain't you? You OK? Ida OK?" Josh gently peeled my hand from his sleeve.

"Yes, yes—you gotta help me, please! This man, Mr. Johnson, he's trapped inside his house—it all fell in on him—and—and—"

"I'm sorry, Penny, but the high school's been damaged and the middle school has collapsed with kids inside—we've got to go there first. All of the other trucks are out on other calls. I'll pass the information on, but we've got a natural disaster on our hands. You're going to have to find some one else to help right now." With that Josh slammed the door and the fire engine rushed out into the street, its sirens screaming.

I ran from the firehouse and into the downtown, searching for a policeman, another adult, somebody— anybody—who could help.

The dream always ended the same. I ran down an endless street strewn with bricks, branches, glass and blood. I would get close to a policeman, a deputy or just another adult and they would fade into the bloodied face of another tornado victim, just as I was close enough to plead for help.

In real life, I came home without help. Grandma never reached Mr. Johnson and after a few hours, his cries stopped. It would be two days before a National Guardsman would pull his body from the remains of his house and three days before Daddy would come home from the patrol post, exhausted and dirty from recovery work.

Mr. Johnson would be among the thirty-five people who were killed and the nearly twelve hundred injured in our town. The tornado made national news as part of more than two hundred tornados that ravaged small towns throughout the Midwest that day. Our town suffered the most casualties; even President Nixon, who came through with the governor, said he'd never seen anything like it.

As the days passed, and the death toll mounted, we learned more about the victims and the random nature of the storm. Ten of those killed were middle school students, practicing for the spring play when the school roof collapsed on them.

Then there was Jimmy Lyle, a junior at Shanahan High School, just like me. We were in English class together, working on a project about Walt Whitman.

Jimmy was on the football team and good-looking in that vapid, muscle-bound jock way. He had longish, brown hair that curled around his ears, a thin, teenaged attempt at a moustache and empty, but pretty, brown eyes.

I knew why our teacher assigned us to work together— Jimmy could use all the help he could get to move on to his senior year and maintain the team's winning ways; I was the brightest one in the class.

His girlfriend, Eve Dahlgren, was a senior and the head cheerleader, who didn't like seeing us working together. She was jealous, pulling him away and starting arguments with him when she saw us together at school.

"You stay away from my Jimmy, you hear me?" she would snarl.

"Baby, it's just homework!" he'd plead, as if I needed defending. Then he'd follow her like a kicked dog down the hall to her locker. We ended up sneaking around, meeting in the library downtown to complete the assignment.

But even my efforts couldn't keep Shanahan High School's record-setting quarterback on the football team.

One of the tornado's odd legacies was the way the swirling wind forced items together, shoving twigs through boards and turning harmless everyday items to weapons. Because of that, nobody ever questioned how Jimmy Lyle's body was fastened to the ground.

Jimmy Lyle's body was found after the tornado, out in one of his grandfather's pastures where he'd been working at replacing fence posts. His skull was crushed from the weight of a tree branch and the posthole digger was embedded in his chest. Everyone assumed he'd taken shelter under the tree when the rain hit and he died when the branch fell on his head. The injuries from the posthole digger had to be just one of the many freaks of the storm.

His name was on a brass plaque recognizing the tornado victims, the fourth one down in the second of three columns.

I didn't see a lot of my classmates as Shanahan High School was rebuilt. Some of them were bused, along with me to a neighboring district, where we finished the school year. A lot of other students' parents were too terrified to rebuild and left for nearby areas not quite so prone to nature's wrath. Eve Dahlgren's wealthy parents stayed, but sent her to a private girl's boarding school in Columbus. She returned each summer after college and I'd see her shopping with her mother at Hawk's, the old department store that used to be downtown. We never spoke, but she seemed to smirk every time I caught her eye.

I took a sip of my coffee and sighed. *What was that little snot's deal all those years ago, anyway?* I wondered.

Like many of the class of 1974, Eve would go on to college somewhere out of state and stay there, where opportunities were more plentiful. She had a big career in California or Texas or someplace. The *Journal-Gazette* did stories on her as she moved up the corporate ladder, then after her mother quit bringing in the news of her daughter's latest promotions, the stories stopped and I happily lost touch in the mid-1990's.

The screen door squeaked opened beside me. It was Duncan, dressed in overalls, his coffee mug in his hand, ready to begin milking.

"You got up early," he said softly. "Bad dream?"

"Yeah," I sighed. His hand rested on my shoulder and I lay my cheek against it.

"Same one?"

"Yeah. Forty years on, it doesn't get any easier."

"I'm sorry." He gestured with his coffee mug toward the barn, where the Holsteins were lined up patiently waiting to be let in. "The girls look like they're anxious for their breakfast. Let's get started. You'll forget about that bad dream soon enough."

I nodded and stood up. He was right: I couldn't live in the past. Duncan had been through the tornado too. He just didn't talk about it.

After milking, the day would go on as any other. I would head into work at the J-G and the sprint toward deadline would begin again.

It didn't matter if the image of Jimmy Lyle, leaning on a posthole digger and reciting "Oh Captain! My Captain!" never left my mind.

Chapter 2: Leland

"So, Dr. Huffinger, I'm trying to decide if I want to be a journalism major."

She was cute in that preppy, in-crowd kind of way as she picked up her iPad from her desk and sashayed toward my desk, wearing one of those cheap, printed cotton sundresses girls found at the stores circling the campus. She must have gotten a head start on her tan in a tanning booth, too: there were no white stripes on her feet beneath the strappy sandals she wore or on her shoulders where a bra should have been.

I blanched inwardly as I realized I was looking at a student like *that*. It really had been too long.

"Why?" I asked. I didn't look up as I walked around the circled desks, picking up copies of the international newspapers I'd brought in that day.

"I dunno," she said thoughtfully. "It seems like kind of a cool job." She was a good student, a freshman. Her writing was clean and she asked great questions in class. She had potential, but then they all did.

"It can be," I answered slowly, scratching at my ever-whitening beard.

"So what's it like working for a newspaper every day? I really like to write."

I shrugged.

I'd heard the questions before. They ask about the pay, they ask about the hours and, sometimes, adult students ask how hard the job is on families. They ask about the opportunities at a major daily and how soon after graduation I think they'll be hired.

My job was to push them toward believing in all those journalistic clichés: keeping a free press free, writing the first draft of history and speaking truth to power.

The way I felt today, I couldn't do that. Today, I felt I was part of some sort of educational stockyard, moving students toward eventual corporate soul crushing.

"More than likely the pay will suck, the hours are worse and, in my experience, even the most supportive partner can get sick of what the job demands," I answered. "And odds are, regardless of how good your grades are, your first job will be at a small-town paper, maybe a weekly, maybe a daily, making minimum wage or a little above, not at the *New York Times* or the *Washington Post*."

"Oh." The bright light went out of her face.

"But don't listen to me," I said quickly. "I'm just a bitter old professor, hiding here in academia. What do I know?" I laughed lightly and she smiled uncertainly.

"It would really be nice to talk to somebody about the reality of the job, I guess, before I make my decision," she said thoughtfully, pressing her thumbnail against the dimple in her chin. "Somebody who's been in the trenches, you know?"

"Yes," I said. My tie closed in around my throat; I loosened it with my finger. This was my last class and she would hopefully be the last student I would deal with until fall quarter began again. The administration, along with its recent memo on dressing professionally while in class, could go screw itself. I was on my own time now.

"My mother says I should go into public relations. She says anybody can write a press release."

"Well, PR is more than that, and, trust me, not everybody can write a press release." I finished collecting the newspapers and shoved them into my worn, scratched briefcase. "Truth is, though, you'll make more money there."

The tanned freshman knit her perfectly arched eyebrows together.

"OK, thanks, Dr. Huffinger. I need to think about this." She held the iPad close to her young bosom and walked from the classroom.

Had she —or any of them, for that rate—learned anything this quarter? Who the hell knows? I shook my head and looked again at the stack of newsprint in my briefcase before snapping it shut. I'd collected the papers up during my travels through Europe last summer.

We'd spent the class period in groups, each one dissecting a particular city's edition and comparing it to US publications and media policies. As part of their final exam, students had a week to look them over and make a group presentation; each person in the class had a paper due by noon today.

Teaching wasn't what I had planned for the second half of my life, but as more and more newspapers closed, my career options narrowed. My reporting credentials—along with ties to the head of the communications department here at Fitzgerald University—got me into academia, first as an adjunct, then as a full-time professor once I finished my doctorate.

Truth was, I hadn't been in the trenches for a lot of years, but, like any veteran, the scars were still there: an ex-wife who hated my guts, a son I could only visit at his grave, and a daily AA meeting to keep me on track.

Today was the last day of final exams; I'd have the weekend to grade papers, close up my apartment and travel, like I did most summers, under the guise of research.

Last summer was a series of interviews with European editors and journalists to see how their newspapers were coping with political and social changes, so I could bring that information, along with an edition of their newspapers, back to my students.

I put the information together, along with some lesson plans, as part of a paper I titled "The Changing Face of Journalism Education: Bringing World Media to Students." The world was shifting every day, but academia still required you to publish or perish.

The interviews took up just a couple hours of the day. The rest of the time I spent seeing tourist sights alone, catching up with old college buddies who were still lucky enough to have the words "foreign correspondent" beneath their byline.

I stepped into the hallway as I locked the classroom door and, in a few steps, turned the corner toward the stairwell that led to the department's basement offices.

My own office was the third door from that stairwell. The latest college president had milked some millionaire alumnus for repairs to the gothic old building that housed the English and communications departments; as the final term of the year wound down, the smell of the newly painted hallway and newly varnished doors had almost dissipated.

I plucked the several students' Post-It notes off the ornate oak door and slipped inside, reading the notes as I sank behind my desk.

"Hey, Huff, did U get my paper? I sent it thru campus e-mail." There was no name on that one, so I tossed it in the trash. Either the paper was in my inbox or it wasn't. I wasn't here to hold hands.

"Dr. H—I can't get into JOUR211 this fall. Can you get me a waiver? Plz call..." The kid who left that note was a go-getter, the editor of the college paper. I stuck that note on my phone. I would make certain he got into the class. I would call him on Monday morning, after AA and before I left town.

I pulled a framed photo of my son Noah and me off the bookshelf. It was taken during a camping trip just before his death. He had just graduated college, before he started on his own career as a spokesman for an environmental organization. We were smiling at the camera as we enjoyed a beer, the fish we'd caught that afternoon frying over the campfire.

His mother, Bitch Goddess of the Frozen North, often commented on how alike we'd looked. Noah's hair was in a long, brown ponytail, much like mine had been. Just like me, he had been tall, thin and tanned from his love of the outdoors. We even shared the same space between our front teeth. On that last camping trip, we'd not only brought our fishing gear, we'd each brought our cameras, to capture the stunning wildlife we saw during the days.

Six months later, life would never be the same.

There was a knock on my door.

"Come in!" I called out.

"Last day of the term!" sang a woman's mellifluous alto voice. It was Audrey Dellaplain, who taught the broadcast classes.

I placed Noah's photo back on the bookshelf before I answered.

"Yes, it is," I said.

"You got plans? Anything exciting?"

"I'm meeting with a series of US editors to assess the state of open records laws around the country." At least that was what I was telling people.

"God, you're a party animal."

"Well, I think that's something a lot of students need to know and a lot of working journalists probably have strong opinions on." I pretended to sift through the papers on my desk so I wouldn't have to look her in the eye. In reality, there would be no article, no treatise, no dissection of facts or conclusions or theories on various open records laws.

This summer, I wanted to find those journalists who, like Icarus, flew too close to the sun and, as their wings melted, found themselves falling all too rapidly toward the ground. I wanted to interview those who hit the ground hard and then couldn't get up again.

I wanted to know the reasons behind the fall. Was it conflict with those further up the food chain? Questionable sources? Expensive lawsuits? Outright plagiarism? And what led up to it? Ego? Fear? Pressure to publish in an increasingly unstoppable news cycle?

In particular, I was looking for one person, someone I wanted to talk to more than anything: the one reporter who flamed out in one spectacular way, then disappeared from sight.

This summer I wouldn't stop until I found her.

Chapter 3: Charisma

"Your name is *Charisma*? Really?"

My reporter's notebook slapped my thigh in frustration at the deputy's question. I pushed my short brown hair (which never seemed to lay right anyway) out of my eyes and tried to sound professional. We were beside the highway, at three in the morning, standing behind an ambulance as EMTs loaded two victims of a car accident into the back.

"Yes. I have a sister named Sunshine. She's twice as bitchy as me." I tried to smile, but my words didn't come across as humorously as I wanted. The deputy's eyebrows rose uncertainly like a farm boy coming face to face with his first big city hooker.

"What happened to Graham Kinnon?" the deputy asked. "He always used to pick up on these things."

Graham Kinnon was the daytime cops reporter. I took the night beat. It kept me away from the demons that came to visit when the moon was high in the sky and sleep wouldn't come.

I glanced at the minivan on its top in the ditch and closed my eyes. The screams begin again, an explosion rocks the ground beneath my feet, but I clench my jaw and shake my head to control what I now know is not real—at least not tonight.

"He's still there, but he's got a baby to care for now," I said slowly, trying to look like I was making notes. "I've been covering nights for a while."

"Oh. OK."

The answer seemed to satisfy him. My vision faded and I got back on track with the story.

"So tell me what we've got here," I continued. "We have two victims being transported, I see…"

The deputy launched into his spiel about the accident: A family—a man, his wife, their nine-year-old son and three-year-old twin daughters—were driving from Delaware en route to Gary, Indiana. Dad was a road warrior: rather than stop for coffee or a hotel room, he was bound and determined to make it to the Hoosier state when he nodded off at the wheel.

Now Dad was dead, Mom and the son were seriously hurt and the only two uninjured parties were the little girls, who'd been safely strapped into their car seats when the minivan went left of center, careened across the oncoming lanes and rolled into the ditch.

I got names, ages and learned the twins would be held at the sheriff's office until Grandma could get here from Indiana. She would be arriving in a couple hours. The injured would be transported to the trauma center in nearby Collitstown.

The ambulance pulled onto the highway. Our interview over, the deputy stepped back to the crash scene to talk to the responding firefighters and to begin his paperwork. I would follow up on the story as it got closer to our morning deadline, checking on the mother and son's condition, but for right now, all I had to do was head to the newsroom and write up the first version of the story and put it up on the newspaper's website.

I walked back to my little red sedan, got inside and closed my eyes, trying to stave off the feral need to run, to scream, to react, building in my stomach.

I was starting over again in Jubilant Falls.

I'd made sure no one could find me. Today, I used the name Charisma Lemarnier, not the one most recognized by the rest of the world.

I sighed, realizing yet again how lucky I was that the editor, Addison McIntyre, even took me on.

As far as she was concerned, I was starting over after losing both my parents and my husband in a horrible car crash, which resulted in the scars that covered my face. Even the résumé I'd given her was false. The references I'd listed were friends and journalists who I could trust to tell the same tale I'd told her, listed as editors of made-up small town newspapers where I'd built my "career."

She bought the story hook, line and sinker, and never called to check my references.

With Graham Kinnon, another young widower on staff, she believed me when I said my need to hide was partially to come to terms with my disfigurement, and to deal with my widowed grief. At least that much was true.

Tonight, out of habit, I flipped the car visor down and touched my late husband's photo, suspended there by rubber bands, before turning the key in the ignition and heading back to the newsroom.

Somehow Addison never questioned the need to hide away and heal in order to begin again.

"I want you to work for me, but you need to understand the risk you're taking," she said. "I can't protect you if anything happens or anyone in your family comes looking."

"Nobody's going to come looking," I said. "I'm off everyone's radar."

Tucked into a largely agricultural corner of southwest Ohio, I thought Jubilant Falls was a good place to hide.

To look at me, they might never know who I'd been, anyway. It took too much plastic surgery to return my face to the confident young woman I once was. It was close, but I'd never match my University of Maryland graduation portrait, even if you could see past my natural brown hair.

A scar ran across my scalp; more started at the edge of my left cheek and puckered back toward my ear, then hopscotched up my temple and across my forehead. There were reminders of shrapnel wounds across my arms, legs and torso. Only pure, hard chance kept me from losing my left eye.

I hid everything with long sleeves, regardless of weather, and professional-grade make-up, the kind broadcasters began to use when their stations switched to high definition—at least during the day. I didn't bother when calls like this brought me out in the middle of the night, where it wasn't likely anyone could see my wounds anyway.

It was a given I would never bare my body to another man again, much less my soul.

I pulled my car onto the highway and waved at the deputy as I headed back to the newsroom, pushing the disaster that brought me here back into the depths of my soul as the white lines on the highway slipped beneath my wheels.

Slowing to turn, I eased my car off the highway. In a few more blocks, I was pulling into the parking lot of the *Journal-Gazette*.

This job was probably the right one for me right now.

Around the corner from the paper, above a downtown lawyer's office, I had a studio apartment with a kitchenette, a tiny shower and a pullout couch. I could walk to work if I wanted, but more often than not I had to drive to some outlying crash or fire, so I just left my car in the employee lot behind the building at the end of my shift.

When I wasn't chasing drug busts or car crashes after dark, I was writing soft stories on the public schools, and Golgotha College, the Baptist school at the edge of town, whatever Addison threw my way. It wasn't anything close to what I was doing before, but that was the point. Sometimes, the stories were boring beyond belief, but that was OK.

Maybe sometime, I reasoned, I could go back to what I'd done before, maybe I could write a book, but right now, as the pieces of my psyche fell back in place, I belonged here.

I picked my notes from the passenger seat and closed the digital police-scanner app on my smartphone as I stepped from my car. I crossed the parking lot and let myself into the J-G through the back door. I passed through the darkened press room and the employee break room on my way to the steps up to the newsroom, marveling at the small town trust which would allow me into this building with just a key at all hours of the day and night. No guards, no alarm codes to punch in, no identification cards to scan, just a single key and my word that the reason I was here was necessary.

It was journalism on a smaller, more intimate scale. Small stories that I wouldn't have looked at twice became our front page.

If I had a story idea, I went to Addison's office at the back of the newsroom, knocked on the door and said, "Hey, I was wondering..." Sometimes she gave me the go-ahead and sometimes she let me know the story had been covered recently, but the pace was slower and that was good.

Upstairs, in the newsroom, I turned on the light and slipped into my office chair, flipping on my desktop computer. Chiming an electronic chord, it sprang to life and the story flowed easily from my fingers to the keyboard: *A Delaware man is dead and his family injured following a one-car crash early this morning...*

See girl? I told myself as I wrote. You still got it.

The story nearly wrote itself. I gave it a quick edit, then copied and pasted it onto the newspaper website, all before four-thirty in the morning.

On the white board behind Addison's copy-editing station, I made a note that the story was there before I left. Back downstairs in the pressroom, I pulled the employee door closed behind me and walked the brief two blocks to my little apartment. I would catch a few hours of sleep before heading back into work at seven-thirty.

I felt confident as I walked up the stairs and into my apartment. Maybe I was ready to take on a story that was a little more substantial. A series, maybe? An investigative piece? I was ready to cover something more substantial, I knew it.

I shook my head. What the hell could there be to investigate here in Jubilant Falls?

I flipped on the light as the ground began to shake beneath my feet again. I clenched the edge of the kitchenette counter as the rumbling became more intense, trying to steady myself.

In those seconds, I wasn't in my little apartment anymore. I was back in the past, cries of the injured and grieving filling my ears. There was another sound, one that I never forgot, screaming over my head and sending me diving beneath the dinette table, curling into a fetal position for safety as voices around me wailed in pain and grief.

Then just as quickly, the shaking stopped and in the distance, I heard the whistle of the four forty-five freight train as it rumbled through town. My cat, Monsieur Le Chat, jumped from his hiding place behind the curtains and rubbed his grey and white head against my leg.

"I get it. I get it," I sighed. I sat up sheepishly beneath my dinette and scooped Monsieur Le Chat into my lap, brushing the floor dust from my hair.

The sobs I heard weren't real. Neither was the screaming sound that sent me beneath the dinette.

I was in Jubilant Falls, in a tiny little apartment with an overweight cat and once again, reminded how damaged I truly was.

There would be no more sleep tonight. I clasped the cat closer and stroked his head as the tears rolled down my cheeks.

Chapter 4: Addison

It must have been a rough night for everybody, I thought as I walked through the newsroom later that Friday morning. The whole staff looked like no one slept the night before.

Charisma's car crash story was her excuse according to the time she filed the story. She rubbed her eyes as she spoke on the phone, getting updates on the victims. Knowing how her husband died, I hoped covering the crash didn't cause her any anxiety. If it did, it wasn't showing on her face.

I tried not to gag as I passed reporter Graham Kinnon. His shirt had a wet patch on the shoulder and he smelled of baby vomit; he had circles under his eyes as he sifted through today's police reports for shorter, page three stories.

Like most fathers, he was smitten with his baby girl; despite his exhaustion, he had a smile on his face.

Marcus Henning, my city and county reporter, attributed his lack of sleep to a late-running West Coast baseball game on TV.

Only Dennis Herrick, my assistant editor, seemed to have slept at all. He whistled through his copy editing and page layout duties and we cheerfully and loudly hated him for it.

Despite the collective lack of sleep, the front page came together easily. Charisma's crash story shared above-the-fold real estate with a preview of the new amusement company that would be providing the rides at next month's county fair.

Beneath that, Graham had a trial story and Marcus contributed a city council discussion of abandoned properties within Jubilant Falls that would be sold for taxes. Photographer Pat Robinette added a shot of the worst weed-infested property to the story.

I was able to put the vision of Jimmy Lyle's body and the terror of my tornado dream behind me as the day progressed. It usually worked that way. I knew it was a door that would stay closed for a while; I would cope with it when the lock broke again and memories of that horrible day swung open once more.

My office phone rang. I slipped behind my desk and picked up the receiver. It was Assistant Police Chief Gary McGinnis.

"You ever watch those TV shows where they dig into those old cold cases?" he asked without saying hello.

"The ones where a case that's sat cold for fifty years is suddenly solved within an hour by the handsome young detective who just started on the force a week ago?"

"Yeah, those." There was sarcasm in his voice as Gary slurped his coffee. "We've got two cases we're taking a fresh look at and maybe if one of your reporters would like to do a story on each of them, it might spark someone's memory. We might get some new tips."

"Let me guess: the kid beneath the bridge in the early eighties, and the dead state trooper a few years later."

Gary murmured his assent as he took another slurp of coffee. "You got it," he said, after he swallowed.

"You guys form a task force?"

"If that means Sheriff Roarke, my brothers Marvin and Harold, Mike Birger and me taking over a conference room to look over the old case notes, then yes, we've formed a task force."

A significant number of the Jubilant Falls' police force had the last name of McGinnis, including Assistant Chief Gary McGinnis, Chief Marvin McGinnis, Detective Harold McGinnis and Officer Jim McGinnis. Mike Birger was the city's other detective. He'd landed in Jubilant Falls after a stint as an Air Force security police officer at nearby Symington Air Force Base. Thanks to budget cuts, a third detective position hadn't been filled after the last guy, Mike Berrocco, retired.

"Let me see who's up for it," I said. "I may be able to farm it out to a somebody."

"That new reporter of yours? The one with the French last name?"

"What about her?"

"I like her. She's sharp—she'd be good at these stories, if no one else is available. I don't know why, but I think I've seen her someplace before."

"Really? I like the job she's done so far, that's for sure." I could have confided Charisma's past but I didn't. If she wanted to share that, she could.

I liked Charisma. I liked her a lot. I went with my gut when I hired her, so much so I never checked her references. In an hour-long interview, I saw she had that sharp edge that told me she would go far. I got a vicarious thrill seeing former reporters go from the *Journal-Gazette* to bigger and better things. Charisma would be one of those whose byline I might see in the *New York Times* one day, I thought. Maybe I could help her get there.

It would just be a matter of getting her confidence back, healing from her wounds. She kept us all, including me, at a distance—it wasn't going to be easy.

Gary brought me back to the conversation at hand. "Well, let me know what you want to do and who you're assigning the story to," he said. "It could be real helpful to us."

"Sure." Without either of us saying goodbye, our conversation was over.

I knew all too well the cases he was talking about.

The first murder happened about seven years after the tornado, after I graduated from college. I had just started my first job at another daily and contemplating a move back to Jubilant Falls when the *Journal-Gazette* ran the story about the body of a young man found in a creek beneath a county bridge; no one ever came forward to identify his tanned body or his killer. A few old-time firefighters and sheriff's deputies were still around to talk to about the night that body was found. Police believed that the young man was killed somewhere else and dumped into the creek. No one ever knew his name.

Five years later, after I'd been at the J-G for a couple years, a state trooper was found lying beside his cruiser, the lights still flashing as it sat on the side of the highway, a single bullet in the back of his head.

In the days before dashboard cameras and in-car laptop computers, dispatchers last had contact with Trooper Robert Martz when he was initiating a 2 a.m. traffic stop on the state highway that then ran north and south through Jubilant Falls. He'd radioed in the plate on the car he was stopping, but either dispatch got the information wrong or the plate wasn't on file. He also didn't give a reason for the stop. When my father Walt Addison, the shift supervisor, found Martz's body an hour later, there were only skid marks dug into the road's soft shoulder in front of the cruiser as his killer escaped into the night.

I revisited the story periodically, mainly because of the family connections between Bob Martz's family, my father and me.

In my last story, his three children, now grown, were each photographed somberly holding a corner of a large sepia-toned family photograph from their childhood.

The pull quote, printed in the white space above their heads was stark: "We're still hoping for justice for Dad."

Martz's widow and kids moved away from Jubilant Falls after the youngest graduated from high school. It was just too damned hard to stay in a town where their father had died and justice hadn't been served. I'd stayed in touch until the last story, but had no idea where to find them now.

Gary was right: reexamining the stories would bring phone calls to us and to the police. Folks always seemed to enjoy, in some perverse way, rehashing the gory details of past crimes. Somebody would call, asking a few questions—most of it not relevant to the story or asking salacious questions we would have no idea about.

People, I thought to myself as Dennis handed me a proof of today's front page.

Who knows what might come up? Maybe some justice this time?

*****

At the staff meeting later that afternoon, I presented the idea to my reporters. I'd found copies of the stories in the morgue and passed them around at the meeting.

"I just got a call from Gary McGinnis who said they were taking new looks at the cases and thought one of the stories might spark someone's memory," I said.

"I'd love to look into these," Charisma said. She didn't look up as she perused the yellowing copy of the paper with Robert Martz's murder screaming across the front page: TROOPER FOUND SHOT.

"Chief G mentioned these to me this morning," Graham said. "I told him I didn't think I could do a whole lot right now until Gwennie starts sleeping through the night. Besides, I've got a couple trials coming up that will keep me pretty tied up for the next couple weeks."

"The Jessop trial?" Dennis asked, making notes. "The woman who is suing the county commissioners for unfair termination?"

"Yes. I've also got that school bus driver picked up on DUI charges. If Charisma wants these cold cases, she can have at it. It won't hurt my feelings at all," Graham said.

Marcus nodded in agreement. "Our son Andrew is coming home on leave from the air force pretty soon. My wife wants me to take some time off while he's here."

Charisma looked up at me with a gleam in her eye, the first I'd seen since she'd started here.

"These stories would help me learn about the town, maybe learn a little history..." Charisma practically begged to cover these stories.

"Go for it," I said. There was a knock on the door; my publisher Earlene Whitelaw poked her head into the office.

"Hi ya'll! You havin' a staff meetin'?"

My jaw clenched. Ever since Earlene had taken over the publisher's chair from her father, J. Watterson Whitelaw, it had been a string of bad ideas born from a woman who had no concept of how to run a newspaper.

In a time when newspaper readership was sinking like a rock and revenue harder and harder to come by, she'd increased the number of special sections advertising had to sell—and editorial had to fill with stories—often on short notice.

Large or small, every newspaper has a yearly plan of special sections. Bridal sections, home improvement sections, tax season, car care, a preview of the county fair and a fair review that ran pictures of champions and lists of results were some of the standard sections we did each year, in addition to what was known in the newspaper business as the "progress edition," which highlighted particular themes or businesses in the community.

Earlene took it to extreme.

Since Earlene had been here, she'd pushed all kinds of moronic ideas—a celebration of barbeque when there were no BBQ joints in town, and the crowning humiliation, an edition printed with the fold on the right hand side of the paper— essentially upside down—for Left Hander's Day, highlighted by a rambling story she wrote about the daily struggles *(really?)* she and other left-handers faced. Of course, she wouldn't let me edit that piece of shit for clarity or content.

I took phone calls all day about that one, including one from Gary McGinnis who was laughing so hard he could hardly speak.

It was no wonder our most consistent advertisers were beginning to feel tapped out after so many requests to advertise—and embarrassed about the advertising product their name was often attached to.

As a result, too, the long-stable advertising sales staff began to turn over on such a regular basis there was talk a revolving door should be installed. We'd been through three advertising directors since Earlene took over. The position was currently vacant; Jane, the department secretary, told Dennis that Earlene's bizarre demands were the reason for the volatility.

When I should have been improving the quality of the journalism in our paper, I was scanning the calendar for made-up holidays, like Celebrate Cabbage Day to head off Earlene's crazy ideas. I staved off International Popcorn Day with a couple wire stories on the food page; I talked her out of a front-page story on National Donut Day that involved members of the police force.

A few of these goofy calendar recognitions did give us ideas for stories, but they never seemed to spark interest for her.

A series on bullying was first shot down, but we went ahead with it anyway. When it won a state Associated Press award, Earlene wouldn't speak to me for days.

Over the last few week's she'd started showing up at my Monday afternoon staff meetings, much to the staff's chagrin.

"Hi, Earlene," I said slowly. "Come on in."

Marcus Henning rolled his eyes at Dennis as Earlene, nearly six feet tall in her turquoise stilettos, with a matching silk flower in her sky-high Miss Texas hair, sat down beside him, hiking her skirt as she did so. Dennis and Charisma bit their lips, hiding their smirks. Only Graham, with all the exhaustion of a new parent, didn't react.

The luckiest member of the staff was photographer Pat Robinette, who had a dental appointment, and was missing this show. At that moment, I wished I were having a root canal, too.

"So what's up?" I asked.

"So next Thursday is National Newspaper Day," she began, twisting her chunky turquoise necklace with her long manicured fingers.

Oh Jesus, how did I miss that? I wondered.

"And I had this *wonderful* idea of doing a front page on the process of putting together a newspaper, starting from when the truck pulls up in back with the big rolls of paper to what ya'll do in the newsroom and what advertising does, right to the end when the paper hits the street."

"Hmmm," I said. This might not be a bad idea, depending, of course, on how it was presented. One of my chief complaints about my readers—and my publisher— was how little they really knew about the news business. This could be, as they say, a teachable moment. "So how would the story run?"

"Well, I would write the story, of course..."

Oh shit.

"And I thought, wouldn't it be neat if it was told from a unique perspective? You know, something different?"

"Like what?" I tried to sound neutral as my stomach churned.

"From the viewpoint of one of the mice that I happened to see down in the press room."

My reporter's heads snapped up and their eyes got big, but no one spoke.

I swallowed. "Earlene, I think—"

"I knew you'd love it! I've got some ideas for photos. Let's talk about it later this afternoon, OK?" She stood up, smoothed her skirt, and left, not quite closing the door as she exited.

I waited to speak until I heard her stilettos no longer clicking down the stairs.

"Close the door," I said softly. Dennis leaned over and pushed it closed. The questions—and the outrage—came all at once.

"Is she out of her mind?" Marcus asked. "And then let people think we do all this in a rat-infested building? She's nuts!"

"She's turning us into a joke!" Graham said. "*Again.*"

"People are still laughing about that stupid left-handed edition," Dennis said.

Only Charisma was silent; whether she was thinking about what an idiot publisher she had or how far she'd sunk following her accident, I couldn't tell. I didn't want to ask.

"I think the photo should be of Addison screaming at someone on the phone—I mean if we're going to paint a realistic picture," Marcus teased, diffusing the frustration. Everyone laughed.

"You all need to get back to work," I answered, smiling as I reached for my cigarettes. "I'm going to have a smoke and then see how far my dignity can sink after I meet with her."

In half an hour, I was downstairs, knocking on the door of Earlene's baby-chick yellow office.

"C'mon in, Addison! Perfect timing!" Earlene's adopted Texas drawl stretched each vowel to its breaking point. A woman in a blue suit sat in one of the frou-frou yellow chairs in front of my boss's Queen Anne writing desk, with her back to the door. She didn't turn around as Earlene waved me into her office. "I want you to meet an old friend of mine from back in high school. She's come to town for a little visit."

The woman stood and turned to face me, extending her hand. The wide, even smile on her face froze as she recognized me.

After nearly forty years, she hadn't changed all that much. She was still in great cheerleading shape; I could see the muscles in her long, lean calves. Her pinned-up hair was tinted fashionably golden; her face was smooth and her jewelry tasteful. Her eyes were still hard and feral behind her stylish bifocals.

As she stood next to Earlene, all I could see were two high maintenance blondes, two women used to getting what they wanted from everyone else around them, regardless of who they stepped on or how badly they botched it.

"Hello, Eve," I said. "Welcome back to Jubilant Falls."

Chapter 5: Leland

I took a few steps toward Noah's grave before I saw her. Her presence halted me in my tracks.

I hadn't planned to stop—it had been an unspoken agreement in the divorce that even in death, visitation would be limited to one parent at a time. Through the low-hanging branches of a nearby willow and the cold, white, upright granite markers, I could see Bitch Goddess sitting cross-legged in front of Noah, brushing the tears from her eyes.

Five years after our divorce, she still looked magnificent. Ever thin and perfectly fit, I wondered if she still ran five miles every morning; even in the worst stages of our mutual family illness, she could get up and push through the hangover by pounding through the streets of our suburban Philadelphia neighborhood. It was an act of supreme fortitude—and denial: *A drunk couldn't do this every morning so therefore I'm not a drunk.*

With her long, perfectly manicured fingers, I watched her brush the curly black hair from her face and gaze upward, her lips moving. I understood: I, too, had long, one-sided conversations with Noah. I took a few steps closer so I could see her face, the strong jaw, the prominent nose, and perfectly arched eyebrows. They all still came together magnificently despite the crow's feet beginning at the corners of those steel blue eyes. I would have called the slight marks from her nose to her red lips "laugh lines" except Bitch Goddess wasn't known for her hilarity.

Not that I left her with a lot to chuckle over.

Bitch Goddess dropped her head onto her chest and, without looking, slipped a hand into the designer leather bag sitting beside her. Sighing, she pulled out what had been a familiar part of our marriage, a silver flask wrapped in tan leather. We'd gotten matching ones as a wedding present from our coworkers in the newsroom at the Philly *Enquirer*, before she'd moved to TV news.

With a flick of the wrist, she opened the flask.

What was in it? I wondered. Our poison of choice had been vodka.

She looked around, stopping mid-swallow when she saw me.

"Hey!" she called out sharply. It wasn't an invitation to join her. It was a warning to leave her alone.

Shaking my head, I turned and walked back to my car, trying to ignore the slurred hate that spewed from her perfect, red mouth.

*****

I spent the weekend at my campus apartment grading papers; Bitch Goddess, after all, got the house in the divorce. Fitzgerald House, named for the founder of the university, accommodated unmarried faculty like myself in one-bedroom apartments and was part of my pay. Most of my neighbors lasted a term or two before falling in love, buying a house or moving on.

I was the only one who'd lived there four years.

By Sunday night, I was done and final grades were submitted. I made myself a ham sandwich and flopped into the brown shapeless recliner in the living room. I grabbed the TV remote and turned on the DVR, pressing buttons to see what I'd watched at least twice a week for the last year.

It was Charisma Prentiss, looming large on the screen behind four panelists. She was beautiful, tan and fit in her blue press helmet, jeans, sand-brown boots and brown tee shirt. I had no doubt she could easily carry the military-issue pack on her back, and probably someone else's, too. She'd been the reporter's reporter—print or broadcast, she could do it all, a Bond Girl with a nose for news.

Among her peers, her ego had been as legendary as the stories she filed, fed by her superiors in New York, who needed someone with flair and panache to keep the world focused on the stories that "mattered."

Her peers may have hated her and the attention she garnered, but the troops she embedded with loved her. She could keep up with the physical demands of an army on the move and painted those stories with words that were more than a little pro-military. In the days following the Sept. 11, 2001 attacks, none of her editors or supervisors seemed to catch that tendency—or, considering the jingoistic times we lived in, if they cared. She took risks other journalists wouldn't consider, a mixture of recklessness and arrogance, spiced with a star power that brought ratings and readers to whatever story she provided.

I never met her, but the world knew what happened.

I watched the panel discussion one more time: The fearless way Charisma covered the wars in Afghanistan, Iraq and Syria put many male correspondents to shame. Her series on underground schools for girls in Taliban-held territories was legend. Charisma's final tale was so ingrained, I could recite it from memory: The car bomb that claimed her husband, her refusal to give in to her injuries and her drive to get back in the game, followed by one wrong story that brought it all crashing down. Then she disappeared off the face of the earth.

I had no idea where to find her, not even an idea of where to begin looking. Was she still working? Had she retired? Changed careers? Was she dead? If the post-traumatic stress syndrome she reportedly suffered was true, suicide was a distinct possibility.

The news business could tear reporters and editors apart; I saw that this afternoon at Noah's grave. While many police and fire departments have procedures in place to help first responders depressurize after traumatic events, many reporters are left to cope in their own way with the horror they'd just seen.

And, face it: the effect of trauma on reporters was something most liberal arts educations never covered. So, we keep showing up at murders, car crashes and worse, go back to the newsroom, churn out the story and come back the next day to do it again.

Along the way, you begin to internalize the horror, to make tasteless jokes about the victim or the perpetrator and after a while you can't turn it off when deadline's past and the adrenaline won't stop.

No one ever tells you to find a therapist, anybody who will listen. Nobody says don't drink at night alone, don't drink at work, or don't drive drunk—because they're all doing it too. No one says you need to do it to save your life, your marriage— or your child. But as you hurtle into that dark night, it doesn't seem to sink in until you're left at the side of a literal or figurative road surrounded by the wreckage of your life. The darkness in your soul builds and builds until the relationship you counted on the most is shredded and you find the woman you're married to having sex in the shower with her co-anchor in the middle of the afternoon.

What they *do* tell you is "suck it up," "be tough," "this job isn't for sissies."

Did anyone say that to Charisma Prentiss? Did she run back out into the field because she couldn't let go of the dragon that was the news? Or were there other pressures—pressures to publish, sources or editors to appease? Did she go back because she didn't know to do anything else? Or was it her legendary ego, knowing that nobody could do a story like Charisma Prentiss did a story and dropping out meant she was no longer at the top of the heap?

If I could find her, just for one interview, one conversation...

I stopped the DVR, and used the remote to scratch at my beard.

What would I do? What would she do? I knew what I wanted to ask her, but what was I trying to prove?

I shut off the TV and moved to the computer desk in the corner of the living room. Shaking the mouse brought my sleek Apple computer screen to life. A quick search on Charisma Prentiss brought up the old news of her collapse. Even in the digital world, where everything was traceable, she'd managed to disappear.

What was her husband's name? I wondered. I typed in the words "French +journalist +killed +Baghdad" and hit 'enter.'

There it was: *Jean Paul Lemarnier.* The most recent entry was a story written when his name was unveiled in the Newseum's Journalists Memorial Gallery in Washington D.C., as part of a ceremony recognizing reporters killed while in pursuit of a story. His name was among eighty-two added to the list which brought the somber total to more than 2,200. I clicked on the ceremony video, watching as the widows and widowers of other reporters came forward to speak.

Charisma Prentiss was the only bereaved spouse who didn't attend.

Instead, Lemarnier's parents came to the podium and in tearful French, acknowledged the honor.

Why wouldn't she come to an event like that? Was she afraid her presence would detract from the event? I had a vision of old Charisma, surrounded by cameras, wearing dark glasses like some Hollywood diva, stiff-arming the circle of reporters who wanted to know where she'd been. I shook my head and discarded that idea. Maybe she didn't come because she was afraid of being a pariah, whispered about as she entered the gallery, with her fellow journalists stepping back in disgust as she passed by, like a leper in church.

I typed in "Charisma+Lemarnier," sucking in my breath as story after bylined story scrolled up. Each one—soft, small-town stories interspersed with the occasional breaking news piece—traced back to a small Ohio daily newspaper, the *Jubilant Falls Journal-Gazette*.

The woman, once arguably the free world's best journalist is in Ohio, of all places? It couldn't be her, could it? I asked myself. *And where the hell is Jubilant Falls?*

I dug through the *Journal-Gazette's* website, looking for a headshot of her. Everyone on the staff except Charisma Lemarnier had one. Unlike a number of small town newspapers, there also was no article or accompanying photo on her first day of work: "The *Journal-Gazette* would like to welcome a new writer..." Instead, her byline just began appearing above stories.

I read through a couple of them: A story on a local college student's upcoming piano performance and her struggle to become the first in her family to graduate from college, a child seriously injured in a horseback riding accident and the family's efforts to raise money to pay the rehabilitation bills, an early morning highway accident where the father was killed and the family seriously injured when their minivan rolled.

The content was so much less than what she'd made her name on, but the writing was still solid. It had to be her.

With a little more Internet exploration, I found Jubilant Falls on the map. A few more clicks on a few more websites and I had a plane ticket to Cincinnati, leaving tomorrow afternoon.

Chapter 6: Charisma

"You look like someone I've seen before."

It was Monday afternoon before I could get time to head over to the Jubilant Falls Police Department. Assistant Police Chief Gary McGinnis made the comment as he brought in a stack of files and a cup of coffee for me.

"Yeah, a lot of people say that," I said, taking the mug from him. I took a gulp before saying any more, letting my brown hair fall in front of my scarred face, hiding it from his piercing gaze.

"No, seriously, you do," Chief McGinnis was insistent.

"Somebody once told me I look like Paula Abdul, only taller," I lied. "I told them they were crazy."

"Maybe that's it."

I had a pretty good weekend. With Monsieur Le Chat curled alongside me, I managed to get a full night's sleep Saturday night on my tiny foldout couch. No bloody bodies flashed in front of my eyes; I didn't wake screaming uncontrollably or crying out his name. It was progress, and I was thankful for that.

On Sunday, I drove to one of the malls in nearby Collitstown, treating myself to what Dennis told me was a local confection: Cincinnati chili, a Greek-inspired dish flavored heavily with cinnamon and nutmeg, served on spaghetti, covered in shredded cheddar cheese, and served with a side order of oyster crackers. I sat in my booth, pouring over the Sunday *New York Times*, concentrating on the lifestyle section and the book reviews.

I felt semi-normal.

Now, with the chief's one question, the walls were closing in again.

I turned to the files on the table beside me.

"So tell me, Chief, what's the deal on this case," I said, tapping the file with my pen.

"Basically, we had the body of a white male, approximately eighteen to twenty-two years of age, discovered by a farmer and his son who were driving over the bridge on Yarnell Road early in the morning," McGinnis began. "The bridge at that time was just inside the city limits, so we got the case. The body was face down in the water, hung up on a tree limb. The farmer sent the son to a pay phone to call the police and stayed behind until they got there. When the fire department retrieved the victim out of the water, he had no identification. He also wasn't in the system anyplace—there were no fingerprints on record anywhere."

"Any wounds?"

"He'd been stabbed several times, twice in the chest, and had several defensive wounds on his hands and arms. His throat was also cut, which the coroner determined was the fatal wound."

"Do you think he died there where he was found?"

"No. We think the crime occurred further up Shanahan Creek and the body floated down the creek toward town. We think he was dead when he hit the water because there was no water in his lungs."

Shanahan Creek was a lot deeper and wider than some rivers I'd seen in my life. I wasn't surprised the body was able to float that distance.

Before coming to see Assistant Chief McGinnis, I drove to the crime scene, parking my car beside the bridge where the body was discovered and scrambling down the banks.

The landscape wasn't the same as what I'd read in the original story, but that didn't surprise me. The fallen tree limb that caught the body was long gone. The photos showed an older bridge, with arching bricks reaching each side of the creek, as police officers lifted the sagging body from the water. Even that was gone, replaced by a modern concrete structure.

I scrambled back up the bank to my car and headed down the roads that paralleled Shanahan Creek, hoping to get an idea of the local geography before meeting with the assistant chief.

Past the edge of town and a slew of newly built homes, Shanahan Creek took a sharp turn and I lost my view of the water. At the next road, I turned, hoping to find it again.

It was a lucky move: there at the bend in the creek sat an older home. Its bricks were painted white; four columns flanked two rows of arched windows with glossy black wooden shutters. There was a row of varnished rocking chairs on the porch and an over-landscaped front yard, lush with flowers at the base of old-growth oaks and maples. A newer three-car garage, also built with painted white brick sat off at an angle from the house. I could see a gazebo in the back yard, near the creek, and further back, a new horse barn with white picket fencing surrounding it. It looked today like a picture from a magazine—and the perfect place to commit a murder.

I didn't stay—my appointment with the assistant chief was in a few minutes. It wouldn't be a good time to pull up the drive to talk to whoever lived there. I scribbled the address down and headed back to the police department.

Now, as I asked my questions, I found myself casting sidelong glances at Gary McGinnis to make certain he didn't recognize me.

"Anything odd about the stab wounds you can tell me?" I asked.

McGinnis looked through the coroner's report.

"The chest wounds weren't at an angle. They were straight in, so likely his killer was the same height, not shorter or taller. The killer probably disabled him with those wounds and then, when he was unable to fight back, stepped behind him and slit his throat. After he died, his killer dumped him in the creek."

"Do you have any idea where the murder actually occurred?" I asked.

Chief McGinnis flipped through a few pages in the file; even though the murder happened thirty-some years ago, it was still considered an open investigation and, as a result, Ohio Sunshine Laws kept me from rooting through the whole file myself.

"We had the sheriff's office walk up both sides of the creek, but they never found anything, so we can't really say for sure where he was murdered."

"How far did they walk?"

McGinnis flipped through a few more pages and shrugged. "Couple miles, I guess."

"Are there houses along there? Anybody I could talk to?"

McGinnis pushed a list of addresses toward me. "Most of it was farmland, so there weren't a lot of houses. A lot of it's been developed since that time."

I tried to conceal my excitement: his list included the address of the white brick house I'd visited. If I were lucky, the place was still in the same hands as it was the day a young man's body fell into Shanahan Creek—a quick check at the courthouse would answer that.

"Anybody else around I can talk to?" I tried to sound casual.

"Believe it or not, it was the old fire chief's first week as a firefighter. He's retired now, but I'm sure he'd still talk about it." McGinnis pulled his cell phone from his shirt pocket and, with his thumb, scrolled through his contacts. "His name is Hiram Warder. Here's his number." McGinnis showed me his phone and I scrawled the information down.

"Anybody else?" I looked at him hopefully.

"Let me check with my brother, Marvin—he's the chief. He was new on the force and on patrol then. He might have some ideas of who is still around," McGinnis said.

"Is there anything else you can show me in that file?" I asked.

McGinnis shook his head.

"I've given you all I can, legally. It's still an open investigation, although we are at a complete standstill. We recently sent the victim's clothing to the state crime lab for DNA testing, but because we don't know how long the body was in the river, I'm not certain if they can pull anything off of it." McGinnis pushed a small folder my way, filled with whatever case file copies I was allowed access to. "If I hear anything, I'll let you know. Maybe we can shake something loose on this thing."

I tucked the file under my arm and we stood up. "Thanks," I said, shaking his hand.

McGinnis nodded. "Glad to have your help. You still look like someone I've seen before."

I tried to laugh it off as I made my way to the door.

I walked the two blocks back to the *Journal-Gazette,* deep in thought. Addison was right—she couldn't protect me if someone came looking for me. But what if that person was someone I worked with on a regular basis? Could I bring them in on my secret and ask them to keep it for me?

On Sunday, while I was enjoying my Cincinnati chili, I read a *New York Times* story about a well-known comedian who stepped away from his Emmy award-winning show to return to the small Illinois town of his youth.

Everyone in that little town knew he was there and, despite the steady stream of fans that came to scout the small business district in search of him, the residents protected his privacy. The comic managed to live a fairly regular life, putting his kids in the public school system, taking his morning coffee—black, two sugars, please—at the local donut shop. The article compared the little farm town to J.D. Salinger's hometown of Cornish, New Hampshire, whose residents rabidly protected the notoriously private author's address and daily whereabouts.

Here in Jubilant Falls, my co-workers in the newsroom only knew me as a young widow coming back to work following a horrible car accident. I wasn't ready to socialize with them, much less tell them the truth about myself. But if the assistant police chief thought he recognized me, other people probably did too. Could I trust anyone, let alone an entire town, to keep the secret until I was healed and ready to tell the world myself?

I stopped at the corner, clutching the file to my chest. My plan was to check in with Addison and then visit the homes along the creek bed, much as the Plummer County sheriff's deputies had those many years ago.

I looked to my right as a man stopped on the sidewalk beside me, both of us waiting on the traffic light. Bearded and tall, he had a gap between his front teeth and wore khaki shorts and a dark, maroon tee shirt. His thin, muscular legs looked like they belonged to a hiker or a runner; on his feet he wore sandals and rag wool socks. His eyes were incredibly sad; white streaks in his beard and hair made their blueness stand out like winter sky.

Without thinking, I swept my hair behind my ear, exposing the pockmarked scars on my arm. I nodded at him and he did a double take. Before he could speak, I felt fear rise in my chest. Maybe it was my scars that horrified him—maybe it was something else. I didn't want to ask. I turned and walked the other direction.

*****

Back at the newspaper, I put my desk phone on 'do not disturb' and disappeared into the morgue, where old editions were kept, and scoured through the stories on the dead man in the creek.

The probing questions of Chief McGinnis and the reaction of the man at the corner destroyed any confidence I had thought I'd built over the weekend.

Times like this made me question the ruse I lived under. I couldn't confide to anyone my fears over Gary McGinnis's questions and the double take of the man at the corner. Until I could calm my nerves, it was best that I just hide. This afternoon, I had the excuse that I needed to research the story. As the newest reporter in the newsroom, nobody would think twice about it.

As the afternoon progressed, I forgot about my fear of being discovered. Instead, I dug deeper into the bound editions, getting a picture of Jubilant Falls in the early 1980s, but little or no insight into the dead young man in the river.

Chapter 7: Leland

That woman at the corner, that couldn't have been Charisma Prentiss, could it? I tugged thoughtfully at my beard as I walked back to my bed and breakfast, the Jubilant Country Inn.

My search couldn't have been that easy, could it? Those scars on her arm were horrible—but that face!

It had to be Charisma.

The hair was brown now, no longer blonde, with bangs hanging over her forehead. Did she hide wounds there, too? The even, high cheekbones I'd seen on the national news looked different somehow, but familiar. I caught a glimpse of more puckered, red disfigurement along her scalp.

Clearly the woman, even if she wasn't Charisma, saw my unfortunate reaction. Who could blame her for the way she'd spun on her heels and walked the other direction? I cringed at the emotional pain I, once again, didn't mean to cause.

But I was at least here in Jubilant Falls.

The drive north from the Cincinnati airport hadn't been too bad. I could see why Charisma (if the woman I saw really was Charisma Prentiss) would choose to begin again here. Once off the highway, I felt calmed by the green farmlands and the slower-moving traffic. As I pulled into town, I thought I'd crossed from reality into the set of a slightly worn Frank Capra movie.

I passed a hotel by the highway without stopping to get a room: the flashing neon sign advertising the bar warned me off.

Instead, I cruised through the historic district close to the downtown and found a bed and breakfast with a room available on a week-to-week basis.

The owner pointed me in the direction of the Methodist Church, where I could find a daily AA meeting, and a diner called Aunt Bea's for lunches and weekday dinners. On weekends, when every room in the B&B was full, there would be large family style breakfasts and dinners I could enjoy.

My room was small and furnished with 1920s antiques. There were reproduction pictures of Abraham Lincoln in antique frames hanging on the flowered papered walls and a novel about Robert E. Lee at Gettysburg on the dresser. Across the double bed lay a quilt with rows of fabric flowers; a lacy white throw lay across the foot of the bed. A small antique desk and chair sat next to the door to my private bathroom.

I flopped onto the bed and wondered what my next step would be.

I couldn't just walk into the newsroom and introduce myself—or could I? There was a possibility that she wouldn't grant me an interview, however I approached her and I would return to my empty apartment at Fitzgerald House with nothing except a few summer weeks in a small Ohio town under my belt.

What would I ask that I didn't already know?

What happened after the bomb exploded and Jean Paul Lemarnier was killed was the subject of endless news broadcasts. In an induced coma, Charisma was airlifted to the military hospital at U.S. Army's Landstuhl Regional Medical Center in Germany, then to Bethesda Naval Hospital in Maryland. After several weeks there, she was released to another hospital closer to her father's home in Washington D.C. for further treatment and cosmetic surgery.

The news went crazy with coverage, making Charisma Prentiss the poster child for traumatic brain injury.

For a while, the woman I sought suffered from aphasia, an inability to use certain words, as a result of her head wounds. There were stories, photos and news clips as she found her way back to speech, first English and then French, the language of her late husband, then the Arabic and Farsi she'd famously used to cultivate her sources. But never any pictures of Prentiss herself. Had she been that disfigured?

There were daily updates on her condition and, when they couldn't get that information, battlefield correspondents talked of nothing else except the hardship they faced, embedded with the troops. Then, thankfully, it all died down.

A year went by before her byline began to appear again, from the usual hotspots. Then came that one badly sourced story that brought it all crumbling down and she was gone.

What should I ask her? *Where have you been? Why come here? Why now?* Those were just the basics. *What made you go back, especially when, in hindsight, you clearly weren't ready? Where did you go? And will you ever come back?*

I picked up my cell phone from beside me on the bed. One phone call couldn't hurt, could it?

I found the number for the *Journal-Gazette* and dialed it, asking the disembodied female who answered to connect me to her extension. The call went straight to voice mail: "Hello, you've reached the desk of staff writer Charisma Lemarnier. I'm unable to take your call right now but if you leave a message at the sound of the tone, I'll return your call as soon as possible."

The phone beeped in my ear and I began to speak: "Hi, this is Dr. Leland Huffinger of Fitzgerald University. I'm looking to get in touch with Charisma Prentiss. If she could give me a call, I'd sure appreciate it."

I hung up. The ball was in her court now. Let's see if she calls me back.

Chapter 8: Addison

"So how was your day?"

Duncan was setting the table for dinner when I walked in the door Monday night. Our daughter, Isabella, was standing in front of the stove, over a skillet of frying pork chops. Potato wedges and green beans simmered in another pan. Of the three of us, she was the better cook and the older she got, the more we relied on her for evening meals.

"I'm not entirely sure," I said, dumping my purse on a kitchen chair.

"What's that mean?"

"Remember Eve Dahlgren? She was a year ahead of us in high school."

"Wasn't she the head cheerleader? A bit of a snot, if I remember your assessment," Duncan said.

"Yeah. She showed up at the office Friday—I don't think I told you. Turns out she met Earlene at that fancy private girl's boarding school in Columbus after the tornado. Earlene went there all through high school, but Eve only attended those last few months of her senior year."

"There's boarding schools in Ohio?" Isabella was incredulous.

"Yes. After the 1974 tornado destroyed the school, a lot of us were bused into the next county to finish the school year. Some parents used that opportunity to send their kids to fancier schools than what we had there."

Isabella wrinkled her nose in hometown school pride.

"Seeing her brought back all those shitty high school memories of Jimmy Lyle and her," I said. "The one they found after the tornado with the post hole digger in his chest."

"Eewww!" Isabella turned from the stove and stared.

"Today, in between Earlene's idiot ideas for something called National Newspaper Day, I got to hear how the two of them went out this weekend and tore up the town." I began pulling silverware from a drawer, helping Duncan to set the table. "Earlene apparently thinks I was good friends with this woman in high school because she felt the need to confide in me everything they did and that the evening didn't end well. They apparently ended up arguing."

"I'm sure you were sympathetic." Duncan smiled, arching an eyebrow.

I rolled my eyes, seating myself as Isabella brought dinner to the table.

"It was an Academy Award-winning performance, I'll say that much."

Before I could say any more, or even take the first bite of my pork chop, my cell phone rang.

It was Gary.

"Penny," he said. "I'm sorry to bother you at home—"

"No, no, don't worry about it. What's up?"

"We found Eve Dahlgren stabbed in her car."

"What?" Like most every one else who stuck around Jubilant Falls, Gary and I went to high school together; we both knew Eve Dahlgren. She was Gary's homecoming date our sophomore year, until she disappeared after the third dance with my date, the basketball team's star center.

"What happened? Is she OK?"

"She's dead, Penny. Eve's dead."

"Oh my god."

"Earlene Whitelaw has been arrested for her murder."

I swallowed hard.

"What? You're kidding me, right?"

"I wish I were."

"Does her dad know?"

"I don't know."

"I'll call Charisma and make sure she gets in touch with you tonight, so we can get the story."

"She can't make it, Penny. That's why I called you."

"What do you mean she can't make it?"

"I just left her—there's a bed and breakfast downtown that's on fire. She's covering that."

"Is it a bad one?"

"It's pretty significant. All the guests are displaced."

"It never rains but it pours." I tossed my napkin on my dinner plate. I'd have to eat later.

Since Charisma came on board, I felt pretty confident at night about turning my police scanner off. As a single parent, Graham Kinnon couldn't catch the late night calls like he used to, but Charisma had been more than competent covering those. It was wonderful to be able to finally know I really could leave the office behind most nights. Tonight would be the first time in a long time I hadn't finished a meal because I needed to go chase a story.

"OK. Where are you?" I asked.

"I'm back at the scene. We're in Shanahan Park downtown."

"Give me fifteen minutes. I'll meet you there."

*****

Yellow crime scene tape stretched from each rearview window of Eve's Lincoln to the closest trees, enclosing the shiny black car in a triangle from which city cops, detectives and coroner's staff stepped in and out of.

I got a shot with my cell phone of Gary lifting the yellow crime scene tape up as Eve's corpse, enclosed in a blue plastic body bag, was rolled on a gurney toward the coroner's van.

God, I hope that's in focus, I thought to myself.

Driving in, I saw the fire truck's flashing lights deep in the historic district as they fought the fire at the bed and breakfast. I would check in with Charisma after I was done here.

I parked my Taurus next to Gary's unmarked Crown Victoria, among in a phalanx of official vehicles. He waved when he saw me, and walked toward me. With a brick-sized radio clasped in his hand, he leaned his elbows on the roof of my car until I was able to pull my cigarettes, lighter, notebook and pen from my purse.

"What the hell happened?" I asked.

"An off-duty officer found Eve in her car about an hour ago."

"I wonder why Charisma didn't hear it on the scanner?" I wondered.

Gary shrugged. "Charisma probably didn't hear it because she's at the fire. From what detectives found, Eve has been stabbed multiple times. It looked like there'd been a fight of some kind while she was sitting in the passenger seat. See the crack in the windshield? We think she might have kicked it while struggling with her killer. She had a lot of defensive wounds, but it was a wound to her side that Dr. Bovir said was the fatal one."

Dr. Bovir was Plummer County's Pakistani-born coroner.

I looked up from my notebook. "You got a time of death yet?"

"Not yet."

"I talked to Earlene today at work. She told me the two of them went out and they argued, but I made the assumption that the two of them were out on Saturday night. That doesn't mean Earlene killed her, though."

"What did they argue about?"

I shrugged.

"Honestly Gary, I tune out about half of what she tells me on a daily basis. I don't know why she felt the need to confide in me all of a sudden. I really didn't listen. If I remember, though, I'll sure tell you. Had Eve been drinking or anything?"

Gary shrugged. "We don't know any of that right now. The autopsy will tell us more. Bovir said he'd have the results to us tomorrow, but the toxicology screen will take a few weeks."

I didn't like Earlene, not by a long shot: she made my days a living hell with her cockamamie promotions and idiot story ideas. What I told her about the news business slid in one diamond-studded ear and out the other on a daily basis. Her sky-high stilettos and her age-inappropriate clothing made her look like a cougar on the prowl.

"I can't see her as a killer, Gary. I really can't."

"Was Earlene at work all afternoon?"

"Oh hell no. She's never at the office past three," I said vehemently. I stopped and covered my mouth with my hand. "Oh my God."

Gary nodded. "We found her fingerprints on the steering wheel, Penny," he said. "We picked Earlene up at home after we got results. Earlene was in the car with her."

"Why were her prints in the system? She's never been convicted of anything."

"Apparently, she was accused by an ex-husband in Fort Worth of vandalism during their divorce. She was on her way back to Jubilant Falls when it happened and this big Texas divorce lawyer tracked her down. She came in and gave us a set of prints at that time and we still had them on file. They exonerated her in that mess, but they hung her on this one. She'll be arraigned in the morning."

"I can't believe this." I shook my head.

"I hate to say it, but it looks like this one is pretty cut and dried," he said.

It didn't look good: an argument that Earlene admitted to, her fingerprints on the steering wheel of the vehicle where the body was found. I couldn't argue with him.

"I can't imagine her going down without a fight, if she's innocent."

"The damnedest things can happen, Penny. You oughta know that."

"I'm going to go over to the old man's house and see if he knows. I would imagine he's already heard from her and got a lawyer hired."

One of the police officers lay on the ground, reaching deep into a storm sewer grate as another held a flashlight.

"We got a murder weapon!" The prone officer pulled out a long kitchen knife, wet from the sewer, its serrated edge covered in blood. He dropped it into a brown paper bag, held by the other officer.

Gary looked at me knowingly.

He was right. This didn't look good for Earlene. I turned to leave; Gary started to walk back toward the crime scene but stopped.

"As much as we both hated Eve Dahlgren in high school, she sure didn't deserve to die like this," he said.

*****

J. Watterson Whitelaw looked even older and even more infirm when he came to the door of his expensive country club house. He waved me inside wordlessly, and showed me to his study, just off the front door. He sank into one of the worn leather Morris chairs that, like him, had been retired from his office at the *Journal-Gazette*.

"This can't be happening, Penny, it just can't be happening!" he said, his old eyes wet with tears. His fat, spotted hands trembled. "She's all I've got!"

"Has she got an attorney yet?"

Whitelaw nodded. "She's not going to be released on bail, not on a murder charge, so my lawyer will be there in the morning for her arraignment. I suppose you need a quote for your story."

"Unfortunately, yes. It's probably going to be our lead tomorrow."

Whitelaw sighed again and hung his head, thinking. After a moment he sat up straight and looked me in the eye. "Here it is: 'There is no doubt in my mind that my daughter is innocent. Our family's attorneys will provide a thorough and vigorous defense to see that Earlene Whitelaw is exonerated. She did not and could not commit this crime.' How's that?"

I read it back to him and he nodded.

"Off the record, what do you think happened?" I asked.

Whitelaw arched a bushy eyebrow. "I have no idea. I never liked Eve Dahlgren from the day I met her when Earlene was in high school. That girl was a problem, plain and simple, and I always had a feeling that she would get Earlene in trouble one day. I just knew it."

Yes, but this time, Eve is the one's that's dead, I thought.

Chapter 9: Charisma

Everyone was gone for the day by the time I came out of the morgue. I sighed in relief as I walked back to my desk, holding old bound copies of newspapers in my arms. Studying the dead editions from long ago was going to pay off.

I felt like I could write a story that not only told about the victim and how he died, but also brought back memories of Jubilant Falls as it used to be. That might be the key to spurring someone's memory that would bring about the one clue that solved this crime.

The voicemail light on my phone flashed on and off. Maybe it was the former fire chief, Hiram Warder returning my call and I could finish up the story on the drowned man for tomorrow's paper. I punched in my code. The message began, a man's voice with words I wasn't ready to hear:

"Hi, this is Dr. Leland Huffinger of Fitzgerald University. I'm looking to get in touch with Charisma Prentiss. If she could give me a call, I'd sure appreciate it."

He started to leave a number, but I pounced like Monsieur Le Chat and hit the phone's delete button. I clutched at my chest and sank back into my chair, terrified.

The message was gone. I was safe.

I took a deep breath and unclenched my hands. *It's OK,* I told myself. *Erasing the message wasn't wrong—you're just not ready. If he calls again, just tell him you're not the Charisma Prentiss he's looking for. He'll go away. He'll go look someplace else. Then your secret will still be safe.*

I exhaled, rocking back and forth as I tried to calm myself down. *It's OK. It's OK. It's OK.*

Across the newsroom, the scanner crackled: "Engine 422, rescue 421, ladder 420, 735 East Second Street, two story building, the Jubilant Country Inn bed and breakfast. Flames are visible through the roof and second story. No entrapment—all the guests have been evacuated and accounted for."

I grabbed the camera from my desk drawer and a notebook from beneath the old bound volumes. This is what I needed—breaking news would take my mind off that message. Second Street was two blocks from the J-G. I could get there on foot in five minutes or less.

This is how you ended up in the mess you're in, by avoiding what scares you. I stopped in my tracks. The words rang like an accusatory shot through my mind. I slipped my camera's strap around my neck defiantly.

So what? I fired back mentally. *I've got a fire to cover.*

I slipped out the back pressroom door and dashed through the employee parking lot toward the flashing lights and smoke that I could see two blocks away.

There were three fire trucks and two ambulances on scene by the time I stepped onto the inn's wide front yard. I was breathing heavily and had a stitch in my side. Stopping to catch my breath, I snapped the lens cover off the camera and began taking pictures: A group of people huddled under a tree across the street, two firefighters holding a large hose as the water shot into a flame-filled second-story window, a woman, presumably the owner, pressing her hands to her face in horror as the blaze reflected in the lenses of her glasses.

I pulled out my notebook and began searching for the incident commander, the fireman in charge of the scene. This evening, it was Battalion Chief Jones.

"Looks like it was electrical in nature," he began as I stepped up with my notebook in hand. "It began in the kitchen and spread up through the walls to the second floor and then into the roof. These old Victorians can burn quick."

A few more questions and I had the basic details I needed: The time the first alarm came in, the age of the house, the number of units responding. The inn's wide yard made the chance of the conflagration spreading to the adjoining historic district buildings small, so those residents hadn't been evacuated from their homes.

With my pen, I pointed to the group of people beneath the tree. "Who are they?" I asked.

"Those are the guests who were staying at the bed and breakfast. There were smoke detectors, so everyone got out safely. The Red Cross will be putting them up for the rest of the night at a hotel, but I don't know where they go after that," Jones said. He pointed to the woman. "That's the owner over there, Susan Jepson. I don't know if she'll talk to you or not."

"Thanks." I stepped over the web of fire hoses crisscrossing the ground and headed toward the guests.

"Charisma!"

I turned to see Gary McGinnis striding briskly across the blocked street toward me. His khaki jacket flared open as he walked, exposing his shoulder holster and the badge on his belt.

A tall, bearded man, one of the guests huddled beneath the tree, turned sharply my direction. Feeling the flow of the situation, the adrenaline of getting the story, I ignored it. I had an unusual name, after all.

"What's up, chief?" I asked.

"I'm glad I caught you here. I didn't even try to call you at the paper—I figured you'd be here," he said. "We've got a homicide."

"Shit," I said. I gestured toward the fire scene. "I have to get this story right now. Can I get a couple interviews and then get back to you?"

The chief grimaced. "This is pretty high profile. You guys will want to have it first, before I send a release to the other media."

'Other media' meant our competition, the television stations and newspapers in nearby Collitstown and sometimes, Cincinnati. I'd learned quickly that while in the past, I may have shared stories across different types of media—the new word was "platform"— here in Jubilant Falls, I was back to the old style of journalism where we competed head to head on every story with other out-of-town newspapers and television stations. It was a cardinal sin to have another news organization beat us on a story.

My insides quivered. I'd handled multiple stories at once before, but that had been a long time ago. *What would Addison do or say? What if I couldn't do it? What if I lost my job?*

Behind me, spectators yelled as more flames exploded through the roof.

"Pull back! Pull back!" I heard Jones call through a bullhorn. Without thinking, I yanked my camera back up and started shooting again.

"I can't leave here right now," I said decisively. "This scene is too volatile and I don't think I ought to leave."

"Don't worry—I understand. I'll call Addison," McGinnis said, resting his hand on his service revolver.

He turned and left; as he did, the tall bearded man stepped from the group of guests and extended his hand.

"Charisma Prentiss? I'm Dr. Leland Huffinger. I left a message on your phone earlier today."

I stepped back as if his words were poison, seeing familiarity in his face: It was the man who had done a double take at my appearance at the corner earlier today.

"I'm not who you think I am. My name is Charisma Lemarnier," I said. I flipped a page on my notebook, defensively firing questions at him as I began to write. "Are you a guest here at the Inn?"

"Yes I am."

"When did you notice there was a fire?"

"The smoke detectors went off and the owner, Mrs. Jepson, came upstairs to make sure we evacuated with our belongings. I wanted to ask you about—"

"Did you happen to smell smoke? See any flames?"

"Um, no. Charisma Prentiss was married to the French journalist Jean Paul Lemarnier. A suicide bomber killed him. I think you're his widow, the wire service reporter who no one has seen since a big story she wrote was found to be incorrect."

"That so?" I looked down at my notebook, staring at my hand and willing it not to shake as I wrote. "What brings you to Jubilant Falls?"

"I'm doing research on some of journalism's more well-known falls from grace. Charisma Prentiss's story was the first one I thought of."

Tears welled up in my eyes and I blinked them back. "That so?" I repeated without looking up. In my former life, I would have punched him.

"Yes. I'd like to sit down with you and talk about your experiences sometime."

"Again, Dr. Huffinger, I'm not who you think I am. My husband died in a car crash, along with my parents. I was injured, but I am not, nor have I ever been, who you think I am. Excuse me, I have a story to complete."

I turned on my heel, put on a brave face and walked back toward Mrs. Jepson. Maybe, as her world was crumbling around her, she'd be willing to talk to me.

If I didn't talk to *somebody* about what was going on *now,* I knew I'd see that bomb explode again in my sleep and my world would do the same.

*****

An hour later, the story was done and I was downloading photos from my camera when Addison rushed in.

"Holy shit," she said, sliding into her seat at the copy editing station. A newly extinguished cigarette was between two fingers of her left hand and she smelled of cigarette smoke.

"I saw Gary McGinnis at the fire," I began. "He said there was a homicide?"

"Yeah." Addison slipped the cigarette between her lips without lighting it and fired up her computer. I don't think she heard me. "Of all the people on this earth..."

One of the things I was rapidly learning about my boss was that she truly was a reporter in an editor's body. If she had a chance to go chase a story, she'd take it in a heartbeat.

"I'm really sorry I didn't go after it when he came and got me..."

Addison looked up at me. "What? You think I'm pissed?"

"Well, yeah."

"Good God! You were at the fire! Don't worry about it!" She began scrolling down her computer's screen. Apparently finding what she wanted, Addison lay the cold cigarette down on the desk beside her.

I relaxed. "So what happened with the homicide?"

Before she could answer, my phone rang and I picked up the handset.

"Newsroom, Charisma," I said automatically.

"Miss Prentiss, this is Dr. Huffinger again—"

"Don't call me that!" I screamed into the phone. "Don't call me here ever again! Do you hear me? That person is gone forever!"

Addison stared at me as I slammed the phone down and burst into sobs.

Chapter 10 Leland

I ended the cell phone call and walked back to the Red Cross van, where a grandmotherly volunteer in a red vest was assembling the displaced, checking off names on a clipboard.

Rooms had been secured for us at one of the hotels on the outskirts of Jubilant Falls, she said.

"I need to stay close," I told her. "I'll go ahead and find my own room downtown. I've got a rental car. I'm fine."

She nodded and scratched my name off her list.

I hadn't unpacked a whole lot, so as we rushed to evacuate, it was easy to grab my small suitcase and lap top computer and run outside. After I got outside, I stashed them safely in the car trunk.

The only thing I'd lost was my bathroom stuff: a toothbrush, toothpaste, deodorant and a pair of scissors to trim my beard. It wouldn't be any big deal to find replacements. I hoped it would be as easy to find a room at the Holiday Inn. Staying downtown would enable me to keep an eye on the woman who called herself Charisma Lemarnier.

Despite what she said, I didn't believe Charisma Prentiss was gone forever. I'd found her. I was going to get her to talk to me, whatever it took.

Waving goodbye to Mrs. Jepson, I jumped in my car and headed the sedan toward Main Street. In a few minutes, I had a room at the Holiday Inn, got settled in and was back out in search of toiletries.

Slowing for the light at the center of town, I saw Charisma again. She was jiggling her keys in a door that apparently led to an apartment above some lawyer's office. A fat cat looked down at her from the window above, whipping its tail. The key was apparently not working well: she stomped her foot in frustration, then turned the key again. She lowered her shoulder and pushed hard against the door. As the light turned green, the door popped opened and she stumbled through the entryway. I slowed my car as she stepped inside and closed the door behind her.

I took a quick turn around the next block and came back to park across the street where I could watch unobserved. She'd pulled the curtain closed by the time I'd returned; I could see her silhouette pace slowly back and forth in the flickering blue light of a television. She had a bowl of something in one hand and was spooning the contents into her mouth with the other.

Cereal? Soup? Ice cream? If she was like a lot of other driven, single professionals I knew, it was likely high on calories and low on sustenance. She probably fared better nutritionally while she was embedded with troops, eating the military's MREs—Meals Ready to Eat—that were issued to troops as they slogged through the mountains of Afghanistan's tribal regions.

The image of the hard-charging reporter came back to me. While she was a pro at the fire scene, there was hysteria in her voice on the phone. She had changed—a lot. But why hide? She had tremendous support from the entire country. She could have come back as the poster girl for TBI, started a foundation, something to make a difference. Certainly the Syrian story could be explained as a result of her torn and damaged thought processes. Or was there more?

Should I knock on her door? I wondered. *Or had I scared her back into her shell?* I leaned back in the driver's seat and caught a whiff of smoke mixed with my own body odor. *Probably best that I don't make contact until I've at least bathed,* I reasoned.

I put the car in drive and pulled into traffic.

*****

Wrapped in a plush hotel bathrobe, I flopped on the queen-sized bed after my shower.

Charisma was still on my mind.

Used to be, when you read her byline on a story, it meant something: troop movements through the deserts of the Middle East or Afghanistan, interviews with generals and presidents, movers and shakers on the world stage.

When she flamed out, she flamed out spectacularly.

It was a single story, asserting the Syrian president was preparing to launch missiles into a Jordanian refugee camp reportedly housing anti-government rebels among the displaced women and children. The story was meant to be the one that could finally convince the western world of the administration's evil. It could turn the tide for the rebels, justify their cause and show the world the true tyranny of the Syrian government.

According to her story, it took Charisma two days to connect with that source, and then through another winding series of connections, down dusty Aleppo back alleys of ancient stone, where she finally met with the man who assured her the story was true.

Instead of seeking out a second source, she filed the story. Whether that was her own ego or pressure from above, no one knew. The world's wire services ran with it—and then her editors fired her in the presence of a US State Department employee when the story, now more than just incorrect, but patently false, became the center of a diplomatic crisis.

Her source, variously reported to be a CIA plant, a government sympathizer or any number of other devils, disappeared into the night.

Her fall from grace was news itself: *Prentiss fired after flaws found in Syrian story* was one headline. Another headline read *PTSD behind Prentiss dismissal.* The more sympathetic Sunday morning cable news shows ran entire episodes about the cost on journalists of covering so much trauma day in and day out; others concentrated on her ego and the dangerous risks she took to get her stories.

There were hearings on Capitol Hill and several high-ranking news officials took early retirements or were fired.

After a few other stories (*Does Prentiss have a future in journalism? Prentiss still on medical leave*), and her refusal to surface anywhere, the interest stopped.

If she was ashamed of the failed Syrian story, I certainly could understand. But continuing to hide? How many national stories had been discredited without the reporter going down in flames? Reporters came back from worse without crumbling. National news figures had careers that continued long after the famous or infamous stories they were part of made it to journalism classrooms across the country.

You didn't, a voice inside my head said.

I sighed and picked my wallet up from the bedside table, pulling out a photo of Noah from my wallet. It was the Stanford University president handing him his college diploma.

No, I didn't, I answered. *But my downfall wasn't something I wrote. It was something I did and kept doing until it destroyed my life, marriage and my family.*

*****

From the day Bitch Goddess and I tied the knot in a Philadelphia judge's chambers, drinking was a part of our marriage. From the matching silver flasks we got as wedding presents, to the mid-day martinis and the after-work beers, our alcohol consumption was legendary. On the weekends, our apartment was the center of the party—whatever party was going on. Sports victories or losses, election night celebrations after deadline, it didn't matter: Come one, come all to the Huffinger household where the liquor flowed like water.

Bitch Goddess slowed down her drinking when she learned she was pregnant with Noah, but never stopped completely. By that time, we'd moved to Boston, where I covered city hall and she was the restaurant critic and features writer. Before long, we were in Phoenix, then Dallas and back to Philadelphia, where Bitch Goddess's perfect looks and unflappable style helped her move from the newspaper to morning anchor at one of the television stations so she could be home from work by the time Noah's school day ended.

Somewhere along the line Noah absorbed our alcoholic ethos, but we didn't see the damage it was doing. A suspension in high school for drinking was funny the first time. By the third time, I was pissed—not that he'd done it, but that he couldn't hold his liquor.

"For Christ sake, if you're going to drink, do it right, and don't get caught," I said.

Of course, that was the wrong message to send. Noah did just what I told him: drank more and hid it better, the same thing Bitch Goddess and I did, day after day.

We switched to vodka when our bosses expressed concern. At the time, rehab wasn't anything that was covered by the newspaper's health care. Even if it was, neither one of us wanted to admit we had a problem.

I wasn't a drunk! I was a *newspaperman*! I yelled at my editor. And my wife doesn't have an alcohol problem either! She runs five miles a day, for god sake. No *drunk* could do that!

Then came the winter night celebrating a scoop on some shenanigans at city hall that brought my life as I knew it to an end.

Noah was home for the weekend from his job. We eschewed the Pen and Pencil, the press club where many of Philly's journalists did their drinking and met at another bar downtown. By midnight, Noah was as drunk as I was when he got behind the wheel of my car and we headed home that awful snowy night.

I passed out somewhere along the forty-minute drive home, I came to as I felt the car swerve. Metal moaned as it smashed against a tree; the car rolled into the ditch, followed by Noah's groan, then sickening silence. Teenage girls screamed from their car, stopped after swerving to avoid us. I pushed my way out through the passenger door above my head as the gas tank caught fire and the vehicle, with Noah in it, burned.

Firefighters found me, broken, bloody and sobbing, by the side of the road, screaming Noah's name as the moonlight and the snow fell around me.

Bitch Goddess blamed me, of course. In many ways, she was right. But in many other ways, we were both responsible. Drinking was the way we celebrated, the way we grieved and the way we coped. After his funeral, we welcomed friends into our home with a shot of their choice of liquor on the rocks. Instead of taking time off, we ended our workdays filling glasses with the contents of the crystal decanters that sat on the sideboard in our formal dining room.

But this time, the liquor couldn't mask our pain.

The words between us got nastier. We were Philadelphia's journalistic equivalent of 'Who's Afraid of Virginia Woolf?' In our grief, we said things to each other no couple should: bitter, drunken, eviscerating words that did nothing to alleviate our grief and everything to intensify the guilt. Our friends, embarrassed by our viciousness, fell away and the parties at our apartment slowed, then stopped completely.

Through it all, Bitch Goddess kept running every morning and she kept drinking. I just kept drinking.

By the time we hit bottom, I was sleeping on the couch and she was sleeping with her morning co-anchor. I came home early from work to find them having sex in the shower. She hadn't climaxed like that with me in years.

I grabbed Bitch Goddess by her curly wet hair and pulled her out of the shower. She screamed when I charged inside and with one punch, broke the bastard's nose. The damage kept him off the air for six weeks.

When he filed charges, it hit the local media with a vengeance. I lost my job, then my wife, and my house. Only then did I go to rehab and realized how powerless I was against alcohol.

A buddy who taught at Fitzgerald University let me bunk at his place while I taught night classes in freshman composition and worked on the doctorate. When he became the communications department chair, I became the journalism professor. If any of my students knew Noah's story, they never said anything and I never volunteered.

Only a few ever asked about the camping photo of Noah and me on the bookshelf in my office.

"Is that your son? You guys sure look a lot alike."

"Yes. That's my son. What can I help you with?" Like Bitch Goddess, I lived by the adage "Never apologize, never explain" and as fast as I could, I would change the subject.

As the memories cascaded around me, for a split second, I considered getting dressed and going downstairs to the hotel bar, then stopped. I'd worked too hard to get to this point. I had five bronze sobriety coins—one for each of the years I'd been sober—mixed in with my small change on the hotel room dresser.

What I'd done was wrong, but you could say I'd come back, at least to a point.

Why couldn't Charisma?

Chapter 11 Addison

Earlene stared back in terror from the other side of the jail's Plexiglas visitor's station.

She wasn't the beauty I'd seen at the office. There were no blonde extensions in her hair, no industrial-strength drag queen false eyelashes framing her eyes and only holes in her ears where fancy diamond studs once were. Orange scrubs, white cotton socks and open-toed rubber sandals replaced the Lily Pulitzer summer dress and Jimmy Choo stilettos she'd worn to work.

Without make up she looked like the fifty-something female she really was, wan, tired and terrified, nothing like the high-maintenance blonde that made my life hell.

"I didn't *do* this, Penny!" she hissed into the phone receiver that connected us. "I *didn't* kill Eve Dahlgren! Yes, we argued but I wasn't—"

"Earlene, shush!" I said, sharply. "These conversations are recorded and they will be turned over to the prosecutor to be used against you if they think it's going to help their case, so shut up."

Earlene clutched the receiver with both hands and her eyes widened even more.

"I've got to get out of here! I can't spend the night here!" she cried. The deputy leaning against the wall behind her looked up from the game he was playing on his cell phone.

"That's not going to happen, not on a first-degree murder charge. You're going to have to just suck it up. You can take it for one night not sleeping on Egyptian cotton sheets. You talked to your dad, I assume?"

She nodded frantically.

"He said your lawyer will be here tomorrow for your arraignment. I'm sure your father has managed to engage the best in the business for you. Do what your lawyer tells you, Earlene." I felt like I was giving the queen of Texas divorce courts a lesson on the criminal justice system.

She nodded again.

"You realize that this is going to have to go on tomorrow's front page." Would I have to say this to anybody else? Sometimes I wasn't sure with Earlene.

"I know." She seemed to recover some of her old aplomb and sat up straight. "Just do me a favor and don't use my mug shot. Use the headshot from my column, please? And I suppose you want a quote from me?"

"The last thing I need is your lawyer chewing my ass because he had no idea you were talking to the press. If anything, it's best that he be your spokesperson, not me."

Earlene frowned. "I didn't do this Penny. I don't need any low-life lawyer to say that for me. There were things that people don't know about Eve Dahlgren and I hope somebody like you can dig it up."

I didn't answer. I wasn't going to give the prosecutor, any kind of ammunition, one way or another.

I hung up the receiver on my side of the Plexiglas and waved good-bye. Dealing with her while she was behind bars was not going to be easy, not for her lawyer and not for me. I may not have liked Eve Dahlgren for all her high-school queen bee crap, but I didn't want to see her dead. I didn't like Earlene either, but I couldn't see her railroaded for a murder she didn't commit.

After I got this first story written and up on the web, I'd start looking into what made these two good friends suddenly so toxic.

*****

Charisma was the only one in the newsroom when I got there a few minutes later. Fogged in confusion and shock over Earlene's arrest, I hardly paid attention to her.

"Holy shit," I said half to myself, as I slid into a chair at the copy editing station.

"I saw Gary McGinnis at the fire," Charisma began. "He said there was a homicide?"

"Yeah. Of all the people on this earth…" I hardly listened as she continued to talk, waiting anxiously for my computer to boot up. Maybe I even answered back, I don't know. I couldn't shake Earlene's terrified face, minus the make-up and fancy clothes, behind that bulletproof glass, but still delusional enough about her own self-importance to make certain I got a quote from her for the paper.

"I'm really sorry I didn't go after it when he came and got me…"

I snapped out of my reverie, remembering that Charisma's coverage of the Jubilant Country Inn fire was the reason I was chasing down the Eve Dahlgren homicide.

Before I could tell her what happened, her phone rang.

"Don't call me that!" she screamed into the phone. "Don't call me here ever again! Do you hear me? That person is gone forever!"

Charisma slammed the phone down and sobbed.

"Addison, I am so, so sorry…" she said through her tears. "I didn't mean to be so unprofessional."

I left my computer and pulled up a chair next to her.

"What's up, kiddo? What's going on?"

"They… found… me," she said, through heaving sobs.

"Who found you?"

She was silent for a moment.

"Some private investigator, hired by my late husband's family. They want to sue the car maker."

"And he wants to talk to you about the accident."

Charisma wiped her eyes and nodded.

I reach over and patted her shoulder sympathetically. "You knew this had to happen sometime, especially with your byline in the paper and on the website every day. I told you that when I hired you."

Keeping her PTSD, her unbelievable amount of medication and the Cincinnati neurologist appointments under wraps was difficult, especially in an atmosphere where working together for years built a team I'd never trade. I kept her secret because I wanted somebody else solid on the staff— and because, I wanted, when she was ready, to see her move on to a bigger and better paper. She might not believe she was ready for it, but I could see in the future she would be.

Now, it looks like someone was getting there before she was ready to talk.

"Honestly, I don't know. I had just hoped that I could come here... and heal." She wiped her eyes again and sighed. "I wanted to let people know on *my* own time, when *I* was ready."

"Where did you meet him?"

"He was at the fire tonight. He was staying at the Inn. He heard Gary McGinnis call my name and introduced himself."

"Do you know that's what he really wants?"

"I don't know. The family blamed me for a long time about what happened. There was a lot of bad blood, part of the reason why I left town," she said. "I need to think about what I want to do, whether it would open up a lot of old wounds to talk to him."

"Let me know what you decide to do. You know I'll support whatever decision you make. Meanwhile, we need to get these stories done and up on the website."

I returned to my computer station and began to bang out the story. The first few paragraphs were easy: the arrest, the murder, her father's quote and how Eve and Earlene met in high school and remained friends throughout the years.

But what else did I have to say about Eve? Why was she in town? Where had she been these last several years and what brought her back? Maybe that was what Earlene wanted me to look into.

I ended the story with a simple sentence: "Whitelaw is slated to be arraigned in Common Pleas Court today." What else could I say? I scribbled a Post-It note asking Graham to cover the hearing and walked across the newsroom to stick it on his desk, which backed up to Charisma's.

I looked over the top of the computer at her. She'd stopped crying and was focused on the fire photos splashed across her screen. Not one of them was a bad picture: I'd have a rough time tomorrow morning choosing which one to use for the front page.

What time is Earlene's arraignment? I wondered. *Maybe I ought to call Graham and tell him rather than leaving a note. That way, if he needs to adjust his schedule in any way, he's gotten plenty of notice.*

I punched his home phone number into the phone on his desk. Two rings on his end and a female voice answered.

"Hi, Mom."

"Isabella? What are you doing at Graham's apartment?"

Chapter 12 Leland

"Why do you want to talk to me?"

I'd fallen asleep watching the television when the electronic ring of my cell phone roused me. The moon was full and shone across my hotel bed; an infomercial for women's skin care flickered in the blue light of the TV screen. I didn't even ask who was on the other end of the phone.

"You know why: You're Charisma Prentiss."

"I'm not. And if I were, I wouldn't talk to you without a lot of conditions. Steep conditions."

"That depends on what those conditions are, Charisma." I swung my feet over the side of the bed.

"If I was who you think I am, why would I want someone to tell the world where I was?"

"It wasn't hard to find you. I Googled your name together with Jean Paul Lemarnier, who was working for the same wire service as you the day he was killed—"

"Why do I have to keep telling you I am *not* who you think I am? Even if I was, I don't want to be found!"

"And I'm saying I don't believe you. If I can find you, so can anybody else!"

Charisma disconnected sharply.

I looked over at the digital clock beside the bed. It was nearly four in the morning. *God, did this woman ever sleep?* If she was wrangling with the same guilt and horror I had, probably not nearly enough.

I flicked through my cell phone with my thumb, searching for her number. I found it and called her back.

"Listen, I know what it's like to feel responsible for the death of someone you love. Let's talk."

She was silent for a moment.

"OK," she whispered.

Within minutes, I stood in front of her apartment door. Jubilant Falls' Main Street was empty. The red, yellow and green lights of the traffic light at the corner reflected off the lawyer's office window beneath her apartment.

I knocked and a light appeared in the stairwell. I heard footsteps come down the steps; the door jerked open and Charisma Prentiss stood in front of me.

She wasn't wearing the make-up I'd seen on her face at the corner or at the fire. There were pockmarks on her face and dark circles beneath her brown eyes. She didn't look like the confident professional I'd seen just a couple hours ago when the inn burned. She was haggard, worn and trembling. She ran one hand through her hair as she reached with the other to shake my hand; puckered scars ran along her scalp and down her neck.

"You OK?"

She sighed. "Hot spots developed at the inn after I left. I had to go back when they sent two engines. The place is completely destroyed now."

"It was hard for you to cover, wasn't it?"

"Not that anyone could tell."

She motioned for me to come inside and I followed her up the stairs. The collar on her summer blouse slipped between her shoulder blades exposing larger, jagged scars as she clutched the stair rails on either side of the faded blue wall.

Once inside her studio apartment, she silently motioned for me to sit down on the couch. She reached inside the half-size fridge, pulled out a soda and offered it to me.

I shook my head as I took a seat. "So why did you call me?"

Charisma popped the can open and took a sip. "I wasn't going to until I came back from the fire the second time."

We were silent. Charisma took another sip from the soda can; her hands shook like a heroin addict in need of a fix.

"When the inn walls collapsed, I'll bet you flashed back," I prodded. "I'll bet when that happens, you go back to those places where you faced the most danger, don't you? Most times it's Baghdad, sometimes it's Aleppo, sometimes, it's Damascus, isn't it?"

She shook her head. "No."

I kept on.

"This time, wherever you found yourself—the tribal regions of Afghanistan, one of the markets in Baghdad, wherever your mind took you—it was all you could do to keep from diving under the nearest fire engine."

"No!" She glared at me.

"The PTSD won't leave you alone, will it? It's hard sometimes for you to cover it up, to not let people see, but you still struggle. The day that bomb went off in Baghdad—"

"Shut up, goddammit, shut up!" she screamed. I ducked as the soda can hit the wall above my head, splattering fizzy brown liquid.

"Admit it. You're *the* Charisma Prentiss. I just want to know how you ended up here, in some dump called Jubilant Falls, Ohio, writing for a third-class paper like the *Journal-Gazette.*"

"It's not a third-class paper."

"C'mon! What's the circulation? Ten thousand, tops? Truth is, it's not the wire service and you're not at the top of your game anymore."

She sighed. "I'm here because I wondered if I could ever do this job again and Jubilant Falls seemed like a good place to hide from my in-law's family."

"I understand wanting to hide, but that's the story you hide behind. It won't work with me."

"Do you?"

"Yes, I do."

Charisma leaned back against the dinette chair and sighed. The fat cat I'd seen in the window earlier came out from behind the couch and rubbed against her leg. Charisma scratched its head as she spoke.

"Nobody, not even my boss knows the truth about who I am, not the people I work with, nobody. Some folks are starting to ask questions, saying they think I look like someone they know, but I'm not ready to tell anybody anything. I wasn't when you left that first message on my phone."

"Are you admitting to being Charisma Prentiss?" I asked. I turned to wipe the soda-spattered couch cushions.

She dipped a shoulder as if to acknowledge her real identity. "What do you want to know?"

"I want to know about your injury, your recovery, about Jean Paul, and how you ended up here."

"If I am who you think I am, you can't reveal where I am. If I need to disappear again, I will."

"Again, I can't do that. If I found you, someone else could, too."

"Then no, I'm not. I'm a widow who happens to have a well-known name. My husband and my parents died in a car crash in Connecticut."

"Give me the date and the location."

She opened her mouth and closed it.

"I didn't think you could. Here's what I'm looking for: Charisma Prentiss was going to be part of a series of interviews with others who are no longer in the news business because of big stories or events that..." I started to say, "blew up in their faces," but glancing at her scars, I reconsidered. "... Fell apart spectacularly. It would be part of an article."

"And that public implosion was the first one you thought about." Her words were flat.

"So you are Charisma Prentiss."

"No."

"You had to have known—"

"*If* I was the Charisma Prentiss you think I am—"

"OK, somehow, the real Charisma Prentiss would have known about all the attention surrounding her injuries and her recovery. The real Charisma Prentiss was too much of a risk-taker and had too big an ego to not want to be in the spotlight again. That's why she went to Syria to get that story."

Charisma shot me a harsh, sidelong glance. She reached down and picked up the cat, scratching it behind the ears. I sensed her emotion building as the cat, irritated at the attention, jumped from her lap. Charisma stood and walked to the window, sweeping the curtain open and staring down at the street.

I followed and stood next to her, watching as the sun began to peek over the horizon and the traffic begin to build in the street below.

She leaned her forehead against the cold glass and began to sob, tears rolling down her cheeks.

"I just want to be able to do what I used to do," she wailed. "I want to be the person I used to be. I don't know if that's ever going to happen again."

I put my hand on her shoulder and without thinking, drew her toward me.

"I know, I know, I know," I whispered into the top of her head.

Charisma clutched my back as she buried her face in my shirt, sobs racking her body. She still smelled like smoke from the fire, but there was a lavender scent I suddenly wanted to find the source of. Her breasts were firm and pressed against my chest; I could feel her short legs against mine.

How long had it been since I'd held a woman in my arms? Entirely too long, apparently. I felt an unprofessional stirring and released her before it turned into a full-blown embarrassment.

She looked up at me and wiped her big, brown eyes. "I didn't want you to see me cry. I'm sorry."

I wanted to take her face in my hands and kiss the scar from its beginning along her temple, down past her ear and into the space I'd glimpsed between her shoulder and collarbone. Instead, I took her hands in mine and stepped back.

"I've been where you are. I was at the top of my game, just like you were, when my personal life imploded and took my career with it," I said. "Remember I said I know what it's like to feel responsible for the death of someone you love?"

"What happened?" Charisma didn't take her hands from mine. My heart skipped a beat.

"I'm an alcoholic. I was married to an alcoholic who was also in the news business and together, we raised a son who probably had a drinking problem."

"Had?"

"Noah and I were coming home drunk from a bar one night. The car hit a tree and he was killed. Noah was driving. My marriage fell apart and I lost my job. I was with the *Philadelphia Inquirer* when it all happened. I was pretty well *persona non grata* there until a friend got me a job teaching journalism." My voice was hoarse.

"I'm sorry, Dr. Huffinger."

"Please. Call me Leland."

"Leland," she whispered. "I'm so sorry you lost your son."

It had been years since my name had been spoken so softly. Perhaps she understood my pain, no doubt she understood my loss, but after more than five years of poisonous invective from the Bitch Goddess, I never thought I'd hear a woman speak so tenderly again. Water crested in my eyes and I turned my face away. Charisma pulled her hand from mine to reach up and wipe away the single tear, but I was quicker. I couldn't let her touch me—not like that, if at all.

I let go of her other hand and stepped back, hoping to recover my professional demeanor and hide my pain. No one, outside of my fellow alcoholics at AA meetings knew my story. What made me reveal it to her?

"So how do you want to do this?" I asked, clearing my throat. "I'd like to talk to you more extensively, maybe shadow you at work?"

"I haven't admitted that I'm the person you think I am."

"Come on! Yes, you are! I can see the resemblance in your face. It's a little different through the cheekbones, but it's still you, Charisma Prentiss! What if I came in and talked to your boss?"

"No you *can't*. I suffered a lot of facial trauma in the accident. Doctors had to rebuild nose and my cheekbones."

"There's video from every major news outlet of your surgeons talking about what they had to do to fix your face. I'll bet I could take your photo back to them and they'd identify you."

"I'd still deny it. I'd say they were wrong."

"You're fighting an uphill battle. Just say you're Charisma Prentiss. Admit it and let me interview you. Let me talk to the folks you work with."

"You show up in the newsroom and start asking questions and I disappear, for good. You can take the blame for it."

"What if I agree to your conditions? What would those conditions be?"

She chewed her lip thoughtfully.

"OK, here's the deal: I'm working on a couple stories about some unsolved murders. The police have formed a task force and they're hoping my stories will spark some clues. You can come with me while I'm working outside of the newsroom and we can talk then. But that doesn't mean you have any input on these stories while I'm working on them. When you publish your article, you still can't tell anyone where I am."

"So you are admitting you're *the* Charisma Prentiss?"

"I'm admitting it to you. You say anything to anyone else—anybody I work with, anybody I know or even come in contact with—and this whole thing is off."

I'd found her.

I nodded in agreement. Awkward silence hung in the air between us, as if something else needed to be said. Was I just overreacting to her body against mine? Her soft words of comfort touched a part of me I'd long buried. Did she want to say something else? What was it? *Leland, would you have coffee with me? Dinner?* I would if she asked, but I wasn't going to scare her off by asking first—not yet. Or was I the one who was scared? *Keep it professional. Just because you think you felt something doesn't mean she did. What woman would want a man who'd killed his own son, even accidentally?*

I started to head for the door.

"Well, you have my cell number. Just give me a call and I can be ready whenever you want me to go with you." My hand trembled as I handed it to her.

By the time I got out the door and back to the street the sun was up. For the first time in five years, I needed a drink.

Chapter 13 Charisma

"Everyone, I need you to come into my office."

It was Tuesday morning, just before we got going on that morning's edition. Addison stood in the center of the newsroom, a coffee cup in one hand, her cigarettes and lighter in the other. There was pain in her eyes.

"What do you think it's about?" Marcus Henning asked me as we filed into her office.

I shrugged. "I don't know. Addison was covering a homicide last night. I was here last night covering the fire, but I left before she did, so I don't know any of the details."

My thoughts centered more on why I said I'd let Dr. Huffinger shadow me.

Watching the inn walls collapse early that morning sent me again to that awful Baghdad roadside, but I wasn't going to admit that to anyone. Back in the newsroom a couple hours later, I was thankful for the solitude as I sat at my desk, rocking back and forth until I was able to update the earlier fire story. After I finished, I tried not to appear intoxicated as I staggered home to my little apartment.

So what made me call him as soon as I got up the stairs?

Graham Kinnon shot a look sideways at me as we each found a place to sit. "It was a big one," he said. "The arraignment is at eight, so I hope this doesn't take long."

Pat and Dennis were the last folks into Addison's office. Pat had two cameras hanging around his neck as he closed the door behind him.

What made me call Leland Huffinger? That wasn't part of my plan at all. I groaned as I settled into my chair. Nobody was supposed to find me. I was going to stay here until I was stronger, until I could step out and let the world know I was back on my own terms.

But he'd found me—and easily. How ludicrous was it that I even thought I could disappear, especially when I was still in the news business?

And *what* happened when I started to cry? Of all the stupid, girly things...

He'd touched my shoulder and then what? Did he draw me into his arms or had I pulled him into mine? I don't remember, but it wasn't the feeling I had when Jean Paul held me, that feeling of first all-encompassing passion, the one great love that was supposed to last a lifetime and then didn't.

This was different, warm and safe, with my head on his chest and his arms around me. I hadn't felt like that for over two years. Was this what safe harbor felt like? Or was I simply so tortured that I welcomed the first man to put his arms around me?

Then, without thinking, as Leland spoke about his son's death, and that single tear began to roll down his face, I'd reached up to wipe it away. How inappropriate was *that*? Thank god he'd reacted the way he did, saving face for both of us.

Addison cleared her throat. Tapping the end of her cigarette on her desk to pack in the tobacco, she began to speak.

I shook my head to clear my thoughts. *Focus,* I said to myself.

Focus.

"Last night, as some of you know, there was a homicide in Jubilant Falls. The body of a woman, Eve Dahlgren, was found stabbed in her vehicle at Shanahan Park. Eve is a native of Jubilant Falls who had just returned home, for what reason I don't know." Addison stopped and flicked her lighter a couple times, staring intently at the dancing flame. "Earlene has been arrested for the murder."

Leland Huffinger was no longer the center of my thoughts as everyone, except Graham, gasped with a collective *"What?"*

"The goofball with all the bad ideas actually killed somebody?" Dennis asked. He took on the tone of a silly teenage girl. "OMG, ya'll! She would have, like, broken a nail or messed her hair up or something!"

Addison held up her hand for silence.

"Apparently, Earlene and Eve were out together this weekend. Earlene told me they argued that night and I stupidly told Gary." Addison continued. "Police also have Earlene's fingerprints on the steering wheel of Eve's Lincoln. Graham and Pat will be covering her arraignment this morning."

"What happens next?" Dennis asked. "Who's acting as publisher while she's in jail?"

"I don't know. Watt could come in while Earlene is in jail, but that's just conjecture on my part. He asked me to go downstairs and round up the rest of the staff and make the announcement to them. But before I do, here are the ground rules: Nobody is to speak to any other media about this case. Only Watt or Earlene's lawyer are authorized to say *anything* about the case. We can't tolerate any speculation or anybody's comments showing up anyplace, not in another newspaper, not on somebody's B roll on the six o'clock news. I don't want the prosecutor or anybody's lawyer screaming about us poisoning the jury pool or having either Earlene or her father coming in here pissed about something someone on the staff said. Am I clear?"

"Do you think that will be a problem?" Marcus Henning asked.

"I'll bet you a dollar to a donut that every one of you will be approached by some out-of-town media. This will be huge news when it hits and we're going to be in the center of it. You all keep your mouths *shut.*"

We all nodded somberly.

"We need to keep going, just like any other day. We keep doing a good job covering the news. And this story gets covered like any other—fair and impartially and without any kind of editorial commentary, however innocuous you may think it is. Graham, I need you to stay on anything that happens in court on this. I have a few things I need to look into on this story, so while I'm not here, Dennis is in charge, as always. Charisma, I'll still need you to keep covering the night police calls. Marcus, you continue on as usual."

"You want me to keep going on those unsolved murders we talked about last week?" I asked.

"Absolutely. Where are you on that?"

"I'm interviewing the old fire chief, Hiram Warder, this afternoon on the first murder. There's also an old house that looks like it could have been there at the time of the murder. I'm going to see if anybody who lives there remembers anything. I should be able to have it for you for tomorrow's edition."

Addison nodded. "You've got the fire story, I've got the Eve Dahlgren murder and what else do we have for page one?" She looked pointedly at Graham.

"I have that story on the Jessop woman who sued the county commissioners," he said. "The suit was thrown out after the jury couldn't agree if the commissioners terminated her unfairly or not. I wrote it after I got home last night and then e-mailed it to myself here at work, so it's done."

She nodded tersely. "OK. I'm going to head downstairs now and talk to the other staff. Let's do this, people. We got a newspaper to put out."

Everyone returned to the newsroom to begin building today's edition. Addison, looking somber and with her coffee in hand, headed downstairs toward the advertising and business offices. The newspaper didn't open until nine—nearly an hour from now—so Addison had time to break the news before the public came through the door. Graham, with Pat Robinette behind him, en route to the courthouse and Earlene's arraignment, followed behind her.

I sat down at my desk and turned on the computer. It came to life at the same time Marcus and Dennis's computers did, the three of them chiming in a disembodied electronic chorus.

I didn't have a whole lot to do that morning, just check in with the fire chief to see if they had a total on the damages, then check in with the Red Cross on where the former guests were housed and add that to my story.

But I was nowhere close to making that phone call.

I couldn't have Dr. Huffinger following me around, not now; especially since there would be a good chance someone else might be dogging the staff about Earlene's murder charge.

How long would it be before those reporters would start looking at me and asking questions about who I was? Could I keep my true identity hidden? Even more important, could I hold up under the stress?

I made him a promise that needed to be broken.

Dennis walked over to the television that sat on a wall shelf next to the police scanner and switched it on to catch the local morning news. The picture came into focus: it was a TV reporter standing in front of the *Journal-Gazette*, near the front door's brass name plate.

"The publisher of an area newspaper is behind bars this morning, slated to be arraigned shortly on murder charges..." A sandy-haired, pie-faced young man looked straight into the camera, glancing down occasionally at his notes. Remote trucks from other stations could be seen in the background of his shot.

"Here we go," Dennis said. "Let the onslaught begin." He shook his head and returned to the copy desk as the pie-faced boy continued to talk and we headed for the center of a media maelstrom.

OK, this whole thing with Huffinger is definitely off, if reporters are already lining up outside the door, I thought to myself. I dialed Leland's cell phone number.

"Good morning," he said, gently. "Get any sleep after I left?"

I ignored the too-familiar tone. "Listen, what we talked about last night, it's off."

"Off? Why?" The soft words were gone.

I turned to face the wall so no one could hear me. "Because the publisher here got picked up on murder charges and there's reporters crawling all over this place, looking for whatever they can find," I whispered. "They'll figure out who I am."

"Murder charges? You've got to be kidding me. I've been through a lot of bizarre things in my career but no publisher I've ever worked with—"

"Yeah, yeah, yeah. I can't talk about it right now—I'm on deadline."

"But you said last night—"

"Forget what I said last night. I was tired and stressed from the fire. I shouldn't have promised you anything." I disconnected the call as I caught a glimpse of Dennis walking toward me with a stack of papers. Quickly, I dialed the fire department to derail whatever conversation he might start.

"Hi, Chief, it's me Charisma Lemarnier. I'm looking for a damage total on the fire at the Jubilant Country Inn," I said. Dennis didn't need to know I was talking to a busy signal as I took the stack of news briefs from him. "Uh huh. Sure. I'll call you back."

My other line began to ring as he walked away. It was Leland.

"You can't do this to me! I came all the way from Philadelphia to talk to you!" he said.

"That's your problem." I hung up.

Dennis and Marcus stared at me.

"What was that about?" Marcus asked.

I shrugged. "Man problems."

"We didn't know you were dating anybody!" Dennis leered. He was single, but apparently had been dating Jane, the secretary down in advertising, for some time. While everyone else in the newsroom seemed to be content living out of each other's pockets, easily sharing the daily details of their lives, I couldn't—and wouldn't—do that.

I heard all about Marcus's wife and their three adult kids, Andrew, an air force pilot, Lillian, a new mother living with her stockbroker husband in New York City, and PJ, a senior journalism major at Ohio University. I knew all about Addison's farmer husband and their daughter Isabella, Dennis's dates with Jane and Graham's baby daughter. I knew Pat's wife Dorothy was close to retiring from teaching and after he retired from the paper, they planned to buy an RV and see all the national parks. When I was here at night, I listened to sports writer Chris Royal sweet talk his girlfriend Amy on his cell phone as he waited on wire copy.

They knew I was widowed. They knew I'd been injured. They didn't need to know more.

How could I tell them on the eve of our second anniversary we'd argued and the next day, he was dead? How could I bring that up without depressing everyone in the room? Only Graham Kinnon seemed to understand why I never talked about it.

"I'm *not* dating *anyone*." I said sharply to Dennis and turned back to my phone. I punched in the fire department number again, this time getting through. "Hi, Chief, it's Charisma..."

The call was short—the chief had my numbers for me, which I plugged into the story. With another phone call to the Red Cross, I checked to see how many guests had taken the offer for a free night in the hotel and the story was done. With a few more computer strokes, I sent the story over to Dennis.

"I'm going out to grab some coffee and breakfast. I'll be back in about half an hour."

"Be careful." Dennis pointed toward the television. "The vultures may still be out there."

I slipped down the stairs and into the newspaper's front lobby. Jane's desk was empty; the meeting with Addison was apparently still going on. Outside, the pie-faced boy reporter had his back to the front door, talking to two other reporters in front of the paper's plate glass window. Maybe it was better if I left by the employee entrance near the pressroom, then walked through the employee parking lot and taking the long way around the block to Aunt Bea's, the downtown diner just a few doors from my apartment.

The pressroom, normally a hub of activity, was silent as well. They must be in on the meeting about Earlene's arrest, too. I tried to be quiet as I slipped out the door, but the heavy metal door slammed.

"Hey! Look! There's someone coming out the door!" The three reporters and their cameramen came around the corner of the building. Instinctively, I turned to run.

A man's long thin arm grabbed me by my shoulders. I screamed as I was whirled around.

It was Leland, drawing me into an embrace as the reporters circled us, firing off questions.

"What do you know about Earlene Whitelaw's arrest?"

"Are you an employee here? What has the administration told you about the murder?"

"Has the newspaper taken any official position on the publisher's arrest?"

Fear bubbled up inside me—I wanted to scratch my way out of Leland's tight embrace, to scream, to run, to hide.

"Ssshhh. Just go with me on this," he whispered into my hair. He lifted his head and glared at the reporters. "Do you mind? My sister and I have just lost our mother and she was here to place the obituary."

"Then why didn't you come out the front door?" The pie-face boy asked.

"Because the staff inside knew you goons would do this. Give us a little private time, will ya?"

I buried my face in his chest, hoping my tremors passed for a daughter's grief.

"We didn't mean to intrude," a female reporter said. "We're sorry for your loss."

The group turned and walked back to the front of the building. When they turned the corner, Leland released me. I felt a surprising twinge of regret that his arms no longer encircled me.

"You OK?" he asked.

"Yes, thank you," I whispered. I stepped back and brushed my hair from my eyes. "What were you doing back here?"

"After you hung up on me, I walked over here, hoping I could talk to you. I saw the group at the door and figured there was no likelihood of you coming out the front door. I took a chance and walked back here, just as you opened the door."

"Well, you were right." I twisted my hands together and sighed. "I was heading over to the diner for a cup of coffee. I guess I owe you one, now, huh?"

"Then lets go get one." Leland smiled.

I looked into his blue eyes and nodded.

Chapter 14 Addison

After speaking with the remainder of the newspaper staff, I returned to my office to finish up today's edition.

The meeting with advertising went as expected. Until Watt came in to lead the show, if he did, I put the senior-most ad salesperson in charge and cautioned them as well about speaking to anyone about the case. The hostility against Earlene was more palpable in advertising; it took more work to convince them to keep their mouths shut.

Graham had returned from Earlene's arraignment by the time I got up the stairs; as expected, she pleaded not guilty, but was not granted bail.

I had a few minutes to looks through the clip files in the back of the newsroom to get some more information on Eve to add to our too-thin story, but what we had ended in the mid-1990s, about twenty years ago.

Charisma's fire story was done; Dennis said she'd stepped out for some breakfast.

I looked over Dennis's shoulder to see how he'd placed the story on the page; the six-column headline screamed *Publisher charged in woman's death* across the top of the page. Despite admonitions to the contrary, Pat shot a two-column photo of Earlene in court, wearing orange jail scrubs, standing next to her lawyer and we were going to use it.

"Is her lawyer going to scream about that placement?" he asked.

Big metro newspapers didn't worry about this crap, why should I? I thought to myself. *We've hung smaller fish from higher heights on stories like this.* But that was the concern of smaller newspapers and I knew it. The editor of a big metro wasn't likely to have to deal with someone who was related to the person in my lead story, somebody who wouldn't think twice about pigeon-holing me about the story—loudly—at Tuesday's Rotary Club's luncheon. I had people who to this day hated my guts for stories I'd done years ago.

I sighed.

"She'll scream about it, no doubt. If her lawyer doesn't like it, her dad definitely won't," I said, chewing on my thumbnail. "We're going to take heat no matter what we do. We play it down low on the page and the phone calls start coming in about how we are minimizing the story. If it's placed like we do any other homicide, no one can say anything."

"The fire at the Inn is just as significant," he said. With a few clicks of the mouse, the murder story was moved to two columns in the upper right hand corner of the page and Charisma's story, along with one of her photos, occupied four columns on the left side. "We can run Graham's trial story across the bottom."

I shrugged. "No. Run the murder big. I'll take the heat from Watt and his lawyer." I patted him on the shoulder and returned to my office. I needed to do some thinking about why Eve Dahlgren died.

Why *would* somebody want Eve Dahlgren dead? And why hang Earlene for it? Where would I start to look? So many folks from high school had moved on; it could be difficult to locate them. Maybe Suzanne Porter would have some ideas.

Suzanne and I had been best friends since grade school. While I went off to college, she went to cosmetology school. When I came back to work as a reporter at the J-G, I'd fixed her up with another new reporter, John Porter.

They'd married and despite some tough times, were still together, along with their five boys. Several years ago, I was forced to fire Porter, the cops and courts reporter, before Graham Kinnon took the job. Like a lot of skunks, John managed to come up smelling like a rose and now worked as the vice president of communications at the Japanese auto parts plant at the edge of town.

As a cosmetologist, Suzanne was as good a source as I could get. Men told their bartender everything—women did the same with their beauticians. I'll bet she knew someone who could tell me a lot about what Eve Dahlgren had been doing all these years.

A desktop picture of Suzanne and her family from a long-ago Christmas stared back at me as I waited for her to pick up the phone.

"Well, sure I remember Eve! She's dead? Oh my God!" she said after I explained what I was after. "Hate to say it, but wasn't she a bit of a witch in high school? I'm trying to think who I know who would still be in touch with her or know what she's been up to all this time. Come on over for lunch and I'll see who I can round up for you to talk to."

"Sounds good. See you then." I hung up and headed back to the newsroom where everyone was winding up today's stories. Dennis had the front page done; he printed out a proof and, after scanning it for errors, I gave it my approval. Within an hour, I had a copy of today's paper in my hand, the tart smell of wet ink filling my nostrils. I searched for a notebook among the stack of crap on the copy editing station.

"Time for me to get out of here. I've got some things I need to look into. Yea verily, thou art in charge," I said, making the sign of the cross with my hand over Dennis like a consecrating priest. "I've got some things to check into on this story. I'll be back later this afternoon."

On my way downstairs, I dialed Gary McGinnis's cell phone.

"Who did Eve Dahlgren run around with in high school?" I asked when he picked up.

"You mean after she dumped me?" Gary asked.

"You forget she left the dance with my date, too," I answered.

"Does it matter now?"

"Gary, as much as I disliked Eve Dahlgren, I dislike my boss even more. But I can't believe that Earlene killed anybody."

"Like I told you, this one is pretty cut and dried, Penny," he said. "We've got Earlene's fingerprints in the car and they're fresh. We believe she killed Eve, drove her car to the park and left it there with the body in it."

I sighed. "I'm going to disagree with you on this one, Gary. I don't think she did it."

"I know you too well, Penny. I know you're going to dig into this and I'm not going to try to stop you, but you're wasting your time."

"I don't think so Gary. I really don't think so." I ended the conversation and slid into my Taurus. Hopefully, Suzanne would have something worthwhile for me.

When I arrived, she had three servings of spinach salad with grilled chicken, strawberries and sliced almonds on the table. The salads looked photo-perfect on her collection of pink Depression glass, with strawberry ice tea in matching pink goblets.

Making an edible meal was hard enough for me—making it pretty was impossible.

In a few minutes, there was a knock at the door.

"That's Angela Perry," Suzanne said, handing me the dishtowel she had just dried her hands with. "She's the only one of those ten cheerleaders still in town. I do her hair and her boys were in Scouts with my youngest."

The girl who had been the tiny top of the cheerleading pyramid had gray streaks in her curly red hair, but was still petite.

"Penny Addison! So good to see you again!" she said as we all slipped into our seats. "Suzanne told me about Eve Dahlgren. Frankly, as difficult as she was in high school, I'm not surprised it happened."

"Why is that?"

"Oh, she had a temper. The rest of the school never saw it in public—she wanted everyone to think she was always so perfect," Angela began. "But she really had a nasty side as I'm sure you remember, Penny."

I laid my fork down and began to take notes.

Angela continued to talk as she cut up her chicken. "Because she was the head cheerleader, it was like she thought she was the queen of the school or something. We were supposed to defer to her, and do everything she asked. She dictated who we were allowed to run around with and if she saw us with somebody she didn't approve of, she'd run to the cheer advisor—what was her name, Suzanne?"

"Mrs. McKnight." Suzanne rolled her eyes.

"Yes—Pearl McKnight," Angela continued. "Anyway, Eve would make up these stories that she'd seen us smoking beneath the bleachers or whatever and we'd end up begging Mrs. McKnight to not suspend us from the squad, that it was all a lie... For some reason, she always believed Eve."

"Did you ever see any violent behavior?"

Angela took a bite of her salad and nodded emphatically. "Oh, god yes!" she said through her food. "Eve was fabulously athletic, more than most of the rest of us. Her strength was unbelievable. If she didn't like how you did in practice, she'd punch you in the arm as we walked off the football field. 'Lousy flip there, Angela!' she'd say, and *pow!* Somewhere where nobody could see her hit you, you know? And if you stood up to her, she let you have it. She could just rip you to shreds— physically and verbally. I've never seen anyone with a temper like that in my entire life. I was never so happy to learn she transferred to that girl's school in Columbus after the tornado."

"Did you ever tell Mrs. McKnight what she did?"

"Why? Eve had her convinced we all loved her and hung on her every word. I had bruises up and down my arms all through football season that year, but I told everybody they were from falling. Besides, after the tornado, we were all going to school in the next county and it was like all the cliques were destroyed along with the school. We could be friends with whomever we wanted and it was wonderful. The rest of the cheerleaders and I all felt like we'd been released from some evil cult when she left."

"Did you stay in touch with her after high school?"

Angela rolled her eyes. "My mother, thinking we were friends, gave her my address and phone at college. She called me at my dorm once and I told her I didn't want to ever speak to her again. Other girls heard from her though, I remember, but it's been so long that I couldn't tell you who."

"Do you remember what they told you?"

"Eve got a business degree and she would go into these companies, con whoever was in charge that she could help them cut costs and operate more efficiently and then slash the staff to the bone."

"That's no surprise. Every company today is doing that," I said.

"Yes, but I heard she really took entirely too much pleasure in ripping people up professionally before she cut their jobs. People were emotionally shredded by the time she was through with them. I'm surprised somebody didn't kill her before this."

"Did she ever get married? Do you know?"

"Not that I know. I never heard of her even dating anybody after Jimmy Lyle died."

Suzanne looked across the table at me and arched an eyebrow.

"Yeah," she said slowly. For years, Suzanne listened to me as I tried to rationalize that the boy's death was anything but the result of a natural disaster. "Poor Jimmy Lyle—killed in the tornado."

Angela took the bait. "I know! That was one of the weirdest things, that post-hole digger through his chest. But I guess there were a lot of weird things that happened when the tornado hit."

I stopped writing. "Did you ever wonder about Jimmy? Whether he really died in the tornado or if somebody killed him?"

Angela put her fork down and swallowed hard. Her words were a whisper. "Tell me I'm not the only one who had those thoughts."

"Are you saying you think Eve put the posthole digger through Jimmy's chest?"

"I've always thought his death was bizarre. I mean, could those high winds from the tornado pick up a piece of equipment that heavy and put it through him? And who could prove it wasn't the tornado?"

"I saw cars thrown through store windows downtown," I said. "The junior high collapsed and you know the damage that happened at the high school. There were houses in our neighborhood reduced to piles of sticks. Theoretically, anything could have happened. With all the other deaths and injuries at the time, it sure would have been easy to blame his death on the tornado."

"Eve hated you, Penny, for tutoring Jimmy on that English project. Can you believe I remember it, all these years later? We all knew she was crazy, but she went absolutely nuts when your name came up."

"She didn't make it easy for me to help the poor dumb kid out, I'll admit that," I said. I wasn't going to share how Jimmy Lyle haunted my dreams, even all these years later.

"You all may think I'm nuts for saying this," Angela said slowly. "But I think Eve Dahlgren was crazy enough to do it back then. You don't seriously think her parents moved her to another school just out of fear of another tornado, do you?"

*****

Back in the newsroom, I had one more thing to do before I could get back to figuring out who would want to kill Eve Dahlgren. From what I'd learned at lunch, there could be no limit to the suspects.

A note from Charisma told me she was about to put the finishing touches on the first cold case story. She'd interviewed the former fire chief Hiram Warder and Police Chief Marvin McGinnis and was working with Pat Robinette to choose photos to go with her words, but was out hoping to interview one more person. There was nothing to identify who she meant, if anybody.

Dennis was on the phone with someone and Graham was leaning back toward Marcus's desk, showing him the baby pictures on his phone.

"Graham, can I see you for a moment?" I asked.

"Sure." He slipped the cell phone into his shirt pocket and followed me into my office and closed the door. "Is there a problem?"

"I don't know. You tell me."

"Huh?"

"I have to say I was really shocked to have my daughter answer your phone last night."

Graham colored to the roots of his sandy hair. "Is that a problem? I anticipated a verdict on the Jessop trial before I left that day, but then they decided to keep deliberating. I had to pick up Gwennie and then find another sitter. I called you to ask how you wanted me to handle it, but you were already gone, so your daughter volunteered to watch my daughter. Did I do something wrong?"

"No," I said. "I want to make certain everything is OK with you and if you need any other help."

How times have changed, I thought to myself. When I started in this business, I would have gotten reamed and even been fired for worrying about my childcare arrangements over a story. It was most of the reason why Duncan ended up raising our daughter.

Graham sighed. "It hasn't been easy since Elizabeth died."

Elizabeth Day had been a reporter with the J-G for a number of years, covering the schools, the college and writing features for me until she left for the *Akron Beacon-Journal*. I didn't know at the time she was pregnant, much less that she and Graham were dating. They married soon after her departure, but she died from an aneurysm while giving birth to their daughter. Graham, once the ace crime reporter I could count on to cover anything at any time, became tied to a schedule dominated by his daycare center.

I wanted the edgy, risk-taking Graham Kinnon back, but knew time, and life, marched on. At least I had Charisma, who, despite her emotional scars, did a fine job.

How did I end up with two relatively young reporters who are also widowed? I wondered.

"I know. Just keep me in the loop if you're having problems," I said.

"Isabella said she'd babysit for me anytime I needed—if that's OK with you."

I nodded. "That's fine."

Graham stepped back into the newsroom and my thoughts returned to Eve Dahlgren. Her mother still lived in a farmhouse outside of town.

How old would she be? In her eighties, maybe? I thought. *How willing would she be to talk about her daughter, particularly now that she was dead?*

As painful as it was going to be, I had to ask.

Chapter 15 Charisma

I'm nuts for doing this, I thought to myself as Leland and I walked toward Jubilant Falls' only downtown diner, Aunt Bea's. Even though he was some twenty years my senior, I couldn't help but stare into those ice-blue eyes that never seemed to lose their sadness.

He told me about his days as a journalist, covering city hall at big metros across the country—Philadelphia, Boston, Dallas, Phoenix—making scouring the halls of city government sound exciting. Like me, he understood the love of the chase that was part of a journalist's DNA. Like every excellent reporter, he could zero in on the essence of a story with the magic of his words. I found myself absorbed in them, in the sound and the rhythm of each one.

Noah was a big part of what he talked about and it was only then Leland's sky-blue eyes sparkled. He talked about their love of camping and hiking, how they'd spent one final weekend in the woods as a family, shooting photos of the wildlife they saw. He mentioned his ex-wife only occasionally and never by name.

It was hard to resist the attraction of a man whose first intention was to expose my secret to the world. I had to remember that, even as I felt a stirring inside I swore would never come again.

"Enough about me," he said as he opened the door to Aunt Bea's diner. "Tell me about you."

I shrugged.

"My dad was a foreign correspondent with Reuters, when he met my mother. She was with Reuters, too. So you could say, I got the bug early—or I was born with it. We lived all over Europe before Communism fell and he settled into a bureau chief's job in Washington D.C."

"Is that how you ended up majoring in communications at the University of Maryland?"

I shot him a sharp look. "You've done your homework on me. Yes."

"What attracted you to covering war? That's a hell of a beat for anyone to cover."

"Is this going to end up in your article?"

The waitress came over to our table and took our breakfast order, giving him a few moments to think about his answer.

"I suppose it could all be fodder for the article," he said after she left. "But right now, I just want to get to know you. Off the record."

I was smart enough to know that the best information could be coaxed from a source "off the record" and then thrown into their face at some point in the future. I wasn't going to give into that, the hell with those dancing blue eyes.

"My bosses needed somebody to cover it. I was single, so I volunteered," I said shortly.

"That's it?"

"I'm not going to open the lid on my PTSD for you to dissect here."

He put down his coffee mug and sighed. "I'm sorry."

The waitress brought our plates, steaming with scrambled eggs, sausage and hash brown potatoes. I let her set them down in front of us before I spoke.

"The truth is, Leland, I like you. I like you a lot. But I have to remember that your first motivation is to find out what makes me tick, what made me disappear, and to tell the world where I am today," I said. "That scares the hell out of me."

What also scares me is the attraction I'm starting to feel toward you, the way my heart skips a beat when I look into those sad eyes... But I'm not going to tell you that. Not yet.

"You're not the entire focus of the article. I'm going to talk to former reporters, too."

"Like that New York Times reporter who got nailed for plagiarism? Or the woman who made up the twelve-year-old heroin addict? I didn't make up my sources. That better be clear—my sources lied to me."

"I know. You were misled. So why do you want to break our agreement?"

"OK, maybe I don't exactly want to break it, but my publisher's arrest changes a lot." The words were out of my mouth before I knew what I was saying. "I promised you I'd talk to you and tell you my story. I'll still agree to that, but you can't work with me. We can meet at my apartment in the evenings. You can interview me there. You still can't tell anyone where I am, though."

"I've told you I found you by Googling you. Anybody else with a little bit of knowledge and a computer can find you."

I lay down my fork. "In the whole time I've been here, the only person who came looking for me is you. One other person said I looked like somebody famous and I blew him off. Nobody else cares until you publish your article and the world suddenly knows where I am. That's only going to happen on my terms, when I'm ready."

Leland looked me directly in the face. This time his eyes were filled with pain. "Nothing ever happens when we're ready, Charisma. When we least expect it, when we least want it to, that's when the other shoe drops—good or bad. Of all the lessons I've learned in this life, that's the biggest one."

*****

After breakfast, I went back to the newsroom and left a note for Addison to tell her about my interview with Hiram Warder. The former chief lived in a little subdivision at the western edge of Jubilant Falls, populated with identical brick box houses built after World War II on streets named after each state. When I pulled up, the retired fire chief was sitting on a lawn chair on his front porch, his fingers interlaced and laying across his belly. A cane leaned up against his knee. He struggled to get to his feet as I stepped from my car and onto the porch. It was painful to watch, since he didn't look too much older than Leland.

Why is that man still on my mind?

"Hello, chief," I said, extending my hand. "I'm Charisma Lemarnier. We talked on the phone about the body in the creek."

"Yes, yes, yes," He nodded and struggled back to his chair. "Hurt my leg at a fire. Got a lot of arthritis in it, so I had to retire." He pointed for me to sit in the other lawn chair.

"I'm sorry to hear that," I said as I sat down. "Can you tell me about that day? What do you remember?"

Warder rested both hands on the top of his cane and thoughtfully looked across the yard.

"It was my first day as a firefighter and medic. I'll never forget it. We got the call about six in the morning, just as the sun was coming up. I drove the squad over to the scene there at the Yarnell Road Bridge, where the body was. There were three police cruisers on scene; we had two fire trucks. I parked on the bridge itself and looked over into the creek to see what was going on."

"What did you see?" I didn't look up as I began to take notes.

"I saw the victim from the back. The body was hanging on a big branch that had fallen into the creek. We thought at first the victim was female because he had long hair, like a bunch of those kids did back then. His face was in the river and one of his arms caught in the branches. That's what stopped him from floating further."

"What was he wearing?"

"He had on a tee-shirt with a peace sign on the front, but I didn't see that till we got the body out of the river. All I could see at first was the back of the white shirt and blue trim on the collar and the edge of the sleeves. He had blue jeans on. One of his black high-top tennis shoes was missing."

"How long had be been in the river?" I looked up from my notebook.

Warder shrugged. "Probably all night, from the looks of the body. He was dead when he hit the water though. I remember that."

"How do you know he was dead when he hit the water?"

"If he'd still been alive when the murderer threw him in the water, he would have sucked water into his lungs. Autopsy didn't find any."

"Who pulled him out of the river?"

Hiram pointed at himself. "Couple of us waded into the river and we moved the body off the branch. I had him by the legs. Marvin McGinnis—he's the police chief now, but he was a patrolman then—he got the victim under the shoulders and we carried this poor kid's body up to the banks of the creek."

"What did you see when you laid the body on the creek bank? What kind of wounds did he have?"

"He'd fought somebody off pretty well—his hands were all cut up and he'd taken a couple good cuts to the chest." Warder moved his hand like he was thrusting a knife.

"What got me, though, was the cut to that kid's throat. He was cut from ear to ear. Before that day, I'd never seen anything like it." Warder's hand sank back onto his cane and his eyes looked off into the distance again.

"No one ever came forward to identify him?"

"Nope. Never saw the kid before or since. Nobody knew who he was and the cops never could find anything on him."

"There has been a lot of speculation over the years about the victim, that he was a male prostitute, or that he was a hitchhiker who got into the wrong car and got killed. What do you think?"

Warder looked pensive. I wondered how much pain and destruction the old chief had seen throughout his career.

"Nah, he wasn't any of that. He wasn't skinny, like he'd gone without meals or he was a drug addict. His clothes weren't tattered or raggedy like some vagrant; they were in good shape. Somebody knew that kid."

We were silent for a moment.

"Who do you think killed him then?" I asked.

"Someone here in Jubilant Falls killed that boy and they've been living with that secret for a long, long time."

"You'd think a secret like that would be hard to keep all these years."

"Not if someone else also knows your secret."

"What do you mean?"

"One person didn't kill that boy. Two people did that."

"Two?"

"I've had a lot of time to think about this and I have a theory: While he was fighting off the first person who was stabbing him in the chest, someone else came up behind him and cut his throat. I saw it, remember? That cut was too clean.

Somebody with a lot of strength came up behind him and did that, then together, they dumped him into the water. And all these years, they've had to keep their secret."

I remembered the farmhouse near the creek. I'd wanted to get there Monday night, to question the folks who lived there and find out if they were around when the young man's body hit the water. I never made it because of the fire at the inn. I wanted to get there—*now.*

I stood up and shook Hiram Warder's hand. "I appreciate your time. You've given me a lot to think about."

Warder looked off into the distance.

"Maybe your story will shake something loose this time. I've talked to reporters every couple of years about this story since it happened. What bothers me the most about the whole thing is somebody somewhere misses that boy. Somebody's been looking for him ever since he went missing and they don't know he's buried here in Jubilant Falls. Maybe you'll be the one who sends him home to his family where he belongs."

Chapter 16 Addison

So I *wasn't* alone in thinking Jimmy Lyle was murdered. Hearing Angela Perry voicing the same scary thoughts made me shiver as I left the newsroom.

But what could anybody have done at the time? Jubilant Falls was in shambles, nearly wiped off the map from the tornado. Students were dead at the middle school and others, adults as well as children, were dead and wounded throughout the city. There wouldn't have been the resources at that time to investigate a homicide. And who would have believed it, anyway? Jimmy could have been dead long before the storm hit, but no one would have been able to look for him until the storm passed. And in the days before cell phones, no one would have been able to make contact with him or warn him to take shelter, not without putting themselves in danger.

Tightly gripping the steering wheel, I made my way through the mid-afternoon traffic as I headed out into the county, toward Eve Dahlgren' mother's house.

I was familiar with the place where Eve grew up. Known as the Shanahan House, it had always been a showplace with its white-painted bricks, arched windows and columns; for many years the Dahlgren regularly opened it for holiday home tours in conjunction with the historical society.

MacGregor Shanahan, the founder of Jubilant Falls, lived there in the early days of Ohio statehood. He was also a fast-talking con man who tried to finance and construct a canal from the creek that now bore his name to the Ohio River. Instead, he built the big brick house using backer's money.

Canal Lock Park contained Shanahan's one 50-foot attempt at building the canal and had been part of his original farm.

When the Dahlgren family bought the place, Eve's father, Ed, was vice president of sales at Traeburn Tractor, the forerunner of the Japanese auto parts plant. I saw his picture frequently on the business pages of the paper through high school and my young adulthood, like when Traeburn made donations to local charities, or held a golf scramble. He was a big man, with wide shoulders and a willing handshake, but I could see, even in those grainy newspaper photos, something was hiding behind his toothy grin.

When Traeburn closed, he'd tried to find work elsewhere that sustained their lifestyle but was unsuccessful. After he committed suicide in the mid-eighties and Eve's mother had never remarried, I made the assumption that Ed, like a lot of others in the greedy eighties, had simply lived above his means.

I was out in the county now. I turned right and the Shanahan House came into view. A red, four-door car was parked on the road, at the end of the home's curved driveway.

That's odd, I thought. *Why is Charisma here?* I pulled up behind her and parked. She looked into her rearview mirror and waved, a shocked look in her eyes. She stepped up to my driver's side window.

"What are you doing here?" she asked.

"I was going to ask you the same thing," I answered.

"I got this address from Gary McGinnis as one of the places that deputies looked for information on that first cold case story. I was just sitting here thinking about what questions I want to ask," she said. "You?"

"This is where our murder victim Eve Dahlgren grew up," I answered slowly. "Her mother still lives here."

Charisma's eyes widened. "Do you think Eve or anyone here had anything to do with the creek murder?"

I looked around. Up the long, curving drive I could see a single person slowly rocking back and forth on the porch, but distance kept me from seeing who it was. The odds of anyone hearing us were slim, but I didn't want to risk it, nor did I want anyone to pull up on us.

"Canal Lock Park is just up the road. Meet me in the first parking lot. I need to share something with you," I said.

Charisma arrived seconds after I did. I parked my car and leaned over to open the passenger door.

"Get in," I said, sweeping the fast-food wrappers and old newspapers from the seat to the floor.

"Do you think these crimes are connected?" she asked, sliding into the seat and shutting the door.

"I'm not sure," I began. "But first, there's something you need to know."

I told Charisma the whole story: tutoring Jimmy Lyle my junior year and Eve's rage at seeing us together, the tornado, my suspicions about his death and how Angela Perry felt the same way. I finished by telling her about Angela's stories of violence and the boarding school connection between Earlene and Eve.

Charisma took notes as I told my tale, occasionally bouncing her pen against her chin.

"So is Eve's mother the only one living in that big old house?" she asked.

"I'm not sure who else could be living there. Her father committed suicide years ago."

"Do you think he knew anything about what his daughter might have done?"

I shrugged. "Who knows? I never put that together."

"I think we ought to go back and talk to Mrs. Dahlgren."

"I agree, but I doubt if we get much. Her daughter is dead and she's no doubt grieving," I said. "This could be a tough one."

There was a slight tremor in the hand that held Charisma's pencil. I wondered what was going through her head, if she was thinking about the accident that cost her parents and her husband their lives.

"So what do you know about Mrs. Dahlgren?" she asked finally.

"Not a lot. She used to come into the newsroom with an announcement every time Eve got a promotion or took a new job. She was wrapped up in Eve's life for a long, long time, then for some reason, she stopped coming in."

"If we don't go back there and ask, we'll never know what happened." She reached behind her and fastened her seat belt. "Ready when you are."

In a few moments, we were driving up the curving drive of Shanahan House. A little old lady sat alone on the porch, rocking slowly back and forth. She was dressed in an expensive, pink running suit with clean white athletic shoes that closed with a Velcro strap. Her trembling hands were misshapen from arthritis, but her fingernails were painted soft, glossy beige. Her hair was white, and perfectly styled. Somebody was taking good care of her. Was it Eve? What would happen now that she was dead?

Betty Dahlgren turned to look at us as we pulled next to the wide porch and stepped from the car. Her eyes were wet and empty.

"Hello Mrs. Dahlgren," I said loudly. "Remember me? I'm Penny Addison, from the paper."

"Oh, yes," she said, reaching out to take my hand, although I doubted if she really recognized me.

Up close, Mrs. Dahlgren was even more vacant and frail. I could see how detached she was from today's world. For her sake, I hoped someone lived here with her.

"This is one of my reporters, Charisma Lemarnier," I said. "We wanted to talk to you about your daughter, Eve."

"Eve. Yes."

"We're terribly sorry for your loss, Mrs. Dahlgren," Charisma began.

Confused, Mrs. Dahlgren looked at her and nodded. "Thank you."

"Can you tell us why Eve came home to visit?" I asked.

"Eve is a good girl. She comes home to check on me."

"Did she stay with you?"

Mrs. Dahlgren nodded.

"What kind of work did Eve do?" I asked.

"Oh, she's a businesswoman. A very powerful one." Mrs. Dahlgren nodded as sagely as only a dementia patient can. She tapped her finger against her temple. "And a smart one."

I decided to jump in with both feet.

"Do you remember Jimmy Lyle?"

Mrs. Dahlgren's elderly face froze. Charisma looked from the old woman to me, her eyebrows arched.

"You remember Jimmy?" I asked again. "Her boyfriend in high school?"

"Poor, poor Jimmy," she whispered.

"What happened to Jimmy?" I asked.

Mrs. Dahlgren looked from Charisma to me, her eyes wide with fear.

"Did Eve know what happened to Jimmy?" I pushed.

Mrs. Dahlgren pulled at a small beaded chain around her neck and shook her head.

"No, no, no," she said. "Not Eve, no."

Charisma pulled a picture from the back of her notebook. It was not the photo we'd run of the stabbing victim being pulled from the creek all those years ago, but one the coroner had taken to send to police stations across the country in hopes of getting him identified. It showed the young man's face, turned slightly to the left, eyes closed in death and his long black hair fanned out behind him on the steel autopsy table. His mouth hung open slightly and a sheet covered the slash across his throat. He didn't look dead; he just looked like he was sleeping.

"Do you know who this is?" She held the photo in front of the old lady.

Mrs. Dahlgren closed her eyes tightly and turned her head sharply.

"Eve didn't like that boy," she whispered, her face turned away from Charisma.

"Did Eve hurt him? Did Eve hurt Jimmy?" I asked, pointing at the picture.

Frantically, Mrs. Dahlgren pulled the beaded chain from inside her running suit and pushed the small white disc on it. Feet clattered on the stairs inside the house and the big oaken door flew open. A middle-aged woman with frizzy gray hair and a polo shirt emblazoned with a home health care logo rushed out.

"Are you OK, Betty? You all right? Who are these folks?" she demanded, taking one of the old woman's claw-like hands. She glared protectively at us.

"These are my friends, Karen," Betty Dahlgren said.

"We're from the paper," I said, as I introduced Charisma and myself again. "We wanted to talk to Betty about her daughter, Eve."

"Wait here a moment." Karen helped the old woman stand and led her into the house. In a second, she was back, closing the big door behind her. "I cannot believe that you would sit here and talk to a poor old demented woman and ask her about her dead daughter!"

"We didn't know she had dementia," Charisma lied. "If she didn't want to talk to us, she could have asked us to leave."

"She doesn't know her daughter is dead—we can't make her understand!" Karen said.

"Who is 'we'?" I looked over Karen's shoulder into the doorway, but the bright sunshine didn't extend to the dark interior of the home's foyer.

"You don't need to worry about that. You just need to leave, right now!" Karen shooed us off the porch with her hands.

"Are you going to tell her?" I asked as Charisma and I slipped back into the Taurus. I slipped my key into the ignition.

"I don't think that's any of your business! Now, go away! Leave Betty alone!"
Karen turned back to the house.

The sun slipped behind a cloud and for a second, I caught a glimpse inside the doorway of a short, stocky woman in a pink ball cap with the words 'Barn Diva' across it. She was short, husky, and middle-aged, wearing jeans, and a dark tee-shirt, her hands jammed in her pockets. Her dirty blonde hair was short and badly cut. She rocked back and forth on the steel-toed work boots as she stared at us.

Who the hell is that? I thought.

*****

Back in the parking lot, I pulled up next to Charisma's car.

"Eve Dahlgren had something to do with both of those boys' deaths," Charisma said.

"For her mother to react that way, I'm betting she did," I answered. "We need to look into where Eve's been all these years, where she worked and when."

"I can do that."

"No, I don't want you to. This town talks, Charisma, all small towns do. Remember what I said this morning about being careful how this story gets covered? You start digging around and we're either going to come across as trashing the victim or poisoning the jury pool to try to get Earlene off. Either way, it's going to make us look bad."

"I have an idea," she said, pulling out her cell phone. She scrolled down on the face of her phone with her thumb, found a number and touched the screen to connect. "It could also solve another problem for me."

She was silent until the person at the other end picked up.

"I need a favor."

Chapter 17 Leland

"My name is Leland and I am an alcoholic. I've been sober for five years, three months, one week and two days."

It was an hour after my breakfast with Charisma and I sat in a circle of fellow addicts at the Methodist Church's Alcoholics Anonymous meeting. We'd gone around and introduced ourselves, ending with me. The attendees were the kind of folks I figured I'd see in a town like Jubilant Falls—an obese police officer, a couple men in suits, several men in work boots and flannel; a woman who looked like someone's grandmother held knitting in her lap. The younger woman beside her had multiple body piercings and looked like she'd just graduated college.

Over the past five years, it was the only place I felt safe. Among my brother and sister addicts, I could be honest and open here. I didn't know these folks any more than they knew me, but we all knew we were powerless over alcohol and served as each other's lifelines to sobriety.

"Welcome Leland," said Steve, the group's leader. "What brings you to Jubilant Falls?"

"I'm a professor. I'm here doing some research."

There was a chorus of "Welcome" and "Glad to have you" from around the circle.

"Would you like to tell us your story?"

"Well, like I said, I've been sober five years, three months and two days," I began slowly.

I closed my eyes and told the story of how alcohol shaped my marriage and then destroyed my family. It wasn't the first time I'd said the words in this environment. When I was finished, I opened my eyes to see the knitting grandmother wipe a tear from her cheek. "But in the two days I've been in Jubilant Falls I'm as close to losing my sobriety as I've been in a long time."

"Why is that?" one of the men in suits asked.

"I've met someone through my research and for the first time, I think I'm..." My words caught in my throat. "I'm having feelings for her."

"Awww, that's wonderful!" the grandmother said.

"Thank you," I said. "When I come to AA, I know I'm among friends, wherever I go. There's something very comforting about being among people who've been shaped by the same demons as I have. It's become a cocoon, someplace I can escape from the world. She's changed all that and it terrifies me."

"Tell us about her," someone else said.

I hesitated before answering. Should I reveal Charisma's secrets here? Everything revealed by members at AA meetings was kept strictly within the meeting room walls, but would that extend to her? I decided to take the chance.

"She came here to Jubilant Falls to hide. She's been through hell and she doesn't want anyone to know she's here until she's ready."

"Is she an alcoholic? We would welcome her here and keep her secret," Steve said.

"She was a war correspondent. She was severely wounded and a suicide bomber killed her husband on a road in Baghdad. She suffers from PTSD."

The policeman, who spent the meeting hanging his head staring at the hat in his lap, looked up suddenly. I kept talking.

"But the truth is, these feelings scare me to death. I'm starting to think that maybe I've used AA to hide from the world. Even if we've just met, you all know me. You know my struggles because you've struggled the same way. I've relied on that to keep me sober. I've never told anyone outside of AA about my story, but for some reason I told her. Now that I have, all I want to do is reach for a bottle."

"Don't do that," Steve said. He slipped his hand into his jacket pocket and handed me a business card. "Reach out to one of us instead."

I nodded and took the card from him. I might be calling him sooner than I thought.

The meeting continued, closing as each one does when we all clasped hands andd said the Sobriety Prayer: "God grant me the serenity to accept the things I cannot change, courage to change the things I can and wisdom to know the difference, living one day at a time, enjoying one moment at a time, accepting hardships as the pathway to peace..."

Back in Philly, I would have taken comfort in those words. I would have returned to my classroom or my apartment, knowing I was strong for another day. Today, however, as I walked back to my hotel at the edge of the downtown, I knew my struggle had just begun.

*****

I knew I wouldn't hear from Charisma until later this evening, so rather than sit in my hotel room and not do anything I changed into running gear and drove out to Canal Lock Park, the state park just outside town, for some exercise.

A red sedan that had seen better days was the only vehicle parked in the lot. To ensure my solitude, I parked my rental car in the far corner.

Being outside gave me time to think. How was I going to handle the situation with Charisma? Keep my feelings to myself and miss a second chance at happiness? Open my heart and risk rejection? And what if she did reject me? Could I take that without crawling back inside a bottle?

More than anything, I wanted to get to know her, not just for her story but also as a person.

The June sun shone through the leaves and danced on the ground. I heard the occasional bird in the trees, but I was alone on the beaten path, which ran along a deep, rocky gorge. I picked up my pace, moving to a jog, hoping the exertion would clear my head and sooth my agitation.

My thoughts began to run as well. What was I really looking for? Companionship? Sex?

She'd been in my arms twice now and I was shocked at my reaction. I shuddered as I remembered the tempting way her collar dipped between her shoulder blades as we walked up the stairs to her apartment last night, her lavender smell and the feeling of her hands on my back as I clasped her to me this morning in the parking lot. Was this the reaction of a horny old prof who found himself ogling female students on the last day of class? Or was I just a man who was all too lonely?

I stopped to catch my breath and clear away the sudden thoughts of Charisma's soft hands clutching my naked back as we moved together in the darkness of my hotel room. I squeezed my eyes shut, trying to block out the fantasies of her naked skin against mine, her legs wrapped around my hips, and how I imagine she'd cry out when we climaxed.

Stop it.

I began running again, harder and faster this time, to further clear my head. I was well down the trail when my cell phone rang. I found a rock to sit down on and answered the call. My heart skipped a beat: it was Charisma.

"I need a favor," she said. Her words were choppy and short and she didn't say hello.

"Anything," I said, instantly regretting it.

"I'm not alone."

"Sorry."

"I'm at an interview, with my boss. I need you to do some research on somebody. She's the victim of the homicide I told you about this morning."

"The one your publisher is in jail for?"

"Yes. This town is really, really small and word gets around quick. There's nothing ethically wrong with us looking into the victim's past, but Addison just doesn't want anybody to know we're doing it."

"Sure. I'd be glad to help. How about we talk about it over dinner?"

This time, Charisma was silent.

"I don't go out to dinner."

"How about I get some carryout and bring it to your apartment?"

"That's fine."

"What sounds good?"

"There's a Chinese place on Second Street, the Mandarin Moon. Their food is good."

"See you at seven?"

"Make it six." She hung up.

I slipped my cell phone back into my pocket and continued my run, hoping the exertion would burn off my growing need—for a drink or for her, I wasn't sure.

*****

At the appointed hour, I was standing on the sidewalk in front of her door, holding white carry-out boxes in plastic bags, waiting for her to come to the door.

The door swung open and I sucked in my breath. Charisma had on a thin, long-sleeved flowered blouse, buttoned up over her bosom; tight jeans accentuated her slim legs and she wore white sandals. Her face was flawless, with makeup covering the scars along the left side of her face.

Had she done that for me?

"Hi," she said and smiled. This wasn't the harsh, all-business reporter I'd talked to the night the inn burned or on the phone this afternoon. The haggard look I'd seen nearly fourteen hours ago was gone. She seemed relaxed and glad to see me.

"I wasn't sure what you'd like, so I brought Kung Pao chicken, beef lo-mein and fried rice," I said. I felt like a sixteen-year-old boy, all fear and hormones. I hoped she couldn't sense that.

How long had it been since I'd been on a date? Or was this really a business dinner? I wasn't sure how to consider it. Bitch Goddess and I married at twenty-seven. Noah was born two weeks before my twenty-ninth birthday; my life effectively ended when he died at twenty-three and I was fifty-two. That meant any dating etiquette I had stored went back least thirty years—when Charisma was in kindergarten.

Her fingers brushed my hand as she took the bags from me and I caught a whiff of lavender. "Come on up," she said.

In the little studio, she had the dinette table set with a pair of china plates, mismatched silverware and iced tea in plastic glasses.

"It's not Martha Stewart, but it works," she said as she placed the carryout containers on the table and opened them. I took a seat across from her as she spooned generous helpings from each container onto each plate.

"So what exactly do you want me to look into?" I asked. "I bought a copy of today's paper, so I know the name of your victim and how she died, and the name of your publisher, but that's about it."

"It's kind of a long involved story," Charisma began. "But here's the basics: Eve Dahlgren and my boss Addison McIntyre apparently went to high school together—Eve was a year ahead of Addison and the head cheerleader. She was also a real bitch, intimidating other members of the cheer squad, physically violent, that kind of thing. During Addison's junior year, there was a really bad tornado that pretty much destroyed Jubilant Falls. From what she told me, there was a boy her age, Jimmy Lyle, who died in the tornado and who was dating our victim. He was found on his grandfather's farm with a posthole digger in his chest."

I grimaced as Charisma continued her tale.

"I'm not all that familiar with tornados, but I guess they are pretty common here in Ohio and some pretty odd things can happen. Addison told me about a piece of straw that got shoved through a tree branch or something like that. So when Jimmy Lyle was found with the posthole digger through his chest, everyone thought it was just one of those weird things that happened in the tornado. There's a bronze plaque in front of the city building with the names of all the tornado victims—his is on it."

"What does this have to do with Eve Dahlgren?"

"Addison told me she always believed there was something fishy in Jimmy Lyle's death—nothing to back it up, just a feeling she had. Since the high school was destroyed in the tornado, the kids were all bussed to a school in the neighboring county to finish the school year. But not Eve—her parents transferred her to a boarding school in Columbus, where apparently she met Earlene, who is now charged with killing her."

"OK. Again, what does this have to do with your victim?"

"I'm getting there."

Charisma was completely focused on telling her story. There was no trace of the post-traumatic stress that sent her into hiding. I could see how she would be a formidable force in the field. But I couldn't understand why something that dated back to her boss's high school days was important.

"Addison met today with one of the other cheerleaders, who told her that she also never believed Lyle died in the tornado, that Eve Dahlgren killed him," Charisma finished.

"Why would Earlene kill Eve? That doesn't make any sense."

"Earlene and Eve went out this weekend and apparently argued, according to what Earlene told my boss. We surmise the argument started when Eve let it slip that she killed Jimmy Lyle back in high school. Maybe Earlene said she was going to the police about it, a fight ensued and for once, Eve got the worst end of the deal. The police say Earlene's prints were found on the steering wheel of the car where Eve was found dead."

"Then why would your publisher walk away from the scene? Why wouldn't she call the police? Why wouldn't she turn herself in or claim self-defense?" I took a drink of my iced tea. "This definitely doesn't rise to the level of some of the stories either one of us have covered in the past, Charisma. Why should either one of us waste time on this?"

"Because we don't know a lot about where Eve Dahlgren has been between 1994 and when she showed up dead in the park downtown."

"And your editor wants to pin a death that clearly occurred during a natural disaster on somebody she didn't like in high school so her boss doesn't hang for murder? No matter what led to this Eve woman's death, Charisma, trashing the victim is pretty tacky. I'm surprised you'd get involved in this."

Charisma slammed her fork on the table and her brown eyes sparked with fire.

"Trust me, none of us, least of all my boss, like Earlene Whitelaw and I am *not* involved in trashing the victim. We have reason to believe Eve Dahlgren might be involved in another crime. You may be used to a big city like Philadelphia, Leland, but here in this little town, before you know it, our efforts will get back to the prosecutor, who will scream that we're poisoning the jury pool and slam a gag order on any kind of coverage. That's why neither Addison nor I can look into it. That's why we need you to do it."

"So your boss knows about me then?"

"Yes." Charisma looked away. "I told her the night of the fire."

"Before or after I called the newsroom to talk to you?"

"After I'd screamed at you and hung up—but I didn't tell her the truth."

"What did you tell her?"

"Addison thinks that these scars came from a car accident, one that killed my parents and my husband, the same story I told you. She thinks you're a private investigator hired by my in-laws' family to look into the accident. It was all I could come up with at the time."

I was silent for a moment. "That's a good one. She doesn't know you're Charisma Prentiss?"

She shook her head and smiled crookedly. She wasn't the blonde beauty the world remembered traipsing through the mountains of Afghanistan or the ancient backstreets of the Middle East. She was permanently scarred, physically and emotionally. Her repaired face wasn't the same one that graced television sets across this country.

That was no doubt what allowed her to hide here in this little town. Something else was different about it—the supreme confidence she was known for, the arrogance and the willingness to risk all for a story was gone.

"No, she doesn't—and I'm not ready for her, or anyone, to find out about it. The résumé I gave her was a fake. Everyone I listed there is a friend of mine, willing to hide my true identity. You spill the beans, and I won't only be known as journalism's most spectacular flame out, I'll be known as a fake. One more condition—I need to know two weeks before your article comes out."

"Why?"

"Because that's the day I'm giving my notice. Do you know what will happen when you expose who I really am?"

"I said I wouldn't tell where you were. What do you think will happen?"

She covered her eyes with her hands. "Everyone will know the truth."

"What truth? What do you mean?"

"That I—no, I'm not going into that right now. You don't get that far inside my psyche, not yet." She lifted her head and glared.

"Let's talk about these stories you're working on, the one you want me to help you with. What other crimes are we talking about?"

"I'm working on a couple stories about two cold case murders that happened several years apart. The first one happened maybe five, six years after the tornado—that's the one I'm focused on right now. A young man was found dead in the creek—no identification, no fingerprints on file. He'd been stabbed. I met Addison out at this old farmhouse today. I hoped to talk to whoever owned the place and see if they lived there when the young man was found in the creek. Turns out it was Eve's mother's house and she may have inadvertently given us a couple leads on the deaths of Jimmy Lyle and the stabbing."

"The time of the creek death would have put Eve out of college, maybe working her first job. Did she go to college locally?" I asked.

"Not to my knowledge."

"Did she work here in Jubilant Falls?"

"No."

"Then where?"

Charisma shrugged. "The story about her murder had a little bit about her professional career. When Eve died, she would have been working at a firm in Texas. We don't know why she was back here, if she came to stay, and if we can connect her to the boy in the creek—or even to Jimmy Lyle. That's what we need you to find out."

I pressed my thumb against my chin thoughtfully. It would feel good to get my hands back into a story. I could tell my students I wasn't just some old academic, I'd been back in the trenches. I'd have the opportunity to once more do what I loved—and it would be an opportunity to work with Charisma.

It would be like starting over.

"I'd love to help, however I can," I said.

"Thank you so much." Impulsively, Charisma reached over and laid her hand over mine, then blushed as she pulled it back into her lap. "I'm sorry. I didn't mean..."

"Don't be embarrassed," I said softly, reaching across the table. "Here—give it back."

She pulled her hand from beneath the tabletop and tentatively laid it in mine. It was soft and she'd painted her fingernails. I wrapped both my hands around hers and looked in those big brown eyes. Her eyelashes fluttered, and, beneath the makeup she blushed, but she didn't look away.

I drew her hand close to my lips and placed one small kiss on the back of her knuckles, drinking in the soft sensation and the heady lavender smell of her skin. It wasn't enough—I wanted more. I pulled her hand nearer to kiss her palm, to hold her cool fingers against my face and savor a connection I hadn't felt in years. Her sleeve slid back, exposing a myriad of jagged scars along her forearm. The scars, some large and irregular with feathered edges, some small and pockmarked, traveled up to her elbow like a snake.

"No! Stop!" Charisma gasped and jerked away, shattering the magic. With her other hand, she pushed the errant sleeve down around her wrist. She jumped up from the table and began clearing the dishes. "I'm sorry. I've just—I mean, since Jean Paul died, I—" she stammered.

I stood and reached for her shoulders.

"No, don't!" she cried, pushing me away. She stopped in front of the sink, hanging her head, fighting for composure.

"Charisma, I—"

She didn't turn around.

"If you come to the paper after ten-thirty, we're off deadline. I can introduce you to Addison then and we can get started."

"I want to say I'm sorry."

"Just go, Leland. Please."

Wordlessly, I opened the door and went down the stairs. Once on the sidewalk, I looked up to her window. The curtains didn't move; I couldn't see her silhouette. What was she thinking? What would she do? Had one small kiss provoked her PTSD? Or had it been something else?

I shoved my hands into my pockets and walked back to my hotel room.

Chapter 18 Addison

I was home early enough to start helping with the evening milking, but that didn't last long.

I was attaching an inflator to the last heifer's udder when my cell phone rang. Duncan, seated on a milking stool at the heifer beside me, rolled his eyes as I pulled it from my jeans pocket.

"Hi, Graham," I said.

"Hey, Addison," he answered. "I've got news. Eve Dahlgren's time of death came back from the coroner. It wasn't Monday afternoon—it was Sunday night. The police are saying her Lincoln was moved to the park and left there."

"You're kidding."

"Nope—and Earlene's been released. She had an alibi for Sunday night. She and her dad were having dinner in Collitstown. Watt provided the receipt, which showed two meals: He had a New York strip and she had a spinach salad. The server remembered their order."

"Yeah, with that hair, she'd be easy to pick out. But what about her fingerprints?"

"I talked to Chief G and he thinks Earlene's prints may not be as recent as they first though. They're back to square one."

"No suspects, no leads?"

"That's not exactly what he said, but I got that impression."

While I waited for Graham to send me the story, I called Gary McGinnis at home. I had mixed feelings on Earlene's release: glad she wasn't going to be hung for a crime she didn't commit, but dreading her return to work and the interference that would follow in the newsroom.

"So it's an open and shut case, huh?" I teased when he picked up his phone. "You told me 'Don't waste your time, Penny.' You said you had her fresh fingerprints in the car."

"Don't get too high on yourself," McGinnis said. "It was the autopsy that got your boss released, not anything you've dug up. And yes, we still have the steering wheel, but we can't explain why Earlene's fingerprints are on it. She just happens to have an alibi for the night of the murder."

"What about the knife? The one that was found in the sewer?"

"Techs can't raise any usable fingerprints because the knife was found in a slight amount of standing water. But the blood type matches Eve's. We're sending it to the state crime lab for DNA, just to be sure."

"You never know what else may come up. I met with Betty Dahlgren this afternoon. She let something slip: Eve may have had something to do with the creek murder."

There was silence at the other end of the phone.

"You can't be serious."

"Charisma showed her the victim's photo and Betty said something about Eve not liking him. She *knows* him, Gary. There's a connection. I can feel it."

"We can't operate on feelings, Penny. We tried to notify Betty Dahlgren about Eve's death, but I don't think it sunk in— and that home health care aide was very protective. We were able to search the house and the barn, though. Wherever Eve Dahlgren was killed, it wasn't at that house."

"I also got the impression that Betty didn't understand Eve was dead. But here's something else weird: I met with Angela Perry today." I filled him in on Angela's account of Eve's high school violence and manipulation. "She thinks Eve had something to do with the death of Jimmy Lyle, and from the way Betty Dahlgren reacted when I asked her, I'm starting to think there's something there."

"Penny, come on. He died in the tornado. Everybody knows that!"

"I'm not sure, Gary. I've always had a weird feeling about how he died, but I've never told anybody. Then Angela said something and I just felt—"

Gary interrupted me. "Do you know how impossible it would be to prove he was murdered? All these years later? I've got a homicide on my hands right now!"

"But you should have seen how agitated Betty got when I asked her about him!"

Gary sighed on the other end of the phone. "How reliable could all this be, Penny, coming from a dementia patient?"

"Maybe not at all, but it could be a starting point. What if Eve Dahlgren was a serial killer?"

"And what if I'm the Easter Bunny?"

Chapter 19 Charisma

The story on the dead man in the creek ran on Wednesday morning. I filled the story with what I hoped was an accurate portrayal of Jubilant Falls in the 1980s—a town still staggering to its feet years after a natural disaster when an unnamed body showed up in the creek.

I found details of his funeral, held a day after officials released the report on his death and attended only by the police and firefighters who were on the scene. Pat took a photo of his grave, marked only with a metal plate with the name "John Doe" and the date of his death and we ran the original photo of Marvin McGinnis and Hiram Warder lifting the body out of the creek.

I included Warder's thoughts that two people had been involved with the death, as well as a comment from Gary McGinnis that anything was possible, but police investigation hadn't specifically determined that.

I ended the article with Warder's quote: "Someone here in Jubilant Falls killed that boy and they've been living with that secret for a long, long time."

Maybe it would spark someone's memory—or guilt. Addison and I agreed we couldn't use Betty Dahlgren's reaction to the victim's photo, due to her dementia. Even if Betty's reaction were credible (and it could very well *not* be), it wasn't enough to do anything with. But if we got that one phone call, that could give law enforcement and us a starting point to finding out who killed the young man in the creek, maybe even enough information to go back to Betty and ask more questions just to gauge her reaction.

Addison and I edited the story in her office, with the door closed.

"I don't think we've got any reason at all to look into Jimmy Lyle's death," Addison said. With a push of a computer button, she sent my story on to Dennis. "Gary McGinnis didn't believe Angela Perry's story or the gut feeling I've had for years."

"Leland Huffinger wasn't real sure about it either," I said. "He thought it looked like you were trying to pin something else on the victim to make Earlene look good, or get her off."

"I can understand why they both said that. On its face, it does look like that. Maybe I ought to just let it die." Addison shrugged sadly, tapping a cigarette on her desktop. "When is Leland coming in?"

Yesterday, she questioned me about the wisdom of having a private investigator looking into Eve's past, but I'd assured her it was one way for me to keep an eye on Leland and away from me. He was also an unknown: nobody could accuse anyone from the newspaper of trashing Eve if he did the research.

That was before we had dinner and I felt his kisses on my hand.

Today, I wasn't sure how I'd respond when I saw him again. I didn't like him seeing the scars on my arms but my overreaction wasn't from my PTSD. That was someone prying my heart open for the first time in years.

I was addicted to my job, to the adrenaline thrill of it all—even this smaller, slower version of what I was doing today. I knew how challenging it could be to have a journalist in the family. Just like my mother, I thought that if I married another reporter, or as in my case of Jean Paul, a photojournalist, we could travel the world tag-teaming our stories: I got the byline, he got the photo credit.

But I wouldn't let my personal story end like hers. I wasn't going to end up like her, stuck at home with two screaming kids in Washington D.C.'s sprawling suburbs while Dad sat in the slot at Reuter's copy desk, adjusting adverbs and inverting triangles all day long. Both of them gave up the chase of that perfect story for the fable of perfect family life—and both were miserable, with their marriage and with their lives. Their expectations of what marriage should be wouldn't let them be the people they wanted to be.

Dad divorced my mother, retired from Reuters and found a new career in corporate communications — as well as Kate, a redhead ten years older than me, to shack up with. She kept him active playing tennis and god knows what else. They had a great view of Washington D.C. from their downtown condo and two over-groomed Shih Tzu puppies they treated like infants.

Mom returned to journalism after my brother graduated from college, but her years at home put her behind the earning curve. Now, she covers the city schools in Salisbury, Maryland to make the rent on her shabby apartment and copy edits deluded, self-published novelists at two dollars a page to fund her retirement.

My parents were why Jean Paul had to work so hard to win my heart and why I honestly told him I wasn't ready for children.

The truth was, I wasn't ready for our nomadic life to end.

I didn't want to end up like my mother.

Maybe, if we hadn't argued, if I'd said yes that night to his advances, I'd have a little one to remember him by.

Maybe, he'd still be alive.

And then last night, a kiss changed everything. Feeling Leland's lips on the back of my fingers, then again on my palm transfixed me. The warmth of his lips, the feel of his cheek, his scratchy-soft beard... How long had it been since I'd touched a man—or let a man touch me? Certainly more in the last three days than I had in the last two years. Then the scars, my damned scars, had to show themselves and I was snapped back to the ugly reality of my life.

I reminded myself his primary objective was to tell my tale, exposing where I was and what I was doing. Romancing me was one way to bring down those walls—I couldn't forget that. Keeping him here in the newsroom was a way to keep an eye on him and protect myself.

Addison repeated her question. "When is Leland coming in?"

"After deadline. I thought we could start him in the clip files or the morgue," I said, coming out of my reverie. "I thought I'd start on the Bob Martz story today, too."

"You need to talk to my father, Walt. He worked with Bob." She slipped from behind her desk and opened her office door. I followed her back into the newsroom. "You can go over to see Dad pretty much any time. Just call first—and remind me to give you his phone number."

The mood in the newsroom was subdued as we finished Wednesday's edition. Graham had the story on Earlene's release and you could smell the fear that she would come back in, furious about the photo Pat took and Addison chose to run. Every time Addison's phone rang, conversation stopped until she picked up the phone and her smile told us it wasn't Earlene. As deadline approached and she didn't show up, everyone breathed a little easier. By the time Sam, the pressroom foreman, brought Addison's still-damp copies up, it looked like we escaped.

Then Leland arrived, dressed casually in khaki pants, a Fitzgerald University polo shirt and athletic shoes. He held a Philadelphia Phillies ball cap in his hand. I sucked in my breath when I saw him. Was it fear—how could he have worn a shirt from his college? Or was it hormones? Sitting across from me, Graham Kinnon shot me an odd look. Was I that obvious?

Dennis stood up and walked his direction; I got to Leland first.

"Mr. Huffinger, good morning," I said, extending my hand.

"Miss... Lemarnier," he stumbled over my name as he took my hand in his.

"My editor, Addison McIntyre, wants to meet with you before you begin." I shepherded him to the back of the newsroom and Addison's office as Graham, Dennis, Pat and Marcus stared. I glared at them before closing the office door behind us.

Exhaling blue smoke, Addison flicked a cigarette out of her open window as we entered.

"Addison, this is Leland Huffinger, the investigator I told you about," I said. "Mr. Huffinger, this is my editor Addison McIntyre."

"Thanks for coming in. Charisma explained what we need you to do?"

Leland nodded. "You need someone not attached to the *Journal-Gazette* to research Eve Dahlgren's past."

"I need you to work as a freelancer, outside of the newsroom as much as possible. You can have access to our files, because we allow the public that access, but you need to make calls on your own phone. No one would probably check, but I just want to be sure. You can have access to the newsroom copier because we allow the general public to do that, too. I figured your background as a PI will get us places most reporters can't go. That will be very helpful."

He nodded slowly.

"I need the information as soon as I can get it," Addison continued. "There's been a change in the case: the time of Eve Dahlgren's death has been revised and Earlene Whitelaw has been released as a result. We have a story coming out today on that. The police no longer have a suspect in the case and are pretty stumped. If we can get any new information, it could be very helpful. Charisma, if you can show him the files and the morgue, we can get started."

"One more question," Leland asked. "What about my rate? I get one hundred dollars an hour, including expenses."

I stared at him. Who did he think he was, Sam Spade?

Addison nodded, not missing a beat. "I'm sure I can talk our former publisher into paying for anything that gets his daughter exonerated. Even though she's been released, until someone is charged and convicted, she's still got this whole thing hanging over her head."

We all stood and I led him back out to the newsroom, to the back wall where a row of file cabinets where the clip files were stored dating back to the 1950s. Back when the J-G had an editorial assistant, part of the job was to painstakingly clip articles on people in the paper and file them for future references. Those articles were cross-referenced by another set of files on events: city council meetings, traffic accidents, business news, social events, and weather stories. The tornado had its own filing cabinet, of course. In the days before computers and the Internet, it made for quick efficient research.

It also made it easy for the general public too, so it wasn't uncommon for someone to be rooting through the files, like Leland would be doing.

I lay my hand on top of the file marked PEOPLE: M-N-O.

"Here you go. If you've got any questions, ask Addison," I said.

"You're not going to be here?"

"I might, I might not. I've got other stories to do."

"Oh." He seemed disappointed.

I leaned in closer to him, close enough to take in the smell of hotel soap. "And if I have to leave at any time, you don't ask anybody I work with about me," I hissed. "Understand?"

Exasperation showed in Leland's face.

"Don't look at me that way. I can't believe you asked for a hundred bucks an hour," I whispered.

"What the hell did you expect me to do? Work for free? You're the one who came up with this private dick story," he hissed back.

"I need to get to work. I've got a couple phone calls to make." I turned, leaving him at the filing cabinet.

For the next hour, I sat at my desk, tying up loose ends and making phone calls. There was a short feature on some of the summer mission programs the Golgotha College students were going on that was easy to bang out, since the college's PR guy sent photos. A few more phone calls and I had an appointment with Walter Addison, and, later that afternoon, with Gary McGinnis.

I watched Leland work out of the corner of my eye. More than once, he went into Addison's office with a handful of clips, and then returned to the filing cabinets, nodding.

Was he asking anything about me? I felt paranoia rise in the back of my throat. He never looked at me or tried to catch my eye. Once he asked Dennis where the men's room was, but otherwise, he played by the rules I established. About lunchtime, Leland closed the file cabinet and gathered his stack of papers.

"Thanks, folks!" he called out as he left the newsroom.

I exhaled, apparently loud enough for Dennis to look up at me.

"You know him?" he asked.

"He's a PI from Philadelphia," I answered. "He's doing some research."

"On what?"

I shrugged. "I'm not exactly sure. Maybe it's some family genealogy."

Dennis looked at me like he didn't believe me. I always was a lousy liar.

My cell phone danced across my desk, buzzing with an incoming text message. It was from Leland: *Lunch?*

Not today, I texted in reply. *Dinner tonight?*

Sure, he answered. *Gives me time to keep working. Maybe I will have info for you.*

I slipped my phone into my purse and smiled. Looking up I caught Dennis gazing curiously at me from across the room. I blushed to the roots of my hair.

*****

Walter Addison lived in a huge old white Victorian house two doors down from the burned out hull of the Jubilant Country Inn. He was pulling weeds in the flower garden when I came up the walk. He stood up and pulled his dirty gloves off before shaking my hand.

He was a short, stocky, barrel-chested man with a head full of gray hair, still cut high and tight as if he was still patrolling the highways of Plummer County with the Ohio State Highway Patrol. I could see the family resemblance; my former editor would have called that "unfortunate."

"Nice to meet you," he said. "Penny said you'd be calling. She's had good things to say about you. Before I forget, here's the phone number for Bob's widow. Penny said you'd want to talk to her."

"Penny? That's Addison's first name?" I took the piece of paper from his arthritic hand.

Walt smiled. "You didn't know that? That's right—she goes by her maiden name at work. So you're here to talk about Bob Martz, eh?" He pointed toward an ironwork table and chairs at the side of the house. He'd been expecting me. A pitcher of lemonade and two glasses full of ice sat on the table, next to a plate of sugar cookies, a softer side I hadn't expected from this former state trooper.

I took a seat on one of the chairs and pulled my notebook from my purse.

"So tell me about the night Trooper Martz died."

Walt Addison poured himself a tall lemonade and repeated the story that I'd read in the newspaper the day after Martz was shot: He'd stopped a car for a traffic violation and either the dispatcher wrote down the plate number wrong or the plate was somehow not in the system. When dispatch called to check up on him twenty minutes later and there was no response, he was the supervisor on duty who found Martz dead by the side of the road.

"What was that like for you?" I asked.

Walt put down his lemonade and looked up into the mature maple trees that shaded us. He was silent for a moment. When he began to speak, he chose his words carefully and slowly.

"Bob Martz was a great trooper. We were good friends. His kids went to school with Penny. After Bob died, I used to go sit with Judith, his wife, and we'd talk about what a great guy he was. I could understand her frustration when they never found Bob's killer. We all did."

"*Was* Bob really a great guy?"

Walt was silent again.

"Did Bob Martz have secrets?" I asked. "Could they have gotten him killed?"

Walt sighed. "Judith knew the truth. I don't want it to be the paper now."

"But what if it uncovers who killed him?"

"I can tell you where to look. How's that?"

"What am I looking for?"

"It's in his personnel file."

"What is it?" I repeated. I couldn't just dig through a cop's personnel file just for the sake of digging—Ohio public records law wouldn't allow it, even if that cop were dead. Current state law now dictated I had to have a specific item to request from the file, something the retired state trooper might not know. The idea was to protect cops and first responders from stalkers and criminals, but it could make unearthing problem subjects or people difficult for reporters. I began peppering him with possibilities. "Was it something at work? His coworkers? Poor judgment? A bad case that came back to bite him?"

Walt sighed. "No."

"Was it women?"

Walt pointed his finger at me. "Bingo."

"You knew that all along, didn't you?"

"Yes, I did. I had my own messy situation at home with Penny's mother years before. Even though that all happened twenty-five years before Bob died, I wasn't going to throw stones in my own personal glass house. I could just commiserate with Judith."

"Was it one particular woman?"

"I'm not saying any more because I don't want anything attributed to me in your article. I've pointed you in the right direction. That's all I'm going to do."

*****

My next stop was Gary McGinnis's office. Maybe he would have some information on Bob Martz's problem with women. What kind of problem was it, though? Sexual harassment? Infidelity? And could it have led to him getting shot? Who would have shot him? An angry husband? If he was harassing a female trooper, she could have pulled the trigger, too. But the case wouldn't have dragged on all these years, too, if this trooper used her service revolver, would it? It would have been solved quickly. There were too many possibilities to consider—I'd have to present them all to Gary McGinnis and see what his thoughts were.

Within a minute or two, I was standing in front of the dispatcher's bulletproof glass at the JFPD's basement offices beneath city hall. She buzzed me through the door and back to Gary's office.

The assistant chief stood when I entered and shook my hand.

"Good job on the first cold case. You're a hell of a writer," he said. "We haven't gotten any calls yet, but the story could shake something loose. You never know."

We walked to the conference room next door to his office, where all the task force files were now assembled. Each case had a separate table; a large piece of paper taped on the wall above identified each one. I pointed toward the Martz table.

"That's the next story," I said. "I got some information that you all may be aware of, or you may not. I don't know if it's relevant to my story, but here's what I know." Briefly, I explained with Walter Addison told me.

"Before I came here, I worked for a year or so with the Highway Patrol," McGinnis said. "It was about a year after Bob Martz died. There was some talk: I heard he wasn't above flirting with some of the female troopers or any of the female office staff, but that was all I knew. I was a new trooper and didn't get involved in a lot of the office politics."

"Can I see his personnel file?"

"You know I can't show you everything, but I'd be glad to look for you."

Gary lifted the lid on one of the boxes and dug through until he found the right file. He chewed on his bottom lip as he silently flipped through the pages. He stopped and whistled low.

"What?" I asked.

Without a word, he handed me a letter. It was dated eight months before Martz's death and addressed to the post commander.

"Dear Commander," it read. "I am writing to file a formal complaint about Trooper Robert Martz, who stopped me for speeding last Thursday. While I readily agree I was traveling over the speed limit, Trooper Martz was neither professional nor respectful of me during that time. I explained to Trooper Martz I was returning to Jubilant Falls, my hometown, to attend my father's funeral. While he was willing to let me off with a warning for speeding, he said he would do so if I met him after his shift for drinks. I refused and received a written warning."

I looked over at Gary McGinnis, who grimaced and shook his head. I kept reading.

"Over the next week, seemingly each time that I was on the highway between Jubilant Falls and Collitstown, I would be pulled over by Trooper Martz, each time because I was allegedly traveling over the speed limit. Twice, I was over by less than five miles per hour. Once I was traveling under the speed limit. Each time, he said if I would meet him for a drink, he would not issue me the warning. Each time I refused, he became more and more insistent I meet him. Finally, last Monday, I gave in and said yes.

"I did not meet Trooper Martz as I promised. On Tuesday night, I was traveling on a dark county road when Trooper Martz again stopped me. He pulled me forcefully from my vehicle, threw me face down across the hood of my car and, as he held my hands behind my back, he kicked my legs apart and pushed himself against my buttocks, as if to make me think he would sexually assault me. I believed at that point that rape was a distinct possibility, although he never removed or opened his pants."

"Trooper Martz told me, '*This* is what will happen next time you don't do what I ask. Next time, I won't stop.'

"At that point, Trooper Martz released me and walked away. I was shaken, but I got in my rental car and drove away. The next day, I left to fly home to Texas. I drove to the airport by an alternate route so as to avoid encountering this predatory man again. After calling the post repeatedly and getting no satisfactory response, I am filing this formal complaint."

The next few paragraphs promised certain legal action and listed the name of her lawyer, who was copied on the letter. The next page was a letter from that lawyer.

"Oh my god," I said.

At the bottom of the letter was Eve Dahlgren's florid signature.

Chapter 20 Addison

"Thanks, folks!" Leland Huffinger called out as he left the newsroom.

I wasn't real sure about using this PI as a freelancer, but he was better than any other stringer I had. He could easily find out the professional trail our murder victim went down and whom she supposedly damaged along the way. His hourly charge would be more than worth it.

I leaned back in my chair and stared out into the alley behind the building.

I wanted to talk to Betty Dahlgren again, despite her dementia. Who was that woman at her home, the woman wearing the 'barn diva' baseball cap? What part, if any, did she play in Eve's life—or death?

The one person I really needed to talk to was Earlene. She would no doubt be madder than a wet hen about the photo, but what had she said to me Monday night in jail?

"There were things that people don't know about Eve Dahlgren and I hope somebody like you can dig it up."

Maybe she knew some of them. She was out of jail now, thanks to a meal she ate with her father—and now that charges against her were now dropped, she also might be willing to talk. I picked up the receiver on my desk phone and dialed Earlene's cell.

*****

I met Earlene at her father's house. There was no hello as she pulled the heavy oak door open.

"You ran that god awful photo of me, despite what I requested," she said. "My lawyer said I should let it go. That doesn't mean I won't forget it."

"I'm glad to see you're back home, Earlene," I answered sarcastically. "Thanks for having me over."

Earlene walked down the hall toward J. Watterson Whitelaw's study, expecting me to follow.

One night in jail didn't do too much damage, I thought, as I trailed behind. The tall hair was back, along with the tight denim pencil skirt that barely covered her ass, along with a ruffled yellow top that showed too much bosom for her age. She wasn't wearing her usual stilettos; today, it was a pair of yellow sandals with a designer logo across the toes. I was more than a little envious of her long, tan legs.

"Daddy doesn't want me to stay at my condo," she said. "He thinks it's safer for me here."

Isn't that ironic? I thought.

She flopped haughtily into her father's heavy leather chair, behind the dark masculine desk that had been in the *Journal-Gazette's* publisher's office my entire career. I took a seat in the same Morris chair I'd sat in two days before.

The desk was covered with all the components for building a high-maintenance blonde: hairbrushes, mascara, powder, bottles and tubes of make-up and creams. A lighted make-up mirror sat in the middle of the desk, reducing the spot where J. Watterson Whitelaw made hard news decisions for years into a workbench of self-absorption.

Without speaking, Earlene picked up a bottle of hair spray. She pulled the narrow cap off with her teeth, like a soldier pulling the pin on a grenade, and began to spray her hair, fogging our corner of the room. When she was done, she sat the bottle down and, staring into the mirror, picked up a tube of red lipstick, applying it with ferocity.

Next, she removed a spot of cherry red from her front tooth with her little finger and wiped excess color from her cheeks with a tissue. She checked her false eyelashes before shutting off the make-up mirror's hard white lights and looking me dead in the eye.

"What do you want to know?"

"I want to know the whole story of your friendship with Eve. I want to know how this whole mess happened."

Earlene folded her long manicured fingers in front of her and began to speak.

"I probably shouldn't do this, but frankly, I don't care about getting clearance from my lawyer," she began. "As you know, I met Eve while we attended boarding school in Columbus. She came up after the tornado. We became friends almost immediately—I mean, how many other people ever heard of Jubilant Falls? Since she was a late term entry, she was one of the few girls who had no roommate and we used to hang out in her dorm room all the time."

"Your dad didn't like her."

Earlene rolled her eyes. "No, he didn't. It was the last six weeks of school, I was a little wild—but that wasn't Eve's fault."

"What do you mean by a little wild?"

"Oh, you know—it was the 1970s. We slipped off campus at night to meet boys, we drank a little beer, smoked a little pot. Everybody did it. Eve knew these boys up at Ohio State and they would pick us up outside the campus fence and take us to the bars on High Street. Nothing serious—I mean, we never got caught and we weren't the only seniors who did that. Daddy just didn't like Eve."

"Did she ever talk about Jimmy Lyle, her old boyfriend from Shanahan High School?"

"She had a brief fling with one of those OSU boys and it ended badly. That was the first time she mentioned something strange."

"What happened?"

"She had a horrible temper   and was horribly jealous. She keyed this OSU boy's new Camaro, broke the windows out, after she caught him exchanging phone numbers with some girl in a bar."

"Was that when she talked about Jimmy Lyle?"

Earlene nodded. "We were about half potted—I never could hold my beer. But Eve, she saw this girl give him her number and she went nuts. She screamed at him, slapped his face and then grabbed my arm and pulled me onto the street. When he didn't follow her outside to beg for forgiveness or whatever, she got even angrier. She found a brick and broke the windows of his Camaro and then keyed it from the front fender to the back. She even scratched 'liar' across the hood. He came outside screaming about the damage she'd done, just as we were hopping in a cab to head back to school.

"She did say something I thought was odd at the time. As we pulled away she turned around to look out the back window and said, 'Well, there's another man who knows not to mess with someone in the Dahlgren family. Jimmy Lyle learned that lesson the hard way, too.'"

"What do you think she meant by that? Do you think she could kill anybody?"

A somber look came over Earlene's face. "There was a part of Eve that really kind of frightened me. She had a horrible dark side—these unbelievable rages, and dark, dark depressions. But when she was at a party, she was the life of the party. She'd dance on the tables; she could outdrink every man at the place. She had no inhibitions whatsoever and always wanted to push the limits. My first husband used to call her Zelda, after some writer's crazy wife, I don't know who. As for killing somebody, I..." Earlene stopped.

Silence hung in the air between us.

"You believe she could, don't you?"

"The Saturday night we went out, Eve got really drunk. She had been caring for her mother for several years by then and it was a horrible stress on her. Betty has dementia so bad. Eve spends half her money keeping up that house and the other half paying for her mother's care. We went out to dinner that night, and then to this bar. I wanted to stay and have a few drinks, but Eve was acting all paranoid, said she was being followed, so we went to the liquor store, picked up a bottle of vodka and we went back to my condo."

"Paranoid? About what?"

"She always got this paranoid streak when she came home."

"Why do you think that was?"

Earlene shrugged. "Who knows? She made so many people angry over the years."

"But you said she lived in Texas. The people she dealt with professionally wouldn't have followed her back to Jubilant Falls, would they?" I thought about Betty's reaction to the photo of the young man found in the creek.

Earlene shrugged. "She wasn't talking about her job. In her line of work, she eliminated the chaff and the dead weight after a company bought another company out."

"So she came in after corporate raiders bought a company and gutted its staff." I made a note to check in with Leland Huffinger for the details on her professional life.

"Whatever you want to call it, there was a lot of weight on her shoulders from a lot of different sources. When we got to my condo, we had more than a couple drinks and that's where she went off the deep end."

"About what?"

"I mentioned that we'd done a fortieth anniversary issue on the tornado and she just went crazy. 'I don't want to talk about that stupid tornado! I don't want to remember that day!' she said. I told you that Monday, remember? She just kept doing shots, one right after the other."

"The tornado destroyed a lot of people's lives," I said, trying to hide the fact I hadn't listened to too much of anything she'd said Monday afternoon. "What else did Eve say?"

"That's just it. That night was the second time I ever heard her talk about Jimmy Lyle."

My stomach tightened in fear. I swallowed hard and looked her in the eye.

"What did she say?" I asked.

"She said there weren't thirty-five people killed in the tornado. There were only thirty-four."

"Did she mention Jimmy Lyle specifically?" My pulse quickened.

Earlene nodded. "I asked her, 'Eve, who are you talking about?' She just kept saying 'Jimmy was going to ruin my life. He was going to ruin my life and he got what he deserved.' I asked her if she knew how he really died and that's when she turned on me."

"What did she say?"

"She said she knew what really happened, but if I ever mentioned this conversation to anybody about Jimmy Lyle, she would destroy me. I tried to convince her to tell somebody, but she wouldn't hear of it. We argued and she left. Then Monday the police find her dead in the park and I'm looking at a murder charge!"

I leaned back in my Morris chair as Earlene checked herself in the make-up mirror.

"Tell me something, Earlene. Did you ever go to her house?"

Earlene leaned to the side the mirror and gave me an odd look. "Of course not!"

"Really? Why not? I mean if you two were such good friends..."

"With her home situation, Eve didn't want me to come over."

"What do you mean?"

"You never knew? The abuse she suffered at that house was horrible. She's an angel for taking care of Betty, after all that happened at that house."

Chapter 21 Charisma

I handed the letter back to Gary.

"She's accused him of GSI—gross sexual imposition. That's pretty damned serious," I said. "Did you know that was in there?"

Gary flipped through a few more pages of Martz' personnel file before answering me.

"If I did, it wouldn't have mattered before Eve Dahlgren was killed. But look at this." McGinnis handed me another piece of paper. "The post did an investigation, as she asked. The commander took the whole thing very seriously—put Martz on desk duty and everything—but it didn't last too long. Apparently, what Miss Dahlgren didn't realize was that warnings—written or verbal—are recorded in the dispatch log. It's a little different than what we do here at the PD. We actually keep all written warnings on file for a period of time. When investigators checked the log for the nights Eve claimed Martz stopped her, they found no mention of a warning or even a traffic stop. They couldn't even find a record of her calling in to complain—and if someone called in to accuse a trooper of a sex crime, there'd sure as hell be a record of it and there would sure as hell be a swift response. Because of that, the post commander said there was no basis for her accusations and dismissed the whole thing. She apparently wasn't happy."

"According to one of Addison's sources, the woman who was the cheerleader with Eve, she had a tendency to fabricate stories to get back at people," I said.

"Looks like that's what happened here," Gary said, flipping through the file. "She wanted to stick to her guns, though. Her lawyer threatened a lawsuit, screamed cover up, but backed down when faced with the truth."

"But why would she target a trooper?"

"I don't know," McGinnis said. "According to the investigation report, this whole thing was 'the result of some unknown personal vendetta.' Bob Martz may have flirted with the women in the office, but he was a professional with the general public, from what I heard while I was there. Eve may have come on to him somewhere or somehow. When he refused her advances, it pissed her off and she wrote this letter. Who knows at this point?"

"Could it have gotten him killed though? Could Eve Dahlgren have shot him?"

Gary shot a sideways look at me. "You're listening to your boss too much. She wants to pin an awful lot on our victim. Eve may have been a badge bunny—"

"A *what?*"

"A badge bunny—a woman who wants to have sex with cops, especially if they're in uniform. Eve may have been a badge bunny, but we don't think she's a killer."

A shadow darkened the door and we looked up as a heavy, almost obese police officer stepped into the room. The epaulets on his white starched shirt had four stars and he carried his hat in his hand. It had the same four stars across the front.

"Hey Marvin," Gary said, nodding. "Charisma Lemarnier, this is my brother Marvin. He's the chief."

"Pleased to meet you, Chief," I said shaking his hand. "I had hopes of interviewing you for the story about the body in the creek, but we never seemed to make connections."

Marvin McGinnis's bear-paw hand covered my hand. "Yes, my schedule can get pretty full. Still, I'm pleased to meet you. It's not often we have a reporter with your qualifications come to Jubilant Falls," he said.

"What do you mean?" I asked, my throat tightening.

"Most reporters who've covered Baghdad probably find Jubilant Falls a very dull place."

I closed my eyes and clenched my jaw. What I'd feared for so long, what I'd tried to hide was somehow known to the world. Who would have done this to me? Why? My hand, still clutched in the chief's heavy grasp, began to shake. I pulled it free.

"Please," I whispered. "Please don't say anything... I can't let anybody find me. I'm not ready."

The chief didn't hear me. "You don't look like I remember you from television, though. Wasn't your hair blonde back then? You're face is a little different, too, but then with the injuries you sustained... I probably shouldn't have said that. I'm sorry. I just remember sitting in front of the television watching that one series you did on girls' schools in Afghanistan. Man, that was powerful stuff, powerful stuff. Then when that bomb went off—"

Gary's eyes widened as he too realized my identity.

"You're Charisma Prentiss!" he gasped. "Oh my God!"

"*Stop it! Shut up!*" I screamed. Dropping the papers from Bob Martz's file onto the floor, I ran from the room, out the door of the basement department and up the stairs into the street.

Chapter 22 Leland

I ordered lunch at the hotel restaurant and carried it up to my room, where I would continue my research.

Thanks to the clip files, I had a list of firms Eve Dahlgren was employed by, either full-time or as a consultant, up until the mid-1990s. Hopefully, I could get folks to talk to me and let me know what she was like, where she went after that and why. A couple phone calls shouldn't take long; although not the most ethical thing to do, being a fake PI was a good cover. There would be plenty of time this afternoon to run that stuff down.

My mind was on Charisma.

As I ate, I thought about everything I'd seen in the *Journal-Gazette* newsroom this morning. They were a hard-working bunch, comfortable working with each other. Although Charisma also gave her job all she had, I noticed she kept herself apart from most interaction with the other staff members. One young man spoke incessantly about his infant daughter; an older male reporter, looking to be in his early fifties, spoke about covering city hall to Addison. From his conversation, he sounded like the most senior reporter there. A photographer was on staff, but he was apparently out on a vacation day. Dennis, the only person whose name I caught, was the assistant editor and functioned often as the one who kept everything running smoothly.

The chatter was typical of most newsrooms I'd been in—loud, profane and politically incorrect—but Charisma didn't take part in any of it. She kept her head down and worked as everything circled around her. It might have been part of her efforts to stay unrecognized; it might have been her single-minded focus, I wasn't sure. As a result, she wasn't really an integral part of the team. The others knew she could be counted on, that she would fulfill her responsibilities, but I sensed that they hadn't bonded with her. She wasn't one of them and until she opened up and put down roots here, she wouldn't be.

I'd seen that in other small newspapers, ones dominated with staff members whose families had been in the community for generations. New employees who were not related to someone in the community were welcomed and accepted, but it was expected at some point they would move on—and they generally did. Was that what was happening here? If so, that couldn't necessarily be blamed on Charisma.

Why had she chosen this particular little Ohio town? Was it the slower pace? Was it the off-the-beaten-path aspect of Jubilant Falls? Maybe she figured both would be make it easier for her to recover. And why choose to hide in plain sight as she had? Why continue to work in an industry like the news that made someone's identity so public, day after day?

When Noah died and my marriage collapsed, I couldn't face the public scrutiny and chose to hide in academia. While I wasn't charged with my son's death, I still had to live with the story on the front page, followed less than six months later by another headline, *Reporter Charged In Assault*, after I punched Bitch Goddess's lover in the face. Philly newspapers, as well as every other East Coast paper had a field day with it, with headlines filled with leering, juvenile double meanings that nearly destroyed Bitch Goddess's career. That was followed a few months later by a brief page 3B story that began: *An Inquirer reporter charged with assaulting a Channel 3 news anchor received probation and will enter alcohol rehabilitation as part of his sentence.*

The story ended with the publisher's statement, "Mr. Huffinger has been a great part of the team here at the *Philadelphia Inquirer* for a number of years and we wish him well on his efforts to regain his health."

The story didn't include a picture of me being escorted out of the building by security, a box of personal belongings in my arms. Management wouldn't fire me until I'd been proven guilty, after all.

No one ever came looking for me and I did everything to keep the story of my own personal and professional implosion to myself. Outside of my AA meetings, I never told anyone the truth about myself.

Like Charisma, I'd found a place to hide, an insular little world of my own.

She said I'd been the first to come looking for her. It hadn't been too difficult. Did the general public really have that short of an attention span? Was that what she was counting on?

Maybe tonight she'd be willing to open up to me about her PTSD. Maybe I could find out more of what was behind her choices.

I swallowed my last bite of lunch, stacked my dirty dishes on the tray, and opened the door to set them in the hall for pick up. A young woman from housekeeping walked by, carrying a stack of towels in her arms. A lavender fragrance, similar to Charisma's, followed in her wake.

I sat the tray on the carpeted hall floor and leaned against my doorframe, struck by the nearly physical reaction I had to the scent.

I had more than veered off the path I intended to follow when I came to Jubilant Falls. I wasn't anywhere near close to looking at this whole situation from an academic or objective viewpoint. Why even pretend I was here to research anything?

After all, it's not like the department chair knew what I was doing, or that I'd received any kind of a grant or stipend to fund this wild goose chase. My meals, my hotel bill and my airline ticket all came out of my own pocket.

Don't lie to yourself, old man, I thought.

I came in search of the world's most sought-after reporter, and suddenly didn't want to expose her secrets. I'd seen her at her best, making sure she got the information she needed the night the inn burned. I'd seen her at her worst, fighting through the after-effects of the trauma she'd endured. Who was I to rip open her wounds again, this time for the public to see?

Charisma held me at arms length for that very reason. I saw that now.

I stepped back into my hotel room and closed the door.

If I was going to gain her trust, I had to keep up my end of the bargain and see what I could dig up about Eve Dahlgren.

Chapter 23 Addison

"Betty Dahlgren abused Eve?" I stared at Earlene, who was back to gazing at herself in the make up mirror, adjusting each one of her false lashes, like Gloria Swanson in 'Sunset Boulevard,' ready for her close up.

An abusive background would make sense of the bullying Angela Perry suffered through, I thought to myself.

Somehow, I couldn't put the image of a raging, abusive parent together with the well coiffed little old lady sitting on the front porch of that old elegant farmhouse, but god knows what secrets lurk inside someone's door. Maybe Eve's father was the abuser. He might not have abused Eve—he might have abused and controlled Betty and Eve was simply a witness. In either case, it would color her relationship with men. It might also explain what happened at the bar near OSU—and even her overreaction to me tutoring Jimmy Lyle.

"I don't know what the exact details were," Earlene said. "She wouldn't talk about it—never, *ever*—except in these cryptic one-sentence declarations when she'd had too much to drink."

"Like what?"

Earlene shrugged. "One thing she would say, particularly when she had been drinking, was 'You don't know what's behind those awful doors.'"

How could a house with such local historic significance have such dark secrets? Suddenly, I thought about the stocky woman in the pink baseball cap, the one I'd seen at Betty's house.

"Did Eve have a sister or a cousin? Somebody that lives at the house with her?"

Earlene grimaced. "Not that she mentioned. Why?"

"I saw this person the other day when I was out at the Dahlgren house to talk to Betty. This woman is short, stocky, maybe a couple years younger than us. She has bad hair, short and dirty blonde. She had a ball cap that said 'Barn Diva' across the front."

Earlene shook her head. "No idea. They've had horses for some time. I'll bet she works with them."

"You and Eve went to college together, too, didn't you?" I vaguely remembered her rattling on and on about tailgating at college football games.

"Yes, Texas A&M. We applied at the same time and everything."

"Didn't you guys room together?"

"Not the first term. Eve didn't show up until January, when winter term began."

"Why not?"

"She said her parents decided to take her to Europe at the last minute, as a graduation gift."

"Did that seem strange to you? You would think that your best friend from high school would want to pick up where you left off, party-wise."

Earlene shrugged. "If my Daddy wanted to take me to Europe at the last minute, I'd sure let him. Anyway, Eve was bright. She made up all the classes she missed during summer term. We had an off-campus apartment together that summer—while I was working retail at the mall, she was studying."

I made a few more notes. Earlene stood up and smoothed her tight skirt.

"You're going to do a story on this, right?"

"What does your lawyer say?"

"Oh, who cares what he says? He did his job."

"As long as you realize the consequences of talking to me. The investigation is still open and you could be charged again."

Earlene rolled her eyes. "That isn't going to happen."

"Can you explain how your fingerprints got on the Lincoln's steering wheel?"

"Of course! I've driven that Lincoln more than once when Eve's had too much to drink! I drove that car just a few days ago."

"What about the knife the police found?"

"Well, *clearly* Eve was right to feel paranoid at the restaurant Saturday night. Somebody was following her, just like she thought. Whoever it was, overpowered her in the car on Sunday and drove her to wherever she was killed. And I'll bet you they wore gloves when they drove the car and when they stabbed her with the knife. I've seen that lots of times on television."

"This isn't television!"

"I know—and I didn't kill her!"

I tried not to shake my head in disbelief as I made a few more notes and we both stood.

"When do you think you'll be back in the office?" I asked finally.

"Daddy wants me to go back to Texas to visit some old friends until this blows over. My lawyer says I need to stay until this whole thing gets resolved. I may not listen to either one of them," she shrugged. "I may go to the Bahamas. I can't go back to that office as long as people think I killed somebody."

*****

I returned to the newsroom for a few minutes to check in before calling it a day. Marcus waved at me as he finished up a story on the annual meeting the county commission held with township trustees. He also had photos of the fair board painting the cattle barns at the fairgrounds in preparation for next month's fair.

Dennis had a whole list of messages for me: Graham was awaiting a trial verdict on the school bus driver caught driving drunk and wouldn't be back in the office until he heard one way or another. Two people called about being left out of an obituary, claiming to be children from their deceased father's unknown first marriage, and the city school transportation coordinator wanted to do a story about two new buses the district purchased but couldn't get in touch with Charisma.

"Where is she, anyway?" I asked Dennis. "I haven't heard from anybody. My cell phone hasn't rung all afternoon."

He shrugged. "I don't know. She's put in a lot of hours over the last few days, according to her time card. She might have gone home for the day."

I nodded and laid the message on her desk. She could get it tomorrow.

"Well, I think I'm going to do the same," I said.

In a few minutes, I was pulling up the long gravel driveway to the farmhouse, past the soybean field where the tiny green leaves were starting to poke through the rich, black soil.

It was one of those perfect Ohio days where white puffy clouds hung in a light blue sky. Today, one of them hovered behind our old red barn; the Holsteins in the paddock outside the barn added to the pastoral scene. Duncan's old Allis Chalmers tractor stood outside the barn, hitched to a hay wagon, which held several plastic-wrapped round bales, the first cut from our hay fields.

They would be used to feed our heifers later this summer and into the fall and winter. A second cutting would come about a month later, and depending on the weather, we might be able to get a third cutting, which could be a source of cash when we sold it to area horse owners.

I am so lucky to be here, I thought to myself as I parked my Taurus next to the side door. *On this beautiful day, on this beautiful farm, who could want anything else?*

The old wooden screen door, which led into the kitchen, was open. As I stepped from the car, a high-pitched angry wail pealed from inside the farmhouse.

"Hi guys," I said, stepping into the kitchen. "Did I hear a baby cry?"

Duncan and Isabella stood in front of the microwave. Duncan turned to face me.

"Oh, hi," he said. "We've got some company tonight." In his arms was a small, red-faced bundle, kicking and crying. The microwave beeped, and Isabella removed a bottle. She took the baby from her father and popped the bottle into its mouth, instantly stopping the squalling.

"Hi Mom. This is Miss Gwendolyn Kinnon, Graham's daughter," she said.

"Ahh, Miss Gwennie," I said, touching her little face. "I haven't seen you in a little while."

Gwennie, now pleased she had something in her stomach, smiled from around the bottle nipple, formula running from her mouth and into the fat folds of her neck. Duncan wordlessly took a dishtowel from the kitchen counter and wiped it away, laying the towel on Isabella's shoulder.

"Graham has another jury he's waiting on, so I'm watching her again," Isabella said. "He said he tried to call you and let you know what was going on, but it went straight to voicemail."

I grimaced and dug through my purse. "Hmmm. My phone didn't ring all afternoon—figures, it's dead. I did hear from Dennis about the trial, though, so we're good. Dad and I will go out and get the milking done while you feed Gwennie."

Duncan and I headed out to the barn as Isabella sat in the living room to finish feeding the baby.

He reached over and took my hand as we strolled across the grass toward the milking parlor.

"Kind of nice to have a baby in the house," he said.

I looked over at him. "You're kidding, right?"

He shrugged and smiled. "Maybe."

"Isabella has a couple terms in college yet and no plans beyond this farm, Grandpa," I said. "Let's not rush things."

Still, after I ran back into town for a pizza, and we all settled into the living room, it *was* nice to sit back and watch Isabella play with Gwennie on the rug. The drooling, now smiling baby kicked both legs and waved her arms as Isabella held a squeaky toy above her. The joyous sound of a giggling baby, the way Isabella—and Duncan— got down on the floor and played with her... I couldn't help but feel warm, safe and calm here in my own home.

But what about Eve? From what I learned from Earlene, she didn't experience the feelings that now surrounded me. The abuse she allegedly suffered at the hands of her parents clearly colored her relationships with others, both women and men. She bullied other members of the cheerleading squad and the men she dated, subjecting them to physical abuse and lies. Jimmy Lyle did something to her that set her off and, if Earlene was to be believed, he ended up dead. She vandalized yet another young man's vehicle when he was caught flirting with another girl in a campus bar.

Her job continued the abuse, if Angela Perry was to be believed, ripping people apart before eliminating their jobs in an effort to streamline corporate efficiency.

Was the young man in the creek one of her professional victims? Betty Dahlgren's reaction was striking: "Eve didn't like that boy." What did that mean? Had they been romantically involved? Had he not taken a break up well? Or had this unknown young man come to Jubilant Falls, begging to get his job back? Had she killed him then?

In Charisma's story, Hiram Warder surmised that two people committed the murder. But who? Eve and her father? He was still alive at the time the boy's body was found. Could he have killed him and then out of guilt, committed suicide several years later? Could it have been someone else who lived in that house? Eve never spoke of any siblings, according to Earlene.

And who was that woman in the 'Barn Diva' hat? Where does she fit into all this? Does she work at the farm, caring for the horses as Earlene surmised? Does she help care for Betty Dahlgren? What's her place in all this?

Who killed Eve Dahlgren? Who had she enraged in her long history of abuse to make her feel paranoid while out to dinner Saturday with Earlene? Was someone following her? And what would push them far enough to want to kill her?

My thoughts on Eve's murder evaporated as Gwennie squalled. Isabella picked her up, patting her on the bottom as the baby sucked ravenously on her fist.

"Time to call it a night, little one," Isabella said. "One last bottle and we're putting you to bed."

Duncan made up another bottle of formula and, when the microwave beeped, handed it to Isabella. Gwennie took the rubber nipple into her mouth, sucking until her eyes grew heavy with slumber.

"Where is she sleeping?" I asked as Isabella walked down the hallway toward the dining room we used as an office.

"Graham brought over a portable crib," Duncan said. "We set it up back there the last time Izzy babysat."

"What, is this going to be a regular thing?" I asked.

Duncan shrugged. "It works out pretty well for everybody. Gwennie seems to like Izzy. Graham knows his daughter is OK, Izzy has a little extra money in her pocket and you have a reporter who can stick with a story until it's done."

There was a knock at the kitchen door.

"Speaking of the devil...Isabella, don't put her down just yet. Graham's here." Duncan walked through the kitchen and let Graham in the door. "Come on in," he said.

Graham waved sheepishly at me.

"Got a verdict?" I asked.

He nodded. "Guilty. Sentencing will be later this month, but guy won't be driving a school bus—or anything else— anytime soon. At least that's what the prosecutor is asking for and the judge indicated he wants to throw the book at him. I can write the story tonight, if you want. We'll need to follow up with the school district, too, and see if he gets fired."

"Go ahead. That way we will have it before the TV stations and the eleven o'clock news," I said. I knew as soon as he got her settled into bed, he'd sit down and write the story. Many things may have changed in his life, but his drive to be first on a story hadn't. He could post it from home to the website.

Isabella brought Gwennie into the kitchen and handed her off to her father. Quickly, we rounded up baby stuff: blankets, toys, bottles, a final bottle of formula from the fridge as Graham fastened his daughter in the car seat outside. Duncan and I handed everything to Izzy, who packed it all in the diaper bag.

"Got everything?" I asked, reaching for the diaper bag. "I'll take it out to him if you want."

"I got this." Isabella smiled and pulled the diaper bag closer to her. "Let me go say goodbye to Miss Gwennie."

Duncan wrapped his arm around my shoulders as she walked out to Graham's minivan.

"It was nice to have a little one around, I have to admit," I said, leaning against him. "Maybe some day."

Duncan drew me close and hugged me. As we parted, I glanced out the kitchen door. I saw Graham lean close to my daughter's face and his arms slip around Isabella's shoulders. Did he just kiss my daughter? What the hell is going on here?

Chapter 24 Charisma

Who could have done this to me? *Who?*

I paced around my studio apartment, shaking with anger and fear. How did the chief of police find out? Who could have told him? Or did he, like Leland, do a simple computer search, dig up my past and was so damned star-struck he had to open his mouth?

Leland. Who else could have done this to me except Leland? But why tell the police chief? Where and how did they connect?

I should have known better. I should have listened to that little voice inside me, the one that said he was only working to get me to lower my guard. The feelings I had, that was all crap—manipulations by a man claiming to know what it was like to be the cause of losing someone you loved. Taking me in his arms to soothe my tears, to hide me from those reporters seeking information on Earlene's arrest, placing a kiss—*that kiss*—on the back of my hand... It was all crap.

I got conned—I was stupid enough to let it happen, to open up my heart. That whole story he told about his son dying in a drunken car wreck, about his nasty divorce? It had to be made up, anything to get him to tell me made up, anything to get him to tell me my story, to get me to say everything that happened that horrible, horrible day when Jean Paul died.

I grabbed my cell from the dinette table and punched in Leland's number.

"You bastard!" I screamed as soon as he answered.

"What?"

"You broke your promise to me! You exposed me!"

"I have not!"

"Bullshit! The police chief, Marvin McGinnis, knows who I am! 'We don't get reporters with qualifications like yours...'" I mimicked. "'Jubilant Falls must seem awfully dull after Baghdad.' How the *fuck* would he know who I am? *Huh?* What did you do to me? What did you do?"

He was silent for a moment. "I was at my daily Alcoholics Anonymous meeting. There was a police officer there, it must have been the chief. I mentioned you." His voice sounded sad, but I wouldn't be sucked into his game this time. I wouldn't feel sorry for him.

"You *mentioned* me? How the hell did you happen to *mention* me?"

"What we say at AA is supposed to be kept within the walls of that meeting. Obviously, the chief didn't do that. I'm sorry."

"You just couldn't wait to tell somebody you'd found me, could you? You just couldn't wait!" My voice shook with rage.

"That's not true. I promised you I'd keep your secret in the article. I wasn't going to reveal your location there. I was going to give you two weeks notice before the article came out, so you could give notice or tell your boss or whatever you wanted to do. I even went along with your ruse that I was a private investigator. I agreed to every condition you set."

"Until you get among your damned AA buddies and you can't wait to tell them who you've found."

"No, Charisma. That's not what happened."

"What the hell did you say?"

Again, he considered his words before answering.

"I said I met someone that I thought I was starting to have feelings for. That I was scared those feelings would impact my sobriety."

"You expect me to believe that?"

"You can believe what you want. It's been a long time since I've wanted a woman in my life. I'm falling for you."

"I may have been born at night, but it wasn't last night, Leland. I'm not going to fall for that crap. You can go to hell as far as I'm concerned."

I disconnected the call and threw my cell phone on the couch. Did he really expect me to believe him? Falling for me, for this scar-covered body?

I picked up one of the couch pillows and with an angry scream, threw it across the room.

It landed in front of the bureau where I kept my clothes, next to the only closet in the apartment. I walked across the carpet and yanked open the closet door. Crammed into a corner was the one duffel I'd brought with me when I came to Jubilant Falls. It was military issue; I'd dragged it from one corner of the world to another. After I got out of the hospital the second time, it held everything I had when I came to this stupid little town.

I yanked it into the middle of the floor and, grunting with each angry movement, began pulling all of my clothing out of my bureau drawers, throwing pants, pajamas, tee shirts and jeans at the duffel bag. When the bureau was empty, I did the same to my closet, tossing dress pants, blouses and my winter coat at the duffel. Some of the clothing landed inside, most of it landed on the floor nearby.

I had to leave tonight.

After I packed, I'll walk over to the newsroom, leave a resignation letter on Addison's desk, get in my car and hit the road. I could leave a note for my lawyer landlord downstairs: I could tell him to keep my deposit, the dishes I bought, the towels in the bathroom and even the art on the wall. The rent was paid through the end of the month.

I needed to disappear now.

The plan had never been to stay here in Jubilant Falls. I was going to get back on my feet here, before moving on to the next step in my career... if there was going to be a career. But where could I go? To my mother's apartment in Maryland? To Dad and Kate's condo in Washington? Neither appealed to me. I couldn't go back to New York. Who would hire me? A newspaper or newspaper service? Not after that Syria article. I couldn't go on camera without someone commenting on my face and my scars. Maybe I could work as a producer someplace? My passport was still valid—maybe an overseas broadcaster, like Al Jazeera? My Arabic and Farsi were a bit rusty, but each would come back, despite my injuries.

It would, wouldn't it?

The intercom from my downstairs door buzzed as I yanked open the bathroom cabinet. I stomped over and pushed the button.

"Fuck you, Leland! Fuck you and all you stand for and all you've done to me!" I screamed.

"Charisma, please. Let me in."

"I think you've done enough for one day."

"What I told you on the phone was the truth. I was telling the members of the AA group how frightened I was because I was falling for you. I was afraid I would lose my sobriety."

"And you just happened to mention who I was."

"Let's not do this on the street. Let me come up. Let me explain myself."

I let my thumb off the intercom button and stomped downstairs.

I threw open the door. Leland stood there, clutching his Philadelphia Phillies ball hat in his hands. Those blue eyes that once drew me in looked sad and filled with pain. It was a good act, anyway.

I motioned for him to follow me up the stairs, but didn't say anything in greeting. Once inside my apartment, I turned and folded my arms.

"Explain yourself," I said.

"I was at an AA meeting, like I told you. I said you were a former war correspondent and your husband was killed by a bomb in Baghdad," he said. "I said you were severely wounded."

"And how many female war correspondents were injured *and* widowed in Baghdad in the last few years? Huh? One— *me.*" Enraged, I pointed at myself, my pulse pounding in my temples. "It's not hard to put all those pieces together, Leland."

He hung his head. "I know. I just counted on the confidentiality of the meeting."

"And I counted on you keeping your mouth shut at all times, which you didn't do."

"I thought I could trust the folks at this meeting."

Suddenly, all my anger evaporated, leaving me filled with an incredible sadness.

"There's a reason I never let anyone tell my story, Leland. You and I know how this business works. I'm the prize 'get' for anyone looking for the next big headline. I know my story will be spun six ways to sunset and I'm not ready for that. Somebody will interview me, then their version shows up in print or on TV slashing me to ribbons for that Syria story. Somebody else will make me the poster child for traumatic brain injury or post-traumatic stress or whatever box he or she thinks I'll fit into. Fact is, I don't want to be spun. I don't want to feed someone's ego—whether that is some big TV reporter or a journalism professor like you. I want the truth to be told, but my way.

"I'm still coming to grips with my limitations. I can't multi-task like I used to. I'm not the pretty blonde I used to be—I cry every time I take off all my clothes and see every scar that marks my body. I have a titanium rod in my left leg and a scar there that looks like I've been filleted. There's blue pieces of shrapnel embedded up and down the left side of my body the doctors couldn't get out, like some kind of buckshot tattoo. How can I let any man see me like that?"

Leland started to speak but I held up my hand for silence.

"Crowds scare me sometimes," I continued. "It's a good thing I'm the only one living in these apartments up here because some nights I wake up screaming. Last week, a freight train came through town early in the morning after I'd been out on a story and I was convinced it was an incoming missile. I dove beneath the table, screaming for Jean Paul. I couldn't find my helmet. All I could see was his camera lying in the dirt and covered in his blood, just like the day he died. Then the train whistle blew and I realized where I was and I broke down."

"I want to make you feel safe. I don't want you to have to go through that alone."

I shook my head and continued my story. "I went back to work long before I was ready and got pulled into the situation in Aleppo through a combination of things: an editor who wanted to be first, the second source I never sought out, and my own ego, which didn't take into account how damaged I really am. I was so damned close to the edge with my PTSD, sometimes I wonder if the whole thing was some kind of hallucination. If that's what really happened, I was psychotic and needed to be in that mental hospital, not hung out to dry on every network and in every newspaper."

"What mental hospital?"

I shook my head. He wasn't going to hear that story now.

"Somebody should have been looking out for me and forced me into treatment, but they weren't. The woman that everyone knew as Charisma Prentiss was a commodity, not the wounded, damaged woman that I am. They needed the ratings, the next story and what about me? What about me?

"So now you know why I came to Jubilant Falls. I thought I could work here. I thought I could hide here. I thought I could heal, figure things out. You want to keep me safe? Well, you're a little too late. You think you have feelings for me? That's too damned bad."

"What are you going to do now?" he asked, gesturing at my clothing on the floor.

"I'm going to disappear. I have to. It won't be long before either Marvin or Gary McGinnis says something to somebody, who says something to somebody else, and then the word gets out and I'm not in control of the situation anymore. It's not ego for me to say that—my own well-being ranks ahead of somebody else's scoop."

"Are you going to tell Addison?"

"I don't know yet."

"What about the Eve Dahlgren information you had me dig up?"

"You can fill Addison in tomorrow and collect your check. I won't be there." I opened my apartment door and showed him the stairs. "You can go now. You've got what you want— spin it any way you see fit. I hope it gets you where you want to go."

Without a word, Leland walked out through the door. I closed the door behind him, sank to the floor and sobbed.

It was nearly one in the morning by the time I had my duffel packed and ready to load into my car. It sat next to Monsieur Le Chat's cat carrier by the door. Monsieur Le Chat sat atop the carrier, his tail whipping angrily.

I tried to call Addison, but the voice mailbox on her cell phone was full. At this time of the morning, I didn't want to call her home phone. Instead, I found myself walking around the corner to the newsroom.

I could leave a note, load my car and be on my way, I reasoned. Where that would be, I still didn't know. Head east and show up on either of my parents' doorsteps? Head west and see what happens? I slid my key into the pressroom door and slipped inside.

Across the darkened room, the light in the employee break room was on, as was the coffee pot. Was somebody here or had both just been inadvertently left on? Who knows, the way staff from all departments came in and out of the building. I switched off the coffee pot, but left the light on as I passed through to the stairs and up to the newsroom. I would need it on my way back out.

I jumped back as a man's tall, hulking shadow passed across the newsroom door.

"Oh hi, Charisma." It was Chris Royal, the sports writer. "What brings you in tonight?"

"Oh, um, I forgot something... My camera."

Royal, holding a stale donut and a cup of coffee, didn't seem to catch my nervousness as he blathered on. "I got a west coast Reds game on rain delay. I'm waiting until two, and then taking what story the AP already has on the wire and getting the hell out of here. You got a police call or something? I didn't hear anything on the scanner."

He leaned back in his office chair, donut crumbs in his scraggly beard. Like most sports writers I'd known, he was a creature of the night. Most of the staff never saw him unless they were here in the evenings. He had on a dirty tee shirt, wrinkled khaki shorts and his hairy legs and feet disappeared, sockless, into a pair of beaten tennis shoes.

He'd apparently been at the J-G for a couple years, and managed to establish a reputation for decent sports writing, but sometimes-questionable hygiene.

His presence meant I couldn't clean out my desk or write my resignation letter. What did I have in my desk anyway that I couldn't walk away from? A stack of notebooks? An old coffee mug? All I had was my camera—Jean Paul's camera, actually. No family pictures, not even a photo of Monsieur Le Chat. Nothing I couldn't leave behind. Besides, Leland would be more than happy to fill Addison in on what happened.

"No, I, um, have an assignment first thing in the morning," I said.

"Oh, OK." Royal brushed the remaining donut crumbs from his hands and beard and turned back to his computer.

Over at my desk, I opened a drawer and pulled out the familiar camera bag.

Could I walk away? In the short months I'd been here, I had gotten better emotionally, at least until this latest setback in the guise of Dr. Leland Huffinger. Addison and the staff had been good to me, never questioning me about my past, but accepting me as a member of the team.

The community had accepted me, too. I'd developed positive relationships with the city school board, the folks at Golgotha College and especially with Assistant Chief McGinnis—at least until today when he realized who I was.

I couldn't face them again.

I held the camera close to my chest and left the newsroom.

Chapter 25 Leland

"So, what can I get you?"

The bartender, a young woman with a pierced eyebrow, wiped the area in front of me with a rag.

The hotel bar was dark, bland, and semi-shabby, probably only used by guests. Booze sat in three rows in front of a mirror, framed in neon. Tonight, I was the only person there.

Thank God.

I pulled a fifty-dollar bill from my wallet and slapped it on the bar.

"Vodka, on the rocks, with a slice of lime," I said. "Top shelf."

Her movements were graceful as a ballerina. She turned to pick up a glass from behind the bar, making sure I got a good long look at her lusciously plump behind filling tight black pants and the full breasts that filled her white tuxedo shirt. In one smooth motion, she filled it with cubes from the ice bin below the bar and poured the vodka. The dance ended when she set the glass in front of me. She caught my eye and gave me a saucy smile with red lips that matched her bowtie.

"There you go."

A few simple days ago, I reprimanded myself for ogling a female student. Today, this juicy, young thing in front of me didn't even merit a passing fancy. My mind was still on the damage I'd done to the one woman I wanted.

Breathing deeply, I wrapped my hand around glass. This devil hadn't come knocking in more than five years. If that glass touched my lips, the slide would begin again.

And why shouldn't I just lift it to my lips and take a swallow? I'd lost the complete trust of a woman I'd wanted in my life—or at this point, wanted to see if she would fit into my life—thanks to someone breaking the code of AA meetings. I'd been let down by those who had for many years kept me on the straight and narrow. Then I'd let down Charisma. Nothing mattered.

Before I knew how opening my mouth at AA had hurt Charisma, I'd spent my time hunting down where Eve Dahlgren had been since the 1990s. What I'd found put some credence behind Addison McIntyre's belief that a person—not a tornado—could have killed Jimmy Lyle. I'd found nothing to connect Eve to the death of the young man in the creek, despite the reaction of the demented old lady, but other information I'd found might start putting the pieces together. I'd found out Eve Dahlgren was exactly the evil bitch Addison McIntyre thought she was, but she still didn't deserve to die. Nothing I found led me directly to her murderer. Or did it?

I was going to tell Charisma tonight at dinner. It was going to be a night of celebration.

Until now.

I made wet circles with the glass on the bar's black surface.

"You gonna drink that?" The bartender leaned towards me, resting on her elbows. She arched her un-pierced eyebrow at me.

"I suppose so. At some point," I said, smiling crookedly.

"Well, I've got some stuff to do in the back. If you need anything, just holler for me. My name's Judy." She stood and smiled.

"Thanks, Judy." I watched her slink away.

I lifted the glass to my lips, and then set it back down. I knew what would happen if I took that first sip. I closed my eyes as if to hide from what I was about to do.

I'd had vodka the night Noah died, too. Just like what sat in front of me now: on ice, with a slice of lime. He'd been the pride of my life and I'd killed him. How many did I have that night? Six? Seven? Probably more. What did Noah drink? He'd learned at the hands of the master: his poison of choice was bourbon. In high school and college, he mixed it with Coke. The night he died, he drank it straight.

I had handed him my car keys before we left that Philadelphia bar.

I clenched my jaw as the memory of tearing metal, the smell of leaking gasoline flooded through my mind.

The car lay on the driver's side, the engine compartment crushed between the tree and the front seat where Noah hung, bloody and silent, over the steering wheel.

"Noah!" I'd screamed. "Noah! You gotta get out, son! Noah!"

I remembered how I wiped blood from my face and pushed myself out of the passenger window. Still drunk, I fell to the ground, feeling my left arm snap. The gasoline odor suddenly got stronger—there was a flash of ignition—and suddenly nothing would ever be the same.

Noah's funeral, the assault, my ruined newspaper career, all of it was the consequences of one ghastly night.

And what I'd done to Charisma was an extension of all that. Telling my story, opening my heart for the first time in years, admitting I'd found someone I wanted in my life to people I didn't know. It was all too much and she, like Noah and Bitch Goddess, paid the price.

Now she was packing to leave, intent on disappearing into the ether. I'd found and exposed the world's best-known war correspondent, a woman who only wanted to hide, and caused her more trauma than what she already suffered.

The ice in my vodka glass clinked as I lifted it to my lips. I took a sip, feeling the familiar burn as it slid down my throat. I had no reason to stay sober any more, no reason to keep my life on track. I could give in to my demons, stay drunk until fall quarter or later and no one would know, or care. What did I have to return to anyway? Visits to my dead son's grave, with its inherent risk of running into the Bitch Goddess, the first woman whose life I'd ruined? An empty apartment that reminded me daily of how much I'd lost?

I tossed the rest of the vodka down my throat.

"Judy!"

No answer.

"Judy!"

She appeared from the back, wiping her hands.

"I'm coming, I'm coming! Want another drink?" she asked.

"I want the whole bottle and a bucket of ice. You can charge it to my room."

She nodded, filled a plastic ice bucket and sat it on the bar. She grabbed the vodka bottle and pushed the receipt, along with a pen, toward me.

I signed and picked up the ice bucket, tucking the vodka bottle under my arm.

"I put your drink on that, too," Judy said. "Don't forget your fifty!"

"Keep it." I said as I headed toward the lobby and the oblivion that awaited me in my hotel room. "It's yours."

Chapter 26 Addison

"Kinnon, in my office, *now!*"

It was Thursday morning and I was still addled from seeing him kissing my daughter the night before.

Graham stepped inside and shut the door quietly behind him.

"Do you hit on all of your babysitters or is my daughter just not as immune to your charms as the others?" I pointed at one of the wingback chairs. "Sit."

"Addison, it's not what you think." Graham sat suddenly, like a Labrador obeying a command.

"Then tell me what the hell it is." Duncan kept me from peppering Isabella with the same question last night.

Graham sighed. "It was just an innocent kiss, Addison. We're going to go out for coffee this weekend, if—"

I didn't let him finish. "I cannot believe that you would have the audacity—"

"She's an adult, Addison," Graham cut me off. "She's twenty-two. I'm twenty-eight. Elizabeth was almost thirty-four when she died."

This time, I sighed, realizing how ridiculous I sounded. If anybody on my staff deserved some happiness, it was Graham.

"OK. It's just..." I stopped. "Isabella doesn't date much and of all people on this earth, I never thought it would be one of my staff members."

"Yeah, well, how do you think I feel? I came to her high school graduation party! She was a kid when I met her. That night she came over to my apartment to babysit, we got to talking and, I think, we really kind of liked each other. We've been talking on the phone every night this week. It's just coffee, Addison, that is, if—"

"If what?"

"If I can get a babysitter."

I threw my hands in the air. "Sure. What the hell."

"Thanks," Graham grinned. I'd been out-maneuvered.

"Just be sure you treat her well. You're used to dealing with me—you've never dealt with her dad," I said. "Now get the hell out of my office. We've got a paper to put out."

Charisma opened the door and poked her head through. She looked haggard and I could see her hand quiver as it rested on the doorknob. Her voice was hoarse.

"I need to talk to you, Addison," she said.

Graham nodded in my direction and pulled the door closed behind him as Charisma stepped into my office.

"What's up? Did my dad have anything helpful for you on the Bob Martz murder?"

"Yes. Yes he did. But there's something else I need to tell you first."

My stomach sank. I'd had conversations like this before—I'd almost developed a second sense as to when a reporter was going to give notice. This was that time.

"This isn't good news, is it?" I asked slowly.

She shook her head and sighed. "I need to leave. This has to be my last day."

"*What*? You're not giving me two weeks' notice?"

I fished in my drawer for my cigarettes. First, I find out my daughter has a date with somebody on my staff and next my newest reporter says she has to quit today? It's not even fucking eight in the morning.

"I've lied to you, Addison. I'm not who I said I was."

"What is going on here?" I asked as I lit up. It was less than three hours until deadline, I had no idea what my front page is going to look like and I'm spending my mornings dealing with personnel problems. God*dammit.*

"Do you remember the reporter who went down in flames over a bad story from Syria?"

"About a year ago? Didn't she suffer a really bad head injury in Baghdad before all that? Like from a car bomb? What does she have to do with you?"

Charisma looked at me straight in the eye, sweeping her hair away from her face and exposing the scars along the left side of her face. There were more scars on her arm.

As I stared back at her, the uneven cheekbones seem to return to symmetry. The hair wasn't brown and shaggy and in need of a good stylist: it was golden yellow, impeccably cut. The face I'd seen on the television and whose byline I'd read came into focus and I saw the blonde television reporter standing familiarly beside a convoy of military vehicles, dressed in jeans and a bullet-proof vest, speaking confidently about the situation at hand.

She was sitting right in front of me.

"Oh my god. You're Charisma Prentiss."

Chapter 27 Charisma

"Yes. I'm Charisma Prentiss."

This wasn't going the way I wanted it to at all.

I didn't disappear like I wanted to. After I left the newsroom with my camera, I walked back to my apartment, intent on loading the car and leaving Jubilant Falls forever. Instead, I cried myself to sleep, waking ten minutes before I was supposed to be in the newsroom to start my day.

I should have just driven off at that point, but something told me to go inside and tell her the truth. I'd faced tribal leaders in the mountains of Afghanistan, Syrian rebels and sat down with the leaders of several nations, for Christ sake. I should be able to face Addison McIntyre. Instead, my hands were shaking and my voice quavered.

Addison leaned back in her chair and glared at me, drawing deeply on her cigarette. Her eyes were hard. "Anything else I need to know?"

"I guess you know now the resume I gave you was fake. Those were all folks I'd worked with at the wire service willing to lie for me and say I'd worked for them once upon a time at a bunch of made-up, small-town newspapers. The fact you didn't check my references made it easier for me to hide. Now my old friends don't even know where I am."

"And this Leland Huffinger, this private investigator you conned me into hiring at a hundred bucks an hour? Who —or what—is he, really?"

"A journalism professor, doctorate and all. He's the one who found me. He's the reason I have to quit."

"Why quit just because he found you? I don't understand that. I told you when I hired you that if someone came looking for you, I couldn't protect you. I didn't expect you to turn tail and run."

"Leland Huffinger exposed my whereabouts at an AA meeting here in town," I sighed. "He's a former alcoholic and attends meetings every day. Apparently he went to a meeting here and told the folks there, in a round-about way, why he was in Jubilant Falls. Marvin McGinnis apparently was at the same meeting and figured out who I was. I saw him at the police station and the first thing he says to me is 'I'm sure Jubilant Falls is pretty boring for you after Baghdad.' "

Addison chewed her thumbnail, but her eyes were still hard. "Marvin's not known for his subtlety. He lost his first wife to breast cancer a number of years ago. His drinking nearly cost him his job until he found AA. I didn't know he was still attending meetings."

I shrugged. "Yeah, well..."

"Why was Leland Huffinger looking for you?"

"I was supposed to be part of a project. He was looking for journalism's most spectacular flame-outs and he wanted to interview them for an article."

"So the story about him investigating this accident that you supposedly were injured in was bullshit, too."

"Yes," I said. "I thought having him investigate Eve Dahlgren's background for us would help me keep an eye on him, and at the same time, maybe, get us some useful information. I thought it would give me a little control over the situation."

"That didn't turn out so well, did it?" Her voice dripped with sarcasm.

"No."

"So what *wasn't* bullshit, Charisma? What *didn't* you lie about to me?"

"The fact that I'm a widow. The fact that I have PTSD and don't know if I can ever work at the same level again. The fact that I came here to Jubilant Falls to hide and to heal and I will be forever grateful for the opportunities you've given me to do both those things." I stood.

Addison chewed her thumbnail a little more, her eyes softening a bit. Nothing worse than an editor's anger. Had I escaped?

"What if I gave you the opportunity to tell your story and we put it on the front page?"

"Today?" I gulped.

"Could you write it this afternoon for tomorrow's paper?" Addison tossed her cigarette out the window into the alley. "Will you stay one more day, just to do that?"

I looked sideways at her, unsure of her motives.

"I'm not ready to talk to anybody about what happened to me."

"If you do it first, you control the story." Her anger evaporated, Addison began to pace back and forth behind her desk, energized. "Of course, I can't guarantee what happens after we put it on the website or send it to the wire—you realize we have to send this to the AP—but the first words the world sees will be yours—not Leland's. Yours."

She had a point. For all his fake promises, I had no idea how Leland was going to tell my story. He could make me look like some ego-driven reporter, burned by my own self-importance and loss of objectivity—or the broken down shell of a person whose emotional and physical wounds keep her from functioning. The truth was, I had been both of those things. I was still somewhere in between, scarred physically and mentally, still slightly brittle, but not nearly as fragile as I'd been when I came here.

"Addison, I can't. I need to disappear. Once the word gets out that I'm here, my story will be twisted in ways I don't even want to think about. When it gets out that I'm here, this town will be crawling with every kind of national media wanting to talk to me—and to you."

"You think I can't handle that? Thanks, but it's not your problem. Just tell your story and tell it first on my front page."

"I can't, Addison. I can't."

Her shoulders sagged in disappointment.

"OK. I'm not going to beg you to stay."

I turned to leave.

"Wait!" Addison called sharply. "What did you learn about the Bob Martz murder yesterday? If I've got to finish that story, I at least need to get that information from you."

Chapter 28 Addison

"Eve Dahlgren accused Bob Martz of attempted sexual assault eight months before he died? You're kidding me."

"Nope." Charisma slowly shook her head back and forth.

"If we present the way her mother Betty reacted to the picture of our drowning victim and the letter in Bob Martz's personnel file, we can tie Eve Dahlgren to both of our unsolved homicides."

"Those two ties are just that—ties. They aren't proof that she killed either one of them." Charisma seemed refocused and less intent on running away. "With her dementia, Betty's reaction could be completely off base."

If I couldn't talk her into telling her own story, maybe I could talk her into staying long enough to write down everything she had learned about Eve. I had a lot to add from my own interview with Earlene.

"No, we can't say she killed either of those two men, but don't you think it's odd that she's connected to both of them? And now she's dead as well? What made you ask Gary about his personnel file?"

"Your dad told me to look there. He wouldn't give me the whole story—he said something about a messy situation with your mother—but he just told me where to look."

I sighed. My mother June was an emergency room nurse at the Plummer County Memorial Hospital when she met my father. She was also bipolar, un-medicated and, when manic, had a proclivity for sleeping with other troopers and spending wild amounts of cash, behavior that nearly cost Dad his career.

She disappeared when I was six, and I was an adult before I learned she died on an Illinois highway, the victim of a drunk driver. My daughter Isabella was her spitting image, down to her red hair and the Lithium she needed to stay on an even keel.

"Yes. He and Bob Martz's widow Judy were very close." No need to say anything else, I thought.

"He didn't want to spill the details of what was going on. Said he didn't want to hurt Judy. I think there might have been an affair going on with Eve and Bob Martz, but I wasn't able to confirm it."

"Tell you what—you write everything down. I'll call Dad and see if he still has Judith's number. She'd talk to me before she'd talk to anyone else. If Bob were screwing around, Judy would tell me. In all the follow up stories I've done, I don't think I ever asked her if her husband was unfaithful. I never thought of it and no one ever suggested it."

The phone call to Judy Martz was painful.

"I never wanted anybody to know," she said. "Every time you called for a follow up story, I worried that someone told you he had been unfaithful, but you never asked. So, I never said anything—it was too embarrassing."

"I'm asking now."

"Yes, he was involved with a much-younger woman for a couple years. Yes, it was Eve Dahlgren. It was an on-and-off thing."

"I'm sorry, Judy."

She was silent. "Your dad called the other day to tell me she'd been murdered. I always thought she had something to do with Bob's death, but nobody could prove anything."

"And our story won't say she killed your husband. We just think it's odd that she's connected to both of the county's unsolved murders."

"You and your staff can think what you want, Penny. I'm going to think there's been some sort of justice served."

A few more questions and the post-high school picture of Eve Dahlgren came more into focus, none of it pretty. Behind the well-done blonde hair and the perfectly made-up face, Eve was a driven, hard-edged businesswoman with no compunction about verbally and physically abusing those around her, whether professionally or personally. She had no second thoughts about sleeping with someone's husband and then sending a fake letter in an attempt to ruin his career when he dumped her.

An hour later, Charisma's story about Bob Martz filled the copy desk computer screen in front of me.

Dennis leaned over my shoulder.

"You want me to hold the front page for this? We've got a little bit of time," he asked.

"Sure. Tell the guys in the pressroom to give us about half an hour, probably less. I want this big and above the fold," I answered.

In short order, I added what relevant information Earlene told me as well as what Judy Martz's phone call confirmed. Dennis shooed me out of the copy desk chair and brought up the front page and page two, quickly rearranging the news hole to accommodate the new story, moving the ends of stories that wouldn't completely fit on page one—called jumps—to the next page.

"Look good to you?"

I nodded. No time to print out a proof and check it. I prayed I hadn't missed any errors.

"Send it."

"Here it goes, then." He pushed the button to send it to prepress.

It was just before lunch when Sam the foreman brought copies of today's edition up to the newsroom. Charisma, Dennis and I jumped, practically snatching them from his hands. Marcus and Graham crowded around as I spread the paper across an empty desk and we all began to read.

Victim linked to other crimes
By Charisma Lemarnier and Addison McIntyre
Journal-Gazette staff

A woman found dead in a local park has ties to Plummer County's two unsolved homicides.

Eve Dahlgren was found dead in her Lincoln Monday. The car was discovered by an off-duty Jubilant Falls' police officer in Shanahan Park; Dahlgren had been stabbed several times.

Before Dahlgren's death, area law enforcement was taking a fresh look at two unsolved homicides: the stabbing death of an unidentified young man whose body was found floating in Shanahan Creek near the Yarnell Bridge in the early 1980s and the death of State Trooper Robert Martz, who was found shot by the side of the road in the 1990s.

Journal-Gazette publisher Earlene Whitelaw was originally charged with Dahlgren's murder, but released when Dahlgren's time of death was found to be Sunday night and Whitelaw had an alibi for that night.

She was reportedly having dinner with her father, former J-G publisher J. Watterson Whitelaw.

Earlene Whitelaw and Dahlgren had been friends since high school, attending Texas A&M together, and shared an apartment during that time.

An investigation by *Journal-Gazette* staff, originally to look into the unsolved crimes has found Dahlgren is a common factor in both.

Dahlgren's mother Betty, who suffers from dementia and is under the care of a home health aide, was questioned recently by J-G staff and identified the man found in the creek as someone who "Eve didn't like," although she didn't give the victim's name. J-G staff members were asked to leave shortly thereafter.

None of this information was included in the creek murder story, which ran Wednesday, due to concerns over Betty Dahlgren's dementia and the validity of her recollection.

The *Journal-Gazette* decided to include the information when investigation into the Martz murder uncovered a letter from Eve Dahlgren accusing him of gross sexual imposition during a traffic stop.

In a letter, dated eight months before Martz was found shot to death on the side of the road, Dahlgren claims that Martz repeatedly stopped her for speeding and, in exchange for not giving her a ticket, asked her to meet him for drinks.

Eve Dahlgren's letter says she repeatedly refused until she finally promised to meet him for a drink, but did not show up.

Dahlgren, who at that time lived in Texas, was home for her father's funeral, according to the letter.

The next day, according to her letter, she was stopped again.

Dahlgren claims Martz "pulled me forcefully from my vehicle, threw me face down across the hood of my car and, as he held my hands behind my back, he kicked my legs apart and pushed himself against my buttocks, as if to make me think he would sexually assault me. I believed at that point that rape was a distinct possibility, although he never removed or opened his pants."

According to his personnel file, Martz was put on desk duty until an investigation could be completed.

Investigators could not find any proof that Martz ever stopped Dahlgren and he was cleared in the matter.

Martz' widow, Judith, who now lives in Indiana, confirmed that Martz had an on-again, off-again affair with Dahlgren two years before his death. The couple would reportedly meet for sex when Dahlgren came into town to visit her family. He ended the relationship in an effort to save his marriage.

"She was very angry that Bob didn't want to see her anymore," said Judith in a telephone interview this morning. "There were phone calls in the middle of the night where she called to beg him to come back to her. I remember he was placed on desk duty for a few days, but I don't think I ever knew what it was for. I never knew anything about a letter."

An interview with Earlene Whitelaw following her release from jail claimed Dahlgren had a long history of anger management problems and physical violence, allegedly stemming from physical abuse she suffered at home.

Dahlgren returned to Jubilant Falls on a regular basis to check on her mother, Whitelaw said. Dahlgren was financially responsible for her mother's care and the upkeep of their historic home.

Dahlgren was also a heavy drinker who suffered from depression and paranoia, Whitelaw claimed.

One factor that had originally tied Whitelaw to Dahlgren's death was Whitelaw's fingerprints on the steering wheel of Dahlgren's Lincoln. Whitelaw claimed she often drove the vehicle when Dahlgren was incapacitated.

Assistant Chief Gary McGinnis called the connection between Dahlgren and the unsolved murder "coincidental" but, because these cases are still open, could not comment further.

"Our investigation into all three homicides continues," said McGinnis. "Anyone with information on these crimes is asked to call us."

The article ended with the police department phone number. Beside the main story was a brief sidebar on the details of Bob Martz' death and a recap of the young man found in the creek. Pat rounded up a couple of the original photographs from the first article on Martz's death.

I looked up at the circle of stunned faces around me.

"How could one woman have so many connections to so many deaths?" Dennis asked, thoughtfully pushing his thick glasses up his nose.

"I don't know," I answered.

It had taken everything I had not to include Jimmy Lyle's death in the story, despite what Earlene told me, but other than the fact Eve dated him, there was nothing concrete to say she—or anyone else—killed him. Eve's comments about him ruining her life and getting what he deserved could have been the drama of an overwrought teen drunk on watered-down beer, not the confessions of a killer.

I pushed those thoughts away and continued. "There's one more thing that Earlene told me: when they started at Texas A&M, Eve didn't enter in the fall with the rest of the freshman. Earlene said she started in January because her father suddenly wanted to take her to Europe that fall. I wanted to put it in the story, but it couldn't be tied to anything else."

"What do you think it was?" Graham asked.

"I have no idea. I have no proof of anything else other than what Earlene said it was: a last-minute trip to Europe."

"Hey, Addison," Charisma spoke up. "Can I see you in your office?"

Here it goes, I thought. *I'm going to lose her.* As I followed her into my office, I tried to remember if I had any fresh résumés in my desk I could dig up.

God, how had I been so deluded? I, who thought I was going to help some young kid move on to a bigger paper and have a great career, had one of the world's most sought-after reporters under my nose for four months and I never had a clue. When it came to personal relationships, I never could see what was going on—just like what was apparently blooming between my daughter and Graham.

I closed the door behind me.

"So, you're leaving?" I asked, sliding my butt onto my desk. "I'm going to hate to see you go, Charisma. You're one hell of a reporter."

"Thanks," she said. Her eyes were sharp and focused; her voice was clear.

If she could get past the PTSD, maybe she could go back to journalism on a world stage, I thought. I could understand her fear of having her story twisted, but I couldn't understand her fear of being found. I remembered watching her on the evening news, reporting from all over the world, often wearing a flak jacket and helmet.

"I think you have accumulated a few days vacation—I'd be glad to pay you for those," I began. "You also have—"

"I'm going to do it."

I was silent for a moment.

"What?"

"I'm going to write my story for you. After I'm done, I'm leaving, just like I said, but you will be the first person to know the truth."

Chapter 29 Leland

My head was throbbing Thursday morning when I lifted my face from the pillow. The red lights of the bedside digital clock told me it was nearly noon. My clothes lay in a sloppy pile on the foot of the bed. When had I taken them off?

God, how much did I drink? I sat up, swung my bare feet over the side of the bed, and slipped into my boxers. I stood unsteadily, rubbing my face roughly with my hands, hoping to wipe away the fog in my head and the dried saliva from my cheeks and beard.

Does it matter? The answer came back quickly. *You're still an alcoholic.*

My mouth tasted like the bottom of an abandoned birdcage as I staggered the few steps from my bed into the bathroom. The vodka bottle was upended in the sink and the cold, white hearts of a few ice cubes floated with the glass I'd taken from the bar in the ice bucket. I leaned my forehead against the mirror's cold surface, trying to assuage the pounding in my skull.

Five years of sobriety down the goddamn toilet. Five years of hard work keeping my life on track and I fuck it up again. First Noah, then Bitch Goddess and now Charisma—once again I'm the one-stop source for pain, disaster and hurt.

I wet my toothbrush and squeezed a shaky trail of toothpaste along the bristles. Closing my eyes to escape the pain in my head, I began brushing my teeth.

"Don't beat yourself up too badly. You at least called me."

I jumped, dropping my toothbrush alongside the empty vodka bottle. It was Steve, the AA meeting leader, leaning on my bathroom doorframe.

"How long have you been here?" I asked.

"All night." He turned to point at the armchair in the corner. "I slept there."

Shaking my head, I picked up the vodka bottle and sat it upright on the bathroom counter. Running water over my toothbrush again, I returned to brushing my teeth, but didn't say anything.

"You really hadn't drank that much by the time I got here. You can get right back into the program and start all over again, no problem. As long as you're here in Jubilant Falls, we're all here to help you."

"Mmm." I jerked my chin up in acknowledgement and spit into the sink. I put my toothbrush back in my mouth and kept brushing.

"Don't beat yourself up too badly. You only had maybe two, three drinks. You called, and I came right over."

I spit into the sink again, this time vehemently.

"Help me? *Help me?*" I said. "If it hadn't been for one of the idiots in your group, I wouldn't have just sent five years of sobriety down the toilet." I wanted to take the empty vodka bottle and sling it at his head.

"Excuse me?" Steve's supportive, rah-rah tone ended.

"After I told my story, that goddamn fat bastard of a police chief went straight to the woman I talked about and told her he knew who she was. Because of his goddamn big mouth, she's packed up and left town."

Steve hung his head.

"I had spent a year researching, trying to find her and others just like her—I'm not even *talking* about falling for her—all it took was one idiot running his mouth to ruin it all."

"Oh my God. I'm so sorry..."

"I'm sure you are, but it doesn't fix a damned thing." I stepped over to the shower, my voice rising over the water. As steam filled the bathroom, I reached for the empty bottle and, holding it like the Louisville Slugger I wished it were, stepped into the doorway. "I would suggest you get the hell out of here before I decide to sling this goddamn thing at your head."

Steve's eyes got large and he scrambled backwards, fumbling his way toward the door. It slammed behind him as he left, running down the hallway.

I tossed the vodka bottle into the bathroom trashcan and stepped into the shower.

The water cascading over my face chased away the fog in my brain. If Charisma was gone, there was no need for me to remain here either. But before I could leave, I had one more stop to make.

Chapter 30 Charisma

"You sure you want to do this?" Addison looked at me with concern. "You're under no obligation. I mean, I'd love to have the story for selfish reasons, but don't do it because I asked you."

"I owe you, Addison. You gave me a second chance, even though I lied to you. You and these folks in the newsroom gave me the chance to start again."

"You're still leaving, though."

Again, I nodded. "You deserve the truth, but nobody else deserves a piece of me. I'm going to write the story for you and then I'm out of here. I don't even know where I'm going. I just know I'm gone."

"Did you want to tell the rest of the staff before the story runs?"

"No. I can't. They're good folks and everything, but I'm... I'm just not up to it."

"OK."

I returned to my desk and sat down in front of my computer, sighing as I did so.

It had been a long, long road. No one knew my story because I was ashamed of so much, responsible for so much and as a result of one single day's events, I'd paid so much.

Now, it was time to tell it, not because I wanted to but because I needed to protect myself with a story that wasn't spun or slanted or playing to anyone's agenda.

I laid my fingers across my computer keyboard like a pianist beginning to pick out the notes of some personal, tragic sonata and, slowly, began to write down the events that changed my life.

*****

Jean Paul's fingers walked up my arm to my shoulder, followed by his lips. We were in bed, in our dingy room at a cheap hotel inside the Green Zone, where US military officials corralled journalists, both foreign and domestic, when they came to Baghdad.

The rooms were basic at best, with tacky furniture and blackout curtains designed to catch breaking window glass should a missile strike close to the building. US troops called the area The Emerald City, a reflection of how the order and security within its walls seemed like part of Oz, not the ugly chaos outside in the real Baghdad.

"Go away. I'm trying to work," I said, running my fingers through his curly black hair and kissing his lips. I smiled at him as I gently pushed him away.

The electricity was currently working and I knew, before the next of several daily blackouts plunged the city into darkness, I needed to get some work done. I was on my laptop, trying to transcribe some of my interview notes from a mother I'd interviewed on the scarcity of food and medicine and the anticipated chaos once US troops left.

Pulling the thin, worn hotel blanket up to his sculpted abs, Jean Paul settled back into his side of the bed, sighing melodramatically.

"*C'est notre deuxième anniversaire. Ma mère veut savoir quand nous allons donner ses petits-enfants,*" he said. Our conversations were an odd mix of French and English. "It's our second anniversary. My mother wants to know when we're going to give her grandchildren."

"Your mother can wait until we quit living out of suitcases."

"When will that be?" he asked.

The lights flickered uncertainly and I quickly hit 'save' on the keyboard to preserve my work.

"Everyone I've talked to says the country will disintegrate into chaos after the US leaves," I said, focusing once more on my notes. "I've got to get that impression across—I think this woman I interviewed today will really convey that: the lack of medical supplies, the food shortages, the feeling of no future for anyone who stays here. Everyone I've interviewed said to expect sectarian violence, especially now that Saddam is dead. The conflict between Sunni and Shiite Muslims is expected to explode."

"You didn't answer my question."

I waved my hand dismissively toward his side of the bed and kept typing.

"Charisma, please. Can we forget about work for one night and talk?" Jean Paul asked.

"Give me a minute and let me finish. I've got to get this done. Did you talk to Lt. Faulkner today?"

Second Lt. Reese Faulkner was the Army press liaison we worked with. Just out of college, this was his first tour in Iraq. He was bright, young and made sure we had plenty of the patriotic stories that the brass clamored for, but seldom put me in contact with real Iraqis who lived with the real results of the invasion. The current story lines always involved Iraqi troops and how, following US training, they would take over.

"When they stand up, we'll stand down," was Lt. Faulkner's mantra and he repeated it often.

"I want to talk to my wife right now, not some kid."

"Just a few more minutes..."

"Voulez-vous s'il vous plaît arrêter de travailler et de me parler?" he demanded. "Will you please stop working and talk to me?"

I slapped the laptop closed and laid it on the nightstand as the lights flickered, then went out for good.

"Quand avez-vous commencer à se soucier de ce que votre mère veut?" I shot back, frustrated at the interruption and the blackout. "When did you start caring about what your mother wants?"

"Don't you want children, Charisma?" Jean Paul shifted back into his heavily accented English.

"How can we have children if we're living out of suitcases, running all over the world?"

"You don't want to do this forever, do you?"

"And what if I do?"

"I just had hopes that someday we'd settle down somewhere. Get a place of our own."

"Where? Some little French village? And I'd do what? Breed like a rabbit? Wipe butts and noses all day? Spend my day in the marketplace looking for the best lamb chops so you have a perfect dinner waiting for you when you come home?"

"Charisma, every time we have this discussion, you say that. Nobody is saying you need to give up your career. We'd work it out somehow."

"So we'd have a live-in nanny while we chase stories? We'd let somebody else raise our children?"

"I didn't say that either. The truth is, it's getting more and more dangerous here for foreign journalists. I'm uncomfortable with some of the reactions we get when people find out who you are. I worry about our safety. I worry about *your* safety, especially since you are so well known."

I ran my fingers through my blonde hair. "That's always been part of the job. You know that. We'd face the same thing if we were anywhere else."

"No we wouldn't, Charisma. You know that's not true. There are big stories in other, safer places."

"Listen, I watched my mother give up her career at Reuters and my father turn into someone he absolutely loathed when they decided after two kids, she needed to stay home and he needed to stop chasing stories. After my parents divorced and she went back to work, she never made the same money because of the time she'd spent at home raising kids. I'm not going to put myself in that situation." I folded my arms resolutely. "I'm not ready to stop doing what I'm doing just to have children. Not now at any rate."

These arguments were more and more frequent lately, although I couldn't think why. I mean, weren't women the only ones with the ticking biological clock? I thought he was as hooked on covering this conflict as much as I was. We promised our folks we'd Skype or phone once a week whenever possible. I rarely took part in his conversations with his stylish, but overbearing mother, so I didn't know if she was really pushing the baby thing that hard or not. I just know the subject of *bébés* kept coming up between the two of us.

Jean Paul reached for me again, burying kisses in my neck and sliding his hand inside my nightshirt. His warm hand cupped my breast.

"*Oh, mais nous ferions de beaux bébés...*" he whispered into my neck. "Oh, but we'd make beautiful babies."

"Stop it." I pushed his hand away and turned over on my side. "Go away."

He snuggled closer and wrapped his arm around my middle. "I love you, Charisma," he whispered into my shoulder. "I want you to be happy, but I want you to be safe, too. You take too many chances."

I punched the lumpy pillow and lay my head on my hands. "I'll be fine. Can we talk about this tomorrow?"

Jean Paul sighed and rolled away from me.

"We'll get wrapped up in the next story and it will get forgotten. We have this same conversation over and over and it never gets resolved," he said sadly. "I hoped after two years together we could have talked more about children without it becoming *un grand combat.*"

I sat back up. "I can't believe you said that."

"Well, it's true, Charisma." Jean Paul stayed on his side, staring at the wall. "This job is everything to you, your heart and soul. All I want is to know, at some point, when you're going to put us first? When will this marriage be the most important thing in your life?"

"You *are* important to me, Jean Paul. I couldn't do this without you." I flopped back onto the bed and turned over on my side.

"Don't flatter me. Another photographer could take the same shots I do. For god sake, I know Kalil can do what I do! I just want to know where I stand in your heart," he said softly.

Kalil was the local man we'd hired as a fixer, something every foreign journalist couldn't do without. A fixer was just that: a translator, social secretary, a driver, security and ultimate source. He was one of the thousands of private security men vetted by the US government and hired by journalists and other westerners that operated within the Green Zone. Just as Jean Paul and I rarely wandered the city without a Kevlar vest and helmet, Kalil was also there to protect us, driving us around in a specially armored Chevy Suburban. He seldom escorted us without a weapon of some kind, most often a high-powered Kalashnikov rifle.

Kalil came highly recommended, having worked with other journalists who rotated in and out of this embattled city. He knew where the action was—or where it would soon happen.

He knew city officials and how to get in touch, through those dusty, ancient streets, with those who would tell us stories of real life, not what those in power would have us believe.

As life in Baghdad got increasingly dangerous, we relied on Kalil to shoot photos or video, even interview somebody, and then put the story together back at the bureau, which was located on a lower floor of our hotel.

If I was doing a print story, I could observe from the armored confines of Kalil's Suburban, but Jean Paul couldn't get the shots he wanted without leaving the vehicle. If we were doing video, we both had to step outside or be content to let Kalil shoot and interview, then edit the piece together with my commentary, shot from the relative safety of our Green Zone hotel roof. It was an odd form of team journalism.

"Don't be so melodramatic." I rolled my eyes.

He was silent for a moment. "I talked to Kalil today."

"Oh?"

"He said he can get us an interview with some of the survivors of that marketplace bombing yesterday," Jean Paul said. Bombings, kidnappings and sniper shootings were so commonplace that they became part of the background noise with which we lived our daily lives and not the stuff of daily news, unless the body count was high.

"Sounds good. I'll stop down by the bureau's office first thing tomorrow and see if the chief wants us to pursue that," I answered.

"What if they say no?"

"We'll probably go ahead and go anyway."

"Charisma, that's suicide. See what Lt. Faulkner can do for us. Maybe we can embed with a patrol in the market. You know they'll be going out to investigate."

"An embed request would take too long. The brass has to sign off on it—you know that. How else can I truthfully illustrate how this country will collapse after US troops pull out?"

"Why do you have to be the only one to get the big story?"

"Because…" I wanted to finish the sentence with "I'm Charisma Prentiss, that's why," but knew that wouldn't carry any weight, not with Jean Paul. Instead, I said, "Nobody can tell the story like I do."

"I'm glad you think so." Jean Paul sighed and the conversation, again, ended on the same frustrating notes.

In a few minutes, Jean Paul's breathing became deep and regular. I sat up and threw off the covers. I pulled the laptop from my nightstand and found a flashlight in the drawer.

Go ahead and sleep, Jean Paul, I told myself. *I've got work to do.*

*****

The next morning, I ran my fingers through my hair in front of the bathroom mirror. The electricity was working for the time being.

"My brown roots are beginning to show," I murmured to myself. "I wonder if I have any Miss Clairol left?"

Down deep inside the military issue duffel bag I carried, I always had an extra box or two of Miss Clairol's Born Blonde, wherever I was in the world. God knows if for some reason the editors wanted me on camera, I couldn't be filmed looking, well, like I'd been bunking in a cheap Baghdad hotel for a month without benefit of a hairdresser. I'd learned how to color my own hair early on in this gig. Only in situations of extreme danger did I leave my helmet on when recording.

"What did you say?" Jean Paul walked past the bathroom door. The tension between us was still thick and his tone was sharp and accusatory.

"Nothing," I retorted, just as harshly. "Nothing at all."

"I haven't heard from Kalil," Jean Paul said, strapping on his Kevlar vest, with PRESS in big white letters across the back and chest. I wore one just like it, along with boots, a pair of jeans that could probably stand on their own, and a polo shirt. We both had blue helmets with MEDIA written across the front.

When I first started embedding with the troops, I wanted a pair of camouflage pants and helmet just the like American troops wore, thinking it might help me bond with troops who clearly didn't want me there. "Why?" the public affairs officer asked me. "You want to be a target or something?"

Instead, I made sure that I kept up with the troops, portrayed them sympathetically and never minced words when it came to the danger they faced.

"Kalil is probably downstairs waiting for us. Give me a damned minute and I'll be ready to go." I applied lip-gloss and mascara, staring open-mouthed into the mirror, as Jean Paul came up behind me, his eyes sad. "What?" I asked.

"We need to talk some more tonight."

"About what?"

"About where this marriage is going."

"Oh, for god sake. We're fine. I'm fine. You're fine. I love you, OK? You just need to get over this idiotic baby thing." I pushed him out of my way and picked up my Kevlar vest and helmet from the chair in the corner. "Let's go."

I didn't stop to check in with the wire service's bureau chief. Downstairs, at the hotel's front door, Kalil was leaning against his dusty Suburban, his Kalashnikov rifle slung over his shoulder. He looked up and down the street before motioning us forward and into the back seat of his armored vehicle.

"What market are we headed for, the Muraidi market?" Jean Paul asked, attaching a large telephoto lens to his camera.

The Muraidi market had been the target of a suicide bomber several years ago when a bomb attached to either a motorcycle or a vegetable cart, no one was exactly sure, killing 69 people, mostly women and children, and wounding 150 others. Sadr City was one of the poorest areas of Baghdad and a hotbed of sectarian conflict.

"No. Muraidi is not safe today, not for Americans. We are going to one of the smaller markets, where the bomb went off."

Kalil shook his head and pulled the Suburban out into the street. Our progress was painfully slow, thanks to the innumerable security checks before we got out of the Emerald City and into Baghdad proper.

"It's never safe for Americans, Kalil," I answered, sarcastically. "I need Jean Paul to get me photos for a story I'm doing and I need to interview some folks, real people, not some puppet from one side or the other."

Kalil looked at me, then Jean Paul in the rear-view mirror, his black brows knit together in consternation. *You need to control your woman*, his black eyes seemed to say. Jean Paul met his gaze and then looked out the window. His body language seemed to say *She's not my problem, not anymore*.

"You take too many risks," Kalil said to me.

"Why is it everybody wants to protect me these days?" I rolled my eyes in disgust. "I'm not some damn delicate flower."

The Suburban drove through streets that were both modern and ancient. He never took a direct route, in case we were being followed. Even if we wanted to, we couldn't have traveled directly. US troops had many streets and roads blocked to traffic due to security concerns; a six-block trip could take hours. We were on one of Saddam's modern highways when traffic slowed to a crawl.

"What's going on up there?" I asked.

About ten cars ahead of us, a group of American troops circled an old Nissan, their weapons drawn. A woman stepped out of the Nissan, her hands in the air.

I tightened the strap beneath my helmet and opened the Suburban's door to get a better look.

"Get back in here!" yelled Kalil.

I ignored him. I stared intently at the young woman, trying to determine her age—she wore a *niqab*, an Islamic face veil that only left her eyes visible, above her burka. Fashionable sandals made me think she was young, maybe in her twenties. Jean Paul stood behind his open door, balancing his long telephoto lens on the open window, waiting for the right shot. He made an unhappy sound and moved slightly from behind the Suburban's door to get the shot he wanted.

She could be harmless, one of many innocent Iraqis singled out in a US security check.

Or not.

One hand clutched a cell phone, a thumb poised above the keypad.

She was a suicide bomber and the phone was rigged to detonate.

"Put it down!" screamed a soldier. "Drop the phone!"

Those were the last words I remembered as everything around me went black and I felt myself being kicked in the gut with incredible force, back into a deep, dark hole.

*****

I have just a few memories of what happened after the explosion: A medic applying a tourniquet to save my leg, feeling someone's fingers on my forehead. My damaged brain thought it was a priest making the sign of the cross as part of last rites. I learned later it was a second medic writing with my own blood the time the tourniquet was applied.

The back of my head felt wet inside my helmet, the bones in my face were smashed, my perfect, white teeth gone and I caught a glimpse of my left leg at an odd angle and the tourniquet above my knee.

"Jean Paul?" my mangled mouth managed to ask.

The younger, wide-eyed medic looked at his more experienced companion, who may have been older by a mere six months. The older medic shook his head.

"He's going to be OK," the young one said. "Let's worry about you." I learned later that little lie often kept a patient calm and kept them from fighting the medics to get to their wounded friends. It worked with me.

When the young woman blew herself and everything around her up, the doors had blown off the Suburban, killing Jean Paul instantly and injuring me. Kalil, who didn't leave the vehicle, survived with serious injuries. We were among the nearly two hundred, including the soldiers working the checkpoint, who were killed or injured.

I must have blacked out then—I don't remember a whole lot after that. I was medevac'd back to the Green Zone, where I was stabilized, then shipped on to a second hospital and finally, with a nurse who never left my side, flown to Landstuhl army hospital in Germany.

By that time, doctors put me into a medically induced coma to control the swelling in my brain. I don't even remember the number of times I went under the knife. There were a couple brain surgeries, multiple surgeries on my leg, surgeries to dig out the larger pieces of shrapnel, facial and dental reconstruction surgery; I only know that I made it thanks to the dedication of my military caretakers.

Some memories slide in and out. At some point, my parents arrived in Landstuhl, with a VP from the wire service and my brother. They were the ones to break it to me that Jean Paul had been killed. Mom and Dad stood on either side of my hospital bed, each holding my hand as they gently gave me the news. My jaw was wired shut, so I couldn't do more than feel the tears slid down the side of my face.

Even if I wanted to, I learned later, I couldn't have. The brain damage I suffered stole the one weapon I'd always used—my words. It took forever for them to come back.

Somewhere through the fog of pain, rehabilitation, and medication, I realized that I alone, in my arrogance to get a story, to stay at the top of whatever heap I thought I was on, was responsible for the death of my husband and Kalil's serious injuries.

When I got Jean Paul's belongings back, the long telephoto lens was dotted with his blood. The final picture on the disc inside the camera was of the young woman in her *niqab*, circled by US soldiers, holding the cell phone detonator aloft.

If my appearance upset my parents, they never let on. Later, I learned both Mom and Dad, who after their divorce would fight over whether or not the sun came up in the east, presented a united front to the media. Ironically, Kate served as the family spokesperson as the insanity to cover my story grew and grew and grew.

None of it was enough to quell my ego.

It was a plastic surgeon's comment that wafted through my fogged brain as I came out from under anesthesia yet one more time, this time for facial reconstruction. I don't know to whom the comment was made. I just know the visceral reaction I had to it, despite the medication.

"Yeah, we did what we could, but I doubt that she'll be in front of the camera anytime soon," he said.

Somebody else murmured something I couldn't make out.

"Well, at least she had a career in print. That can always continue," the surgeon said. "There's always radio, too."

I knew at that moment I had to come back. I would show them *nobody* could keep Charisma Prentiss down.

I had one more lesson to learn—or did I?

*****

My stomach was roiling by the time I stopped writing. I stood up and stretched, hoping no one could see my hands shaking. Addison, working at the copy desk with Dennis on tomorrow's advance pages, looked up and caught my eye, arching an eyebrow as if to ask, "Are you OK?"

I shook my head imperceptibly and walked from the newsroom to the ladies room, where I stepped into the last stall, locked the door and vomited.

Back at the row of sinks, I poured a splash from the communal mouthwash bottle on the counter into a paper cup, rinsed and spit.

I stared at myself in the mirror with eyes ringed in exhaustion. I looked as emotionally spent as I felt. I pushed my bangs back from my forehead and turned my head to more clearly see the scars that ran along the side of my face and into my natural brown hair.

Once, that line was an angry red incision, held closed with shiny metal staples across my shaved scalp, but not now. Once it defined everything that limited me—physically, verbally, and emotionally. I'd come far in many ways, but in others, I'd barely taken a step, like the night the freight train came through town, sending me diving beneath my dinette table.

I could have left right then, and Addison wouldn't have said a word, but my promise to her wouldn't let me. The second half of my story needed to be written—and today. I owed that to Addison before I disappeared from Jubilant Falls.

I stepped back into the newsroom and ran right into Leland Huffinger.

Chapter 31 Addison

"Dr. Huffinger, I presume?"

The tall, bearded man standing in my newsroom stepped back awkwardly, nearly knocking into Charisma, barely keeping his hands on the folder he clutched. His eyes widened in further shock as he realized who was standing behind him.

"You were supposed to—" he began.

"Lets finish this conversation in my office, shall we?" I said sharply. I pointed toward the door. My reporters stared as the three of us walked by.

Once inside, I slammed the door.

"So you're the reason I'm losing a reporter?" I pulled a cigarette out of the package on my desk and tapped it hard on the desk surface. "Does that mean I don't have to pay the private investigator rate you quoted me?"

Huffinger looked at Charisma and then back to me.

"She knows the truth," Charisma said sharply.

"Yes, I know the truth," I repeated.

"Mrs. McIntyre, you have to understand it was not my intention to expose Charisma Prentiss. We had talked on several occasions, and I had agreed that I would not expose her whereabouts without her permission."

"Until you opened your mouth to Marvin McGinnis," Charisma shot back.

"What is said in an Alcoholics Anonymous meeting is supposed to be kept confidential. Chief McGinnis broke that confidence, but I still plan on holding up my end of the bargain.

My article will not expose your location and I will give you two weeks advance notice prior to publication," Huffinger said in sad acknowledgement.

"You gonna guarantee that McGinnis might not run out and call somebody at, oh I don't know, CNN?" Charisma shot back. "Fox News and MSNBC would love to chew me up and spit me out again. They both did their part to trash me while I was recovering."

"Charisma, I have already apologized to you."

"At least MSNBC waited until I was out of the mental hospital."

"Calm down everybody, calm down," I said, holding up my hands. I could be cool about the situation. By noon tomorrow, I'd have my revenge. Dr. Leland Huffinger would be scooped— provided the chief kept his mouth shut. "While I don't like losing Charisma, I understand her anger. However, I specifically asked you, Dr. Huffinger, to do some research on our murder victim, Eve Dahlgren. What did you find out?"

"Here's the biggest item." He opened the folder he was holding, and handed me a piece of paper. "It's a birth certificate. Eve Dahlgren had a baby boy in October 1974."

"What?" I snatched the paper from him. So, there was no trip to Europe after all, despite what Earlene told me. Thanks to the Texas Department of Health's Vital Statistics Unit, I held the real reason Eve Dahlgren didn't show up to the fall term at Texas A&M. I showed the paper to Charisma.

"She named him Andrew, Andrew William Dahlgren. It says it was a live birth, but there's no father's name listed," she said.

Huffinger nodded.

"I'm going to bet it was your tornado victim, Jimmy Lyle. If he died in April 1974, that's about the time she would have just found out she was pregnant. With Andrew's October birth date, she would have been about a month and a half, two months into her pregnancy before the tornado hit."

"Where is this child today?" I asked.

Huffinger shook his head. "I don't know. There are no death records in Texas or here in Ohio and no school records in Austin or here in Jubilant Falls."

"That means that kid is still out there," Charisma said.

"He's not a kid now," Huffinger said. "He'd be close to forty. He had to have been educated somewhere, gotten a job, maybe even had a family. I couldn't find anything. It's like he was a blip on somebody's radar screen and then disappeared."

"Eve told Earlene that Jimmy Lyle ruined her life. I'm going to bet that child is the reason Jimmy Lyle was killed," I said. "What if she brought the baby home from Texas and killed it? Or the baby died, for whatever reason?"

They both cringed.

"Well, it's a possibility!" I said, exasperated. "We've tied her to Bob Martz's murder and the boy in the creek. What's one more murder? Nobody here even knew she was pregnant—she could have gotten away with it easily."

"But a baby?" Huffinger asked.

"Seriously, think about it, you two," I continued. "Wouldn't the kid have had to generate some kind of records *somewhere*? As an adult, there should have been a Social Security card issued, some tax records or proof that he had a job. *Something.*"

"If he was adopted by someone, the records would have likely been sealed," Huffinger said. "I checked some of the online forums where adults were looking to connect with birth parents and didn't find anything. It's possible he realized how good he had it and never searched for his mother."

We were silent for a moment, pondering the bombshell information.

"If Earlene and Eve were such good friends, how could she not know her friend was pregnant?" Charisma spoke up.

I shook my head. "It's not like today. An unplanned pregnancy was a mark of shame in the mid-seventies, although attitudes were starting to change. And somebody with the social standing Eve's family had here in Jubilant Falls, they would have done anything, I mean *anything,* to hide that fact."

"So she could have not known—or she could have kept Eve's secret all these years," Charisma said.

I shrugged. "She could have done either of those things, yes. As self-involved as Earlene is and always has been, I can't see her stepping outside her comfort zone to help anybody, not now, and not in college. And as concerned as she was with appearances and control, Eve probably kept the information to herself."

"Giving birth in Texas would have kept anyone back home in Ohio out of the loop," Huffinger said. "She could have come home, left the baby there—or whatever—and returned to college without anyone being the wiser."

"What else did you dig up on Eve?" I asked him.

Huffinger flipped through a few more pages in the folder.

"She was at a number of different Texas firms and did exactly what you said she did: she went in and cut the fat from companies that had just been taken over. I let the folks I talked to think that I was doing a story on her, following up on her murder. She didn't leave a whole lot of friends behind. A number of people filed complaints against her with the company and a couple times with the state after she fired them."

"Anybody ever track her down and try to talk to her after she canned them?" I asked.

"Like our creek victim?" Charisma echoed.

Huffinger shook his head. "Not that I could find out. I couldn't get the names of anyone she'd canned to speak to them directly, or cross-reference them with missing person reports. There wasn't time. Even the long-time HR folks I talked to didn't have a high opinion of her."

"You know the one person who had a high opinion of Eve?" Charisma asked.

"Her mother, Betty Dahlgren," I said.

"That home health care worker won't let us get within a mile of that place, and especially now, since our story is on today's front page," she said.

"We've got to try, though," I said.

There was a knock on the door. It was Marcus, holding a fast-food milkshake in one hand.

"What?" I asked.

"A missing senior citizen just came over the scanner," he said. "Graham went out to chase it, but I thought you might want to know."

"Who is it?" I asked.

"It's Betty Dahlgren, the same woman you mentioned in your story. She apparently had a GPS attached to her ankle. The 911 caller said she found it cut off and laying on the front porch and the car, a Buick, is missing."

"Charisma, I need you and Leland to get out to that farmhouse *now*," I said, gathering up a notebook, pencils and tossing them, along with my cigarettes, into my purse. "Pat and I can chase down Gary McGinnis or the sheriff and see how they are doing, get a photo. Who made the 911 call, Marcus?"

"The daughter."

"*Daughter?*" Charisma and I chorused.

"Yes. Betty Dahlgren's younger daughter, Julia, called 911. Why?"

Chapter 32 Leland

"Just shut up and get in the car." We were in the employee parking lot. Charisma pointed her key fob at her red sedan. The lights blinked and, with a soft click, the doors unlocked.

"Charisma, you have to understand..."

"I don't have to understand shit. We're on an assignment, OK?" She slid inside, quickly buckling herself into the driver's seat. I followed suit, belting myself into the passenger seat.

She turned the key in the ignition, unconsciously reaching up to touch a photograph rubber-banded to the sun visor above her head. It was a European-looking young man with curly black hair smiling confidently, holding a camera with a long telephoto lens as he half-leaned, half-knelt against an ancient crumbling wall. His chambray shirt, dirty jeans and work boots looked as suave as only a Frenchman could make them look. It had to be Jean Paul Lemarnier.

"Is that your husband?"

"Shut up." She put the car in reverse and pulled out of the parking spot. "I'm not telling you squat."

We were not en route to the Eve Nil's family farmhouse as originally ordered. After Addison McIntyre learned murder victim Eve Dahlgren had a sister, she insisted on going there with the photographer Pat Robinette. Instead, Charisma and I rushed to the scene where Mrs. Dahlgren's abandoned Buick had been discovered, nose down in a ditch on a two-lane road somewhere on the east side of Plummer County.

Within minutes, we arrived at the lonely country road surrounded on both sides by old-growth woods. A wrecker was pulling up to the Buick's up-ended bumper as a collection of sheriff's deputies and volunteers stood in circles, examining maps as they planned to search for the old woman.

Charisma pulled off the side of the road and shut off the car. Covered in her icy silence, we walked toward a man in a black uniform. He was medium height, slightly younger than I, with a weightlifter's bulk through his shoulders. He wore a black ball cap with the word 'SHERIFF' across the front; one hand rested comfortably on his service revolver, the other hooked around his belt. He was speaking to Graham Kinnon, the young man I'd seen previously in the newsroom, who nodded as he took down what the sheriff said.

The sheriff, whose name was Judson Roarke, nodded as Charisma introduced me.

"This is at the back side of Canal Lock Park, which is not too far from our missing subject's home," Roarke said. "While it's a good thing that she isn't posing a danger to others while she's behind the wheel, I am concerned that she may be injured from the accident. We haven't found Mrs. Dahlgren walking along the road and deputies have checked in both directions. If she's not injured and wandering through these woods, my other concern is that the gorge is two miles due east from here. We've got to find her before she falls into the gorge. We're organizing groups of people for a grid search through the woods."

"I'd be glad to help search," I said.

"So would I," Charisma chimed in. "If this goes late, I can take over for you, Graham. Just call me on my cell."

Graham nodded.

"What do you think was the reason Mrs. Dahlgren fled her home?" Charisma asked Roarke.

Roarke motioned us over to the Buick and asked the tow truck driver to stop pulling the car onto the back of his flatbed. He pointed through the window to the front seat of the car.

"There's your reason right there," he said.

It was today's issue, laying flat across the upholstered seat; the headline 'Victim linked to other crimes' screamed across the page.

"It's likely she read the paper and, in an instant of clarity, realized what was going on," Roarke said. "Sometimes that happens with dementia patients. If what you and Addison wrote is true, who knows what's gone on in that family? She might be running for her life. We just need to find her before she gets hurt."

Charisma shot the sheriff a sharp look. Did he know her secret? Was his comment a reference to her disastrous Syrian story?

"We wouldn't publish it if we couldn't verify it, sheriff, " she said. "Twice."

Within the hour, three groups of volunteers, each with a deputy leading, spread out along the side of the road and began walking through the woods. Charisma and I were in the group walking to the east. I was the last searcher on the deputy's left, with Charisma the next searcher in line next to me. Each person was about ten feet from the other, too far to hold an intimate conversation, but close enough for him or her to hear a yell if Betty was found.

I swept the underbrush along with the rest of the walking group, catching glimpses of Charisma out of the corner of my eye. She never looked at me—at least I never caught her looking. Instead, I listened as her steps, like mine, crackled on the fallen sticks and branches underfoot and she called out the old lady's name.

The alcohol fog in my head began to clear the more we walked, thanks to the cool clear air. The smell of the deep woods reminded me of that final camping trip in southwestern Pennsylvania with Noah and his mother. I still loved her then— *we* still loved each other—and we were looking forward to a new stage in our lives, one where Noah was officially launched and we could go back to that time where our lives were our own.

The further I walked among the thick, heavy trees, the more that last family weekend came back to me. Eschewing tents, we'd slept in hammocks strung between the pines— Noah in his and his mother and I in another. I'd held my wife close in my arms as we stared up at the stars. The campfire's embers crackled and sputtered in the night, sending up golden sparks into the sky and I wanted our weekend in the woods to last forever.

Pamela. Her name was Pamela, not Bitch Goddess. I hadn't spoken her name in years, even in my thoughts. But that night as we hung suspended between the pines, we couldn't leave the alcohol behind. My speech that night was slurred as I spoke her name into her hair.

I looked to my right. Charisma and the line of other searchers were still walking deliberately through the woods. Their steps were purposeful, but not fast. No one wanted to miss anything—a piece of jewelry or clothing, the contents of a purse—that could tell us we were on the right road to finding Mrs. Dahlgren.

The trees grew closer together and soon, a green, leafy archway obscured the sun. As I walked, I lost track of the real reason I was here. In my mind, I was following Noah as he walked ahead of me, his brown ponytail hanging down the back of his fishing vest and his fishing rod clutched in his hand, down a barely marked path. We were headed toward the Youghiogheny River from our campsite in Pennsylvania's Ohiopyle State Park, toward a calm place on that rushing river where we'd fished since Noah was little.

It was a trek we made every summer until everything fell apart. I had a series of memories of Noah as we walked this way each year, from the little boy with chubby legs, tightly clutching a chunky-handled, plastic, fishing pole, to the surly teen who would rather have died than go camping with his parents, and finally to that last family outing as I watched the young man, just beginning his career, leading the way on this familiar path one final time.

Last night's shame came back to me. Steve was right—I hadn't fallen completely off the wagon. Maybe I'd been the one to pour the vodka into the bathroom sink—who knows? I didn't remember. But I knew all I needed to do was to get back on, work the program again, and embrace the sobriety that came at such a cost.

Noah would want me to do that.

It looked like I'd lost Charisma before I'd even had the chance to connect with her. But if nothing else, I'd learned from the experience. She'd shown me that after four painful years, I was ready to step out again, maybe find someone who would be willing to take me into her life, somebody who just might be the reason to move out of Fitzgerald House.

You could even say, then, my trip to Jubilant Falls hadn't been a complete loss. After all, I'd found the one war correspondent the world was searching for, the woman no one could find—even if my actions (and I knew I had to take the responsibility for them) would send her back into hiding.

After this was over, I'd drive my rental car back down to Cincinnati and catch the next plane back to Philadelphia. I'd write my story—as much as I had of it—and then settle back and wait for another fall quarter to begin.

And I would do it sober.

A bird called overhead and I stopped to listen, encircled in the dark green bower. I looked up in the trees, but couldn't see it. I looked around for the other searchers. I had wandered farther than I should—the line of searchers was in the distance, out of voice range, but still visible. I'd have to work to catch up with them. The sound came again, this time clearer.

"Help me! Help me!"

It wasn't a bird. It was Betty Dahlgren.

"Hang on! I'm coming!" I ran toward the feeble, female voice.

She had fallen, tripping over a fallen log and into the swale of a small creek. Her left leg hung at an odd angle in the cold water and mud streaked across her expensive pants and shirt.

"Betty? Betty Dahlgren?"

"Yes! Yes! Please help me!" Her claw-like hands reached out for me and her face was wild with fear. "Please, help me!"

Carefully, I hooked my arms beneath her shoulders and pulled her from the cold water. I pulled my cell phone from my pocket and dialed Charisma's number. "Come quick! Bring a stretcher! I've found her!"

In the distance, the woods exploded with voices and the sound of footsteps crashing through the underbrush. I rubbed her arms vigorously to keep her warm.

"It's going to be OK, Betty, it's going to be OK," I said. "Help is coming."

She looked up at me with her ice blue eyes. "I know who killed that man. I know who did it. I just had to get away before she could find me and do the same to me!"

I stopped rubbing her arms. *She doesn't know Eve is dead.*

"What man? The state trooper?" I asked.

"Yes. That one."

*****

Wrapped in a blanket, Betty's damning story kept coming, even as the EMTs splinted her leg and lifted her onto a stretcher. Charisma and Sheriff Roarke were beside me, both frantically taking notes as we walked her back toward the road and a waiting ambulance.

"I told her she shouldn't see him," Betty said, her fingers picking at the blanket. "It was wrong, he had a family. She was so young and so pretty back then—she could have anybody she wanted and I don't know why she insisted on seeing a man twenty years older that she was."

"What kind of relationship was it?" Charisma's questions came like rapid fire shots from a machine gun. "Did they see each other a lot? Were there any plans for the future? Did Eve have hopes of Bob Martz leaving his wife?"

"Yes. She was going to do anything she could to break up that man's family and keep him for herself. She doesn't care about anything else." Betty shook her head as she lay on the stretcher. She reached a claw-like hand up to Charisma's shoulder. "She has to have what she has to have... That's because..."

Betty's sentence drifted off and I wondered if she was sliding back into her dementia—or thinking about the baby her daughter had. Like a slingshot, the old woman's acuity was back.

"When she doesn't get what she wants, look out. She will destroy anything in her path."

Roarke stopped the EMTs and knelt beside the stretcher. "Tell me what happened that night," he said.

Betty looked upward, tears beginning to crest in the crow's feet around her eyes.

"It all started after her daddy killed himself. I told her she should haven't gone to see Bob Martz, that I needed her at home that day, but she didn't want..." Betty's attention faded, whether from the pain in her leg or the pain in her heart, I couldn't tell. "That was when he told her he was going to stay with his wife. She came home so angry—she said she was going to ruin him."

"She wrote a letter saying Trooper Martz tried to attack her that night, didn't she?" Charisma asked. "Did you know that?"

Betty nodded. "Yes, yes, I did. I told her not do to it, that it was a lie and it was wrong to send something like that. 'There's enough lies and secrets in this house, Mama,' she said. 'What do you care if we add one more?' So she mailed the letter and went home to Texas."

"When did she come back to Jubilant Falls?" I asked.

"It was a little while after her daddy died, maybe six months? I know when we talked long-distance, she told me she was still trying to call Mr. Martz and he kept refusing to see her again. She was very, very angry."

Judson Roarke reached over and took her hand. "Tell me what happened next, Betty."

"The night she came home, Eve told me she was going out with friends, but I didn't believe her. People in this town don't appreciate Eve—she's too smart and too beautiful. Small towns are always like that—there isn't anyone here who likes Eve. But I can tell when she's up to something—she's like her daddy that way."

"What did you do?"

Pain from Betty's broken leg made her face contort.

"We need to get you to the hospital, Mrs. Dahlgren," one of the EMTs said.

"No, not yet. Let me finish," she said. "I was waiting up for her when she came in—it was almost two-thirty in the morning. 'You met Bob Martz again,' I said. 'Eve, that is wrong. It is so wrong.' She just smiled and wouldn't say a word. I saw the story in the paper the next morning, after she'd gotten on her plane back home."

"Did you ever find a weapon?" Roarke asked.

"In her drawer, after she left." Pain contorted Betty's face again.

"Did you know she had a gun? What was it?" Roarke asked.

"No. I called her at home in Texas and asked her if she shot that man. She said if I ever told anybody, the same thing would happen to me. Eve still scares me."

The sheriff looked at Charisma.

"She doesn't realize that Eve is dead," Charisma whispered. "The home healthcare worker told me that when Addison and I were out at her home."

Roarke turned back to the old lady on the stretcher. "What did you do with the weapon?"

Betty finally lay back on the stretcher, covering her eyes with her arm. The group began moving again. The ambulance was in sight, its red lights flashing at the side of the road.

"It's buried in the flower garden, out by the gazebo."

Charisma leaned over the stretcher as our group came to the back of the ambulance. The driver was waiting at the open back door.

"You did the right thing, Betty. It's OK now," she said as the wounded woman was lifted into the back of the ambulance.

Betty groaned. "No, no it's not. Eve is going to come get me now. I know she is."

"Eve can't come get you, Betty," Charisma said. "You're safe. Eve's dead."

"She's dead?" Betty sat up on her elbows as the door of the ambulance slammed shut, her eyes wide.

Judson Roarke smacked the side of the ambulance with the flat of his hand. The sirens screamed in response as the medics pulled onto the pavement and the vehicle headed down the road.

He stepped back from the pavement to respond to a voice squawking from his shoulder microphone.

"Good job, Charisma," I said, stepping closer to her. "You got her to talk."

Her eyes followed the ambulance as it disappeared from view, but she didn't answer, chewing her lip in consternation. Was she revisiting the day Jean Paul died? Was she planning where she'd run to next? Did she hate me as much as I hated myself? Or was she focused on Betty Dahlgren's sad confession?

I started to reach for her shoulder, but Roarke jumped between us.

"We've got a suspect barricaded back in the Dahlgren's house—and she's got Addison with her."

Chapter 33 Addison

Julia Dahlgren held the gun against the side of my neck, just below my ear.

She'd grabbed me when I walked onto the porch. Pat Robinette waited in the yard to snap the deputy sheriff leaning on the fender of his cruiser, a photo for which I could have written the caption myself: *Deputy So-and-So, along with Julia Dahlgren, wait to learn the results of the search for Dahlgren's elderly mother, Betty, a dementia patient who removed her GPS ankle monitor and left in the family Buick Friday morning.*

Instead, it went bad—fast.

"Julia, I know Eve's secret," I said.

She reacted with the speed and strength of an animal, grabbing me around the throat and pushing the gun against my neck. Her other arm, surprisingly muscular despite her sloppy appearance, wrapped around my throat, nearly cutting off my oxygen.

"You move and I'll kill you. You won't be the first, either," she hissed in my ear.

"Let her go! I'll shoot!" the deputy called out.

"No! Don't! Don't!" I cried. The barrel pressed against my neck and I was pulled backward into the house.

Julia kicked the big white door closed and I fell against the mahogany staircase, her gun inches from my face.

Standing above me, she was the exact opposite of her late, poised and well-coiffed sister. Julia's brown boots were crusty with dirt and the knees of her jeans were dusty. Her green John Deere tee shirt emphasized her fat, middle-aged frame and her sagging breasts. She wore a pink camouflage ball cap that covered her choppy hair.

When I saw Eve in Earlene's office, her clothing was expensive, yet tasteful. Eve had been thin and trim—the day I saw her, I knew it took a village of beauticians, estheticians and personal trainers to preserve that high-maintenance blonde.

Why hadn't Julia been afforded that same attention?

"You want to see what all the secrecy is about? I'll show you. Move!"

I scrambled up the stairs; Julia's steps close behind me. I missed a step, and stumbled, gasping as I felt the gun barrel against my back.

"Last door on the left," she snapped.

I walked past three bedrooms, filled with oversize antique bedsteads and dark bureaus, their windows darkened with heavy Victorian-style curtains, all designed to put a glossy image over a tawdry truth. Double-globed antique oil lamps sat on small bedside tables; intricate carpets covered the floors. A claw-footed bathtub with copper fixtures caught my eye as we passed the bathroom, toward a closed door at the end of the hall.

As we approached, I could hear the sound of medical machinery, the rhythmic sound of an oxygen pump.

"I open this door and you don't say a thing, you hear me?" She leveled the gun at my face.

I nodded. She lowered the gun and turned the doorknob.

Any other patient, like the man before me on the hospital bed, would have been pushed into a nursing home or a state facility years ago, except for the money Eve—or someone—spent to care for him at home.

He was severely brain-damaged; his eyes were wildly askew; his yellow teeth were ragged and crooked as his mouth hung open. A tube was attached at his throat to help him breathe and two others beneath the bed collected urine and feces. A monitor beside the bed kept track of his heartbeat and his oxygen levels.

"This is Andy," Julia said, taking one of his thick hands. He turned his head slightly toward her and groaned in greeting.

I reached over and patted his leg. It felt misshapen and shrunken beneath the hospital blanket. I remembered Earlene's comment about Eve having to spend much of her salary on healthcare for her mother and this house. A good chunk of it had to go to caring for this poor man.

Earlene's words echoed in my head: *"You don't know what's behind those awful doors."*

Despite the warning, I had to speak.

"Why keep him such a secret?" I asked. "Your sister could have had help from the state. He could have been cared for someplace that wouldn't have been so stressful on her or your family."

She shoved me out the door into the hallway. I tumbled against the wall and sank onto the floor. My arm popped as I hit the hardwood floor, shooting pain up my arm. Julia slammed Andy's door shut. I tried to sit up but her wide, thick hand pinned me by the neck against the flowered wallpaper.

"I told you not to say anything!" she screamed, waving the gun in my face.

"But what about Andy? What about him?"

"And let the world know the Dahlgren family weren't the most perfect in Jubilant Falls?" Julia's words were bitter and sarcastic. "No, we couldn't let the truth about this family and its golden girl get out."

"But you love Andy, don't you?" I gasped, despite the pressure on my throat. "You're the one who protected him, aren't you?"

She leveled the handgun at my nose. "What do you care?"

"This is Jimmy Lyle's son, isn't it?" I continued to rasp. "Jimmy didn't die in the seventy-four tornado, did he?"

Outside, I could hear the deputy shouting, demanding we come to the door, but Julia didn't react. In the distance, sirens blared. *I hope help gets here in time,* I thought. If I could keep her talking, it might buy me some time.

"Yes, he's Jimmy's son. My parents wanted to let him die in that Texas hospital. Eve said if we didn't take him back to Jubilant Falls and care for him, she would tell the whole world how his father was murdered."

She released her grip on my neck. Holding my broken arm close to my chest, I pushed myself into a sitting position with my feet and my one good arm.

"How did Jimmy die?" I winced in pain.

Julia sank against the wall next to me, the gun in her hand, hanging between her heavy legs. Fear kept me from running— fear of what her feral, quick reflexes would do to me and fear that, with my injury, I couldn't react quick enough. But I also wanted to hear the story that kept me awake nights for the past forty years.

"When Eve came home and said she was pregnant, our father threw a fit. He'd worked his way up at Traeburn Tractor from the line, where Grandpa Dahlgren started, to vice president and he wasn't going to have anything like a pregnancy, or some disgusting teen-age shotgun wedding, ruin how he thought he should be perceived. That night before the tornado, my father, Eve and Jimmy got into this horrible argument. Dad was convinced Jimmy had ruined Eve's life and by extension, his. My parents pushed Eve into everything and when she didn't succeed, Dad beat her. He was reaching up to hit Eve that night, but Jimmy grabbed his arm and told him to never to that again."

So her dad hit her, just the way Eve would physically abuse the other cheerleaders, like Angela Perry. That also explains how and why she led Jimmy Lyle around by the nose. But it sounds like Jimmy stood up for his girlfriend that night and it cost him his life.

"Did he ever beat you?" I looked over at her.

She shrugged. "Why do you care? I got my share for being the stupid and ugly one—they sent me away to boarding school early, hoping to hide me. I flunked out before the tornado and never graduated from high school. It doesn't matter anymore. The day of the tornado, Dad went looking for Jimmy. He wanted to settle it once and for all. Nobody was going to make him look bad, like Jimmy did the night before. Dad found him working in his grandfather's pasture, just as the storm came up. Dad got into it with Jimmy again and he killed him, simple as that. Dad got home just before the tornado struck. He was covered in blood and soaking wet from the rain."

"Jimmy was found with a posthole digger through his chest and a tree branch on his skull," I said.

"I heard Dad tell Mom he knocked him out and shoved the posthole digger into his chest. The branch must have fallen on his head during the tornado. For the rest of his life, Dad was terrified he'd get caught. But Eve, little golden girl Eve—she turned the tables on the situation. She'd always been like that—if she could turn something to her advantage, she would.

From that day forward, we all danced to Eve's tune. Even though we both wanted to keep Andy, nobody ever paid two cents worth of attention to me because I wasn't as pretty as Eve. And look at me today. I'm the only one left in this miserable place. I'm the one holding everything together."

"Did Eve pay for everything?" I pressed my arm against my chest as more pain radiated to my elbow. If I could keep her talking, maybe I could get out of this, somehow.

"Oh, yes. After Traeburn Tractor closed and Dad couldn't find a job to pay for Andy's medical care, Eve threatened to expose him, even though she was already working and sending money home. So he took the coward's way and blew his brains out. Unfortunately, that left Eve as the only income and god knows we couldn't move from this house without exposing the biggest, nastiest secret of all. She declared that somebody in the family has got to stay here with Andy, so here's Betty and me, stuck in this house once again. She paid me well to make sure I'd keep my mouth shut."

"Does Karen know the truth about Andy?"

Julia smirked. "Of course not. She thinks he's my poor retarded brother."

"Who killed Eve?"

Before she could answer, Judson Roarke's voice blared through a bullhorn: "Let your hostage go, Julia. Come out with your hands up and we can end this without anyone getting hurt."

She jumped to her feet and yanked me up by my shirt, pushing me toward the window. I screamed in pain. Her arm hooked around my neck again and she shoved the gun perilously close to my face.

Down in the manicured circular driveway, there was a line of sheriff's cruisers, a township fire department ladder truck, and an ambulance. The county's SWAT team, with weapons drawn, had assembled in front of those vehicles. At the back of the cruisers, Charisma stood next to Dr. Huffinger and Gary McGinnis, who wore a Kevlar vest.

"Do as they say, Julia, let me go," I said. "Please. Let me go."

"Shut up!" She pressed the barrel against my cheek. She turned to the window and kicked it out, the glass tinkling on the concrete below. Weapons—service revolvers, automatic rifles—pointed toward the window in one synchronized movement. Judson Roarke waved them down.

"I'm not coming out!" Julia screamed. "If you come in, I'll kill her. You hear me?"

She pulled me away from the window and pushed me back down the hall, toward another narrow door.

"Who killed Eve, Julia? Did you do it?" I demanded as I stumbled against the wall.

"Don't feel too sorry for my darling sister. She got to go out on Saturday night with that idiot Earlene and I'd just about had it. *Eve* got to go out, *Eve* got to do what *she* wanted, live where *she* wanted and I'm stuck here with *her* child and *our* mother.""So what did you do?" I leaned against the wall long enough to catch my breath and hold my broken arm close again. Intent on telling her story, Julia kept talking as she held the gun close to my face.

"I told her I'd made an appointment on Monday to get the oil changed in my truck and we needed to drop it off at the mechanic's Sunday night. She followed me in that Lincoln. She gets a fancy car that sits here when she's back home in Texas and what do I drive? A piece of shit Franken-Ford I got to baby every step of the way. After I dropped my truck off, she decides she doesn't feel like driving and hands me the keys, like I'm some peasant here to serve the queen. We were sitting behind the mechanic's shop and she started bitching about how much sacrifice she makes and how hard her life is and I'd had it. I'd just had it."

"You stabbed her, didn't you?"

"Not before I choked the shit out of that bitch. She fought me though—kicked through the damned windshield."

"Did you drive her car to the park then?" It was Monday afternoon before Eve's body was found. The murder occurred Sunday night. A dead woman wouldn't have lain unnoticed in a public park on a hot June day until after three. She would have been seen sooner.

"No, I drove home and parked the car in the air conditioned garage. On Monday, I left it in the park and walked over to the mechanic to pick up my truck."

"Why didn't they find your fingerprints in that car? My boss did a night in jail because police found her prints."

Julia grinned at me. "Of course, my fingerprints were there—and they should be! I'm Eve Dahlgren's ever-supportive sister, like I told the cops. I'm staying home with my poor mother and retarded brother to care for the family farm. And they bought it. Just because my sister let that gullible Earlene Whitelaw drive her car isn't my problem. They won't find any prints on the knife, though. I wiped it before I threw it in the sewer."

So Gary McGinnis knew Eve had a sister? How did I not know that? Why didn't he tell me?

"You were going to let Earlene Whitelaw take the fall for killing your sister, weren't you?"

Julia smirked. "If you and your reporter hadn't gone digging, my family would have continued doing what we do best: getting away with murder."

Still pointing the gun at my face, Julia turned the knob and pulled open the narrow door. Curving stairs led up to a dark attic.

"Get up there." She pushed me from behind and I fell across the wooden stairs, screaming with pain. The door slammed behind me. I gasped as I heard the old skeleton key turn in the lock.

"Let me out! Let me out!" I pounded on the door with my good arm.

There was the sound of sloshing outside the door. I stopped pounding as a familiar odor filled the air.

Gasoline.

"Julia! Don't do this! Please! Let me out! Let me out!"

My eyes adjusted to the darkness and I found the light switch near the stairs. A single yellowed bulb glowed at the top of the stairs and I quickly made my way up into the attic. The attic was filled with old furniture and holiday decorations. I ran to the narrow triangular window at the front of the house and began pounding on the glass with my good arm, hoping the folks in the yard could see me.

Did they? I couldn't tell—all I could see was Roarke speaking on the bullhorn, trying to connect with Julia.

There was a *whoosh* of fire igniting in the hall; smoke began to curl through the wide cracks between the door and the frame.

Two shots rang out on the other side of the door. Had Julia just shot Andy and then herself? Was the twisted history this family had kept inside these doors now finished? Or was it the police, using a flash-bang grenade to gain access to the house?

I ran back to the window to see law enforcement rush toward the porch and into the house.

Down the stairs again, I began to pound on the door, despite the growing smoke. I needed to get out before the fire found Andy's oxygen tank.

I groaned in a combination of pain and frustration, running back to search for something to get police attention. Could they come through the flames on the second floor? I didn't know. In one corner was an old kitchen chair, but it was heavy. I would need two arms to pick it up and shove it through the window.

Smoke grew thicker in the attic, stinging my eyes and burning my lungs. My head spun with the chemical smell of the burning varnished wood. I tried to make my way back to the window, feeling my way as I crawled along the old wooden floor. Flames flashed through the attic door and at my back, knocking me on my face.

The attic window shattered—it was a firefighter at the end of the bucket truck.

Chapter 34 Charisma

"Are you OK? Did she shoot you?" I rushed up to the gurney carrying Addison to the waiting ambulance. I'd heard two gunshots and assumed—like the assembled law enforcement—that one of the victims was my boss.

I'd never been so happy to see someone who'd gotten the raw end of any deal of mine. Her arm was in a splint, but she reached up with her good hand to pull off the oxygen mask from her face and grabbed my sleeve. Her voice was raspy and jagged from the smoke.

"Julia killed Eve—she told me so herself! She also told me Jimmy Lyle didn't die in the tornado—her father killed him when Eve told him he was pregnant." Addison started to cough and gasp. The EMT beside her placed the oxygen mask back over her face.

"Betty told me that Eve killed Bob Martz, too," I said. "I've got it all written down."

Addison pulled the mask off again. "Get back to the newsroom. Get this story written and up on the website. Nobody else has this story. We need to be the first," She began to cough again.

"Please don't talk any more, ma'am," the EMT said, reaching to place the mask on her face again.

She waved him off and swung her legs over the side of the gurney. "Let me finish! Don't forget the rest of your story, too," she rasped. The coughing began again; this time, she lay back and allowed the EMT to replace the oxygen mask.

"Of all people, you didn't think you could shut her up, do you?" Gary McGinnis grinned at the medic. "Let me ride with you guys and get her statement. I have a feeling she won't stop talking even on the way to the hospital."

I stopped to watch, as Addison was loaded into the back of the ambulance and Gary jumped in the back of the ambulance with her.

How could one house contain so much destruction for so long?

I turned to watch the firefighters fight the fire in the old house. Would it survive the flames or would it collapse in on itself?

I looked over at Leland, who was talking to Judson Roarke. Maybe he was filling the sheriff in on what he'd found out about Eve's son, Andy. Maybe he wasn't. Maybe he was telling Roarke about me. I didn't care. I needed to tell this story of these three murders.

Then I needed to leave town.

I had half of my story left to tell, but right now I wasn't sure I could do it. *Maybe Dr. Bigmouth could fill Addison in on the rest of what he'd found out about me,* I thought sourly.

I stood in silence watching the firefighters contain the upper-story flames. The lower story looked like it might survive, but flame were now shooting out of the attic, where Addison was found. As the water hoses bombarded the old brick home, Leland sidled up beside me.

"Hate to see a place like this go up in flames," he said tentatively.

"Uh-huh." I stepped away in self-protection.

"Charisma," he began softly. "We're both a lot like this old house. We've seen some serious injuries; we've seen some grievous pain. But we need to go on despite the scars we carry. This house may be burned, but it will be rebuilt. You can, too,

Charisma. You performed like the pro the world remembers just now. We just solved three murders, one of them forty years old! You can't hide forever, and, despite what I did to you, I want you to be whole again. I want you to be happy."

"Well, that's your problem isn't it?" I shot back. "I'll be happy when I don't have to look at you anymore."

"Charisma, I'm so sorry."

"Sorry won't fix this."

I turned to see the coroner's van pull up the drive and pulled a notebook from my pocket. Leland could apologize forever—I had a story to finish. I stepped away from him and touched the fire chief on the sleeve, pointing to the coroner's van.

The chief nodded. "We have two victims: A female in her fifties, believed to be the suspect who took Mrs. McIntyre hostage and a male, late thirties, maybe early forties, who was found in a hospital-style bed, so probably unable to fight back. It looks like a murder-suicide. We don't know if she shot him before she started the fire or after. I suppose Mrs. McIntyre could tell us that. We've got the state fire marshal on the way."

"Addison could have been the third victim," I said simply.

"Yes she could have."

I made a few notes and walked back to my car.

Andy must have lived in the house; the male body had to be his. Eve must have brought her son home to care for him, then left town to get her degree and follow her career, leaving her sister here to care for their home, their mother and her son. What kind of life had Julia Dahlgren led?

I needed to head back to the newsroom and get started on this story, before the TV stations from Collitstown showed up. I had the fire chief's cell phone number. I could call him later for the final details.

Shit. I have to take Leland with me.

I walked back to the fire truck, where he was watching the flames and tapped him on the shoulder.

"If you want a ride, I'm going back now," I said bluntly, gesturing toward my red sedan.

Without speaking—or perhaps realizing I wouldn't respond to anything he said— Leland got into the car and buckled into the passenger seat. We drove silently back into Jubilant Falls; I stopped the car in front of the Holiday Inn and he got out without saying goodbye.

In two blocks, I was back in the employee parking lot behind the newspaper. Putting the car in park, I leaned my head on the steering wheel and began to sob.

*****

It was nearly nine o'clock at night by the time I finished the story of Julia's and Andy Dahlgren's sad deaths and the fire that nearly destroyed their home. It only took an hour to gather myself together and get the story done and up on the website.

Gary McGinnis wasn't able to give me much on the deaths of Jimmy Lyle and Eve Dahlgren—the hospital was keeping Addison overnight and they kept him from talking to her. I filled in everything else I'd learned from Betty about Bob Martz' death.

A more complete version would come tomorrow morning before deadline. Someone, not me, would have to finish it.

I pushed myself back from my desk.

I owed Addison the story of what happened to me in Syria.

The newsroom was empty. Chris Royal, the sportswriter, was taking a vacation day—he'd left a few canned features on tomorrow's sports page and Dennis was going to fill the remainder with wire copy. I could work all night and not be disturbed.

Get it done, a voice inside told me. *Get it written and then get out.*

I rolled my chair back to my desk, ready to begin again.

*****

I'd covered stories in third-world countries, seen how hard-scrabble life could be, but Aleppo, where every building was marked by bombs or bullets, was the worst.

Syria was a country bent on sending itself over the edge of oblivion: incoming missiles from government jets, the screams of the wounded, the god-awful smell of burnt plastic mixing with burnt flesh, and blood. I've never seen so much blood.

The day I'd gone to meet my source had been hot. I hadn't slept—I'd spent the night curled under the table in my hotel room as bombs, both manufactured and improved, fell into the streets.

The barrel bombs, dumped by pro-government forces, were the worst. A barrel was packed with simple explosives and any shrapnel they could find. Carried aloft by a helicopter, they would be pushed out over populated areas and the craft would hover to watch as those below in the street were killed or maimed.

They wait ten minutes for the rescuers, medics or anyone who might want to bring aid and then drop another one.

No one runs in to help the wounded for at least half an hour, now.

As I stepped into the street that day, the bodies from last night's bombing were being taken out into the streets. It was mass murder on a governmental scale. I gasped as survivors picked among the dead and their destroyed homes, scavenging blankets, pillows, and shoes. A woman with a dented toaster in her hands met my eyes and shrugged as she stepped over the body of a dead child. His own brown eyes stared back at me, permanently begging from the other side for someone to do something. The people around him, those picking shoes off dead bodies or stealing pots from bombed homes knew no one ever would.

Those sights must have tipped the delicate balance of my sanity. Between Aleppo and Baghdad, I'd simply seen too much.

My source, a Syrian man with a red scarf over his face, claimed the government had plans to bomb a refugee camp in Jordan filled with women and children. He opened his jacket to show me the uniform of the Syrian air force—but not the side with his name. It should have been my first hint.

"I've seen the orders," he claimed. "The raid will happen next week."

Reeking with arrogance and pushed from above to run the story, I didn't double-check my source, just to show Charisma Prentiss was back in the saddle.

But I wasn't, not by a long shot, and this time, I paid the price.

After the wire service fired me, I locked myself into Dad and Kate's spare bedroom. Memories of Aleppo, Baghdad, Kalil and Jean Paul ricocheted through the frilly white room until sleep or wished-for death wouldn't bring peace. I began waking up at night, combative and screaming. Dad and Kate brought me to George Washington Hospital's mental health wing, signing me in under a false name.

I came back slowly. After a couple months, Dad and Kate brought me back to their condo, set me up again in the guest room.

Kate found me watching one of the Sunday-morning news shows with tears pouring down my face. There were three talking heads, discussing my future in journalism. On the screen behind them was a huge picture of me, full of bravado and purpose, yellow hair sticking out from beneath my blue helmet, in my bulletproof vest and jeans. Behind me, a convoy of armored trucks headed into the Afghan mountains. To them, I wasn't a person, someone who'd been horribly injured. I was a has-been, an ego-driven blonde bimbo who wanted face time more than the truth, someone who ruined her career in particular and seriously damaged journalism in general.

One commentator turned toward the camera, his script clutched self-righteously in his hand. One eyebrow arched and he began to speak.

"I don't know what news organization would be either brave enough—or conversely, irresponsible enough—to take on a journalist like Charisma Prentiss. What do you, our viewers, think? We'll be taking your questions, right after these messages."

Kate pulled the remote from my hand and clicked off the television.

"You don't need that," she said, wrapping her arms around me more like an older sister than the stepmother she nearly was. "You've got to get out of here, Charisma."

"But where could I go?" I wiped my nose with the heel of my hand. "Maybe these guys are right. Who would hire me?"

"You're still a good journalist, Charisma," Kate said. "You can do this job again. What if you went someplace where you could start again?"

"Like where?"

"I don't know. What about a smaller newspaper someplace, a small-market TV station?"

"As Charisma Prentiss? You're kidding me, right?"

"How about under an assumed name?" Kate suggested.

"I'm not sharp enough up here to react to a new name," I said, tapping my finger on my temple.

"What about your married name? Charisma Lemarnier? You and I know most Americans have an attention span of about thirty seconds. They didn't know who Jean Paul was and wouldn't know who you were unless you told them. And face it, since you've quit dyeing your hair, with all your surgeries, you don't look the same. I'll bet you could pull it off. I *know* you could."

And so it began. Kate and I came up with my new backstory, the young widow who lost her parents and her husband in a car crash in Connecticut. I got my brown hair styled; the medications I took to keep the demons at bay added a few pounds. A few of my friends said they'd vouch for me without revealing my identity on a new fake résumé. I used my mother's address in Salisbury, Maryland, came up with a new e-mail address and sent out inquiries to any small newspaper seeking a reporter.

Within six months, I was moving into my studio apartment in Jubilant Falls and praying no one would recognize me as I struggled to get back in the saddle.

*****

There you have it, world. You wondered whatever happened to Charisma Prentiss? Here it is.

I hit the 'save' button on the computer and stood up.

I rustled through my desk drawers one more time. There was nothing in particular I wanted to keep with me, nothing I'd become attached to.

I found a small Post-It note on the copy editing station.

"Thanks for everything," I wrote. "I'm gone."

I signed my full, real name—Charisma Prentiss Lemarnier— and stuck the note on the computer screen where Dennis would sit tomorrow morning. I pulled my key to the employee entrance off my key ring, laid it on the computer keyboard and walked out.

Chapter 35 Leland

By the time I got home to Philadelphia, she was national news.

It was a horrible flight. I got bumped off the flight from Cincinnati, then found myself in the wee hours of the morning in the Detroit airport, trying to sleep in unnaturally-formed plastic seats, rather than park myself in the airport bar, before catching a dawn flight home to Philly.

My apartment at Fitzgerald House smelled slightly musty, as if I'd been gone months rather than a little over a week. I set down my bags and flopped into the shapeless recliner, picked up the TV remote and turned on the TV.

"A reporter who disappeared following a story that sparked a diplomatic crisis has resurfaced briefly in Ohio," the newsman said. "Charisma Prentiss has been working under her married name Christina Lemarnier for nearly a year at the *Jubilant Falls Journal-Gazette...*"

My forefinger hovered over the remote's power button, tempted to shut it off, ignore the whole thing.

Addison McIntyre was sitting at a table in front of a cluster of microphones, one arm in a blue sling, tapping the fingers of her other hand. A woman with big, blonde hair and a leopard print blouse sat next to her, smiling inanely. That must have been publisher Earlene Whitelaw, because Addison looked like she was in pain or wanted a cigarette, or both.

"Yes, Charisma Prentiss worked here as my education reporter and my night police reporter," Addison said. "I knew her as Charisma Lemarnier."

"Was she a good reporter for you?" a disembodied male voice asked.

"She was an excellent reporter," Addison answered. "I've had a number of reporters come and go through this newsroom and I could always pick out the ones who I believed would go on to bigger and better things. I thought Charisma was going to be one of those reporters. I had no idea who she really was."

"Why did she decide to reveal her real identity to you?" a female voice asked.

Addison was silent for a moment. I sat up straight and leaned closer to the TV.

"It was a personal decision," she finally answered. "After she told me who she was, we decided it would be beneficial for the community to know the story."

I felt like a game show contestant cheering on a team member and shouting *"Good answer! Good answer!"* when I knew we'd just lost the big jackpot. She kept me out of it entirely, made it look as though a reporter on her staff just happened to wander into her office and reveal she was a long-missing national reporter. Sure, it could happen.

"And where is she now?" another voice asked.

Addison shrugged. "I have no idea. I came in to work and her office key and her resignation letter were on the copy desk."

The interview ended; there was some old familiar B-roll footage of Charisma in the field, blonde and brash as the world remembered her, followed by a few seconds on her injury, her husband's death and the Syrian story. That followed with some self-righteous chest pounding about the state of the media today.

Nothing about the murders that Charisma helped to solve through her work in Jubilant Falls. Nothing about me, the nosy professor who came into town on a hunch based on a name I saw on a byline on a small Ohio newspaper and who inadvertently blew the lid off everything.

I pushed the power button and the television clicked off.

Like she told me the first time we spoke, that woman is gone forever—and apparently gone again.

Unlike her, my question wasn't 'Where would I go next?' I knew where I was headed.

I was going back to rehab.

I'd made the phone call from the Detroit airport in the middle of the night, right after the bartender hefted an empty beer mug my direction and waved me toward the army of cleverly labeled craft beers standing at attention behind him. I knew then if I didn't get a little fine-tuning I'd be right back where I started—and soon.

I couldn't do that to Noah's memory.

I visited his grave on my way to the clinic.

Four weeks later, I was back in my apartment, feeling stronger, more centered. I still, though, hadn't decided what good it would do to tell my part of the Charisma Prentiss story. Maybe my second-year students would hear the story in a couple weeks when fall term started. Maybe I wouldn't say a word.

Maybe, too, I'd start venturing back out into the dating world. I couldn't have Charisma, but she'd shown me I was ready to dip my toe in the waters again. Broadcast instructor Audrey Dellaplain's office was just down the hall from my office. We'd worked together for several years now. She was divorced, like myself. Maybe she'd have dinner with me. I could drop by her office after the first day of class and ask.

There was a buzz from the intercom downstairs. Who could that be? Probably someone was looking for one of the new professors who I saw moving into one of the other apartments. I walked over to the box by the door and hit the button.

"Hello?"

"Hey. It's me. Can I come up?" The voice was soft and warm and familiar.

"Oh my God." I leaned on the button until I heard the door unlock. In a moment Charisma was at my door. She wore tight jeans, and beneath a white gauzy blouse, her breasts swelled inside a pink tank top.

Without speaking, I pulled her into my arms, drinking in the familiar lavender smell, holding her as tightly as she held me. She looked up into my eyes, a moment of uncertainty in her face. Her hands slid into my graying hair, drawing my face to hers. Our lips met in a deep, passionate kiss.

"You're here," I whispered as we parted.

I pulled her inside, closing the door behind us.

"Yes, I am."

Once again, her fingers slipped into my hair and her lips softly touched mine. I took her face in my hands and swept her brunette bangs away from her face, exposing the angry red scar along her hairline. I brushed my lips across it, following it down her neck. She gasped as I slid the gauzy blouse off her shoulders, exposing pocked scars along her arms and between her shoulder blades.

I looked deep into her eyes, uncertain of what would happen next. This time, I saw no fear, no pulling back. She laced her fingers through mine and brought them to her lips.

"You terrified me the last time you kissed my hand," she said. "Back in my apartment in Ohio."

"Was that it?" I asked. "I wasn't sure what I'd done."

"I didn't want you to see how I really looked. When you pulled my hand to kiss it, you could see the scars on my arms. I wasn't ready for that."

Don't ruin this, not now.

"What are you ready for?" My voice was hoarse.

"Oh, Leland," she said.

I kissed her, sliding my arms down her back, feeling the softness of the tank top, clutching her firm bottom in my hands. Wrapping her arms around my neck, she moaned as I buried my head on her shoulder. In one quick jump, both of her legs were wrapped around my waist; I held her tightly and walked us into the bedroom.

*****

The sun was setting when she awoke. I smiled at her as she stretched like a cat.

"Hey there," I whispered, running my finger across her collarbone and down between her breasts.

She snuggled closer, tucking her hands beneath her head.

"Hey there," she purred.

"So I have to ask. Where have you been?"

She hooked her left leg across mine and I caught a glimpse of the long thin reminder of one of her first surgeries in Frankfurt. Blue shrapnel lay just below the surface of her left leg and among the scars on her arms. She sighed, contentedly this time.

"I drove around for a couple days, staying in hotels. Then I couldn't stand traveling with Monsieur Le Chat any more, so I spent a couple weeks with my parents—some with my mother in Maryland, some with Dad and Kate in DC."

"What made you come to see me in Philly?"

She propped herself up on her elbow and laid her hand on my cheek.

"Something you said, about rebuilding that old house. I decided that it was time to tear down some of those old walls. I want to start again. I've come to terms with the fact I'll probably never be like I was before, and that's OK. I just know I want to start again with you."

"That's what I want, too," I whispered, drawing her into my arms. "That's what I want, too."

Chapter 36 Addison

I stood next to Gary McGinnis as a city worker ground Jimmy Lyle's name off of the tornado memorial in front of city hall.

"So, the next time I have suspicions about a murder, are you going to listen to me?" I asked.

We shoved our fingers into our ears as the periodic scream of metal against granite interrupted the conversation. There was a brief silence. Gary opened his mouth to speak as the grinder started again. He shook his head.

A month after the story ran, Jimmy Lyle's parents asked that his name be removed from the memorial; city council had quickly agreed. The event was going to be our lead story tomorrow, and I wanted to be the one to write it.

Pat Robinette circled the monument, shooting photos as the name was ground off.

"Go ahead, Penny, rub it in," Gary finally managed to say. "You and I both know we wouldn't have ever known about half of that stuff if Julia Dahlgren hadn't confessed to you and Betty hadn't told that reporter the other half. How's the arm, by the way?"

I moved my fingers to demonstrate. "Now that I'm out of that damned cast, I'm feeling a lot better," I said. "I'm almost completely back to normal."

Gary shook his head.

"I still can't believe all that stuff happened in one family. We had the sister in mind as a suspect, all along. When we thought the time of death was Monday, and you said that Earlene Whitelaw had left work early that day we had to check her out. The fingerprints, we thought, sealed the deal at the time."

"I never knew Eve had a sister, all through school. And *you*, damn you, never told me you had a suspect."

"I don't have to tell the press everything, even when it's you. You know that. If I'd said anything, you'd have had it all over the front page the next day."

I punched his shoulder gently. "Probably."

We stopped talking as the grinder began screaming against stone again. My mind wandered back to what had been happening behind the brick walls of the old Shanahan house.

How long had the horror continued there? A murder, conveniently covered up by a natural disaster, a handicapped child raised in secret; no wonder Ed Dahlgren committed suicide. Eve's rages had been a problem since I knew her in high school—that was evident. Was that abusive behavior learned from her father or something else? Who knows, now? Another question: how and why did Eve's involvement with Bob Martz start? Too much time had passed on that one. She was accustomed to keeping many mysteries, and the murder of a married man was just one more.

That same rage apparently burned in sister Julia. Forced by Eve's own controlling anger and financial puppetry to stay behind, watching over her mother and nephew, would be more than galling. No wonder she snapped.

The mysteries of Jimmy Lyle and Bob Martz's long-forgotten deaths were now solved. The horror of three more deaths—Eve, Andy and Julia, by her own hand—all came at the expense of keeping family secrets, making certain that no one outside their doors knew of any imperfections.

There was one more death I still had questions about. Betty's reaction to the picture of the young man found dead in the creek.

"Do you think the Dahlgren family had any connection to our other unsolved murder?" I asked. "I told you how Betty reacted to the photo we showed her. That and what she said: 'Eve never did like that boy.'"

Gary shrugged. "She's been moved to an Alzheimer's unit by a family member, her sister I think. Those few things she told Charisma on her way out of the woods were the last coherent things anyone got out of her. The DNA profile we asked for from the state came through, but it had no matches in any of the federal or state databases. We may never know the truth about that one."

I sighed. "Well, we tried."

"I guess. What's going on with the house where they lived?"

"The historical society that supports activities at Canal Lock Park expressed interest in purchasing the ruins of the home and surrounding land, hoping to rebuild it and use it as a local museum," I said. "Marcus had the story in this morning's paper."

Gary nodded. "Do you hear anything from Charisma? That was the damnedest thing. Who would have thought a reporter of that caliber would have chosen Jubilant Falls?"

I shook my head. "I know I didn't believe it when she told me. I'd bought it all along that she was widowed as a result of a car accident."

"You never were very good about normal people and their relationships."

"Yeah, rub it in." I shook my head. Tonight, Duncan and I would be babysitting Gwennie Kinnon as Graham and our daughter went out again. It was their second date this week.

"But nothing from Charisma, huh?"

"I haven't heard a word, but then I didn't expect to. Most of the time, when reporters move on, they are gone for good. I just hope she can come back to be the national reporter she used to be."

Gary nodded again. "So do you have anyone in mind for her position?"

"Not yet. I'm still working my way through a stack of résumés. I've heard from every new college graduate and has-been in three counties. I just have to decide who looks like the best candidate. Then the interviews begin." I rolled my eyes in mock disgust.

The grinding stopped suddenly. The city worker stood, removed his safety glasses and brushed the dust from the now-flat surface. The rectangle looked odd in the middle of list of tornado victims.

Pat shot a couple more photos.

"I think I got what I wanted," he said. "I'm going to head back to the paper."

"I think I need to get back to my office, too," Gary said. "See you later?"

"Sure," I said, waving as both men walked off in separate directions.

Once I was sure they were gone, I stepped closer and ran my finger across the now-smooth surface.

The touch of the cold stone beneath my fingers told me Jimmy Lyle wouldn't be waking me up anymore at night. Memories might return of that awful day the tornado struck, but I knew now when they did, I could have no fear.

"Rest in peace, Jimmy Lyle," I whispered. "I hope you can now rest in peace."

I lit a cigarette and walked back to the newspaper.

Acknowledgements

As always, my thanks go to that supportive team of professionals, friends and family who make this journey possible.

For Mary McFarland and Doug Savage, who aren't afraid to tell me when I write crap and who guide me, sometimes gently, sometimes not, toward a better book.

For Paul Schaffer, copy editor extraordinaire, who treated my comma deficiencies, misspellings and odd sentence constructions like the grammar professional he is.

For Greg, Scott and Becky who believe in me.

But most of all, this book is for all the journalists who live every day with the horrors they've seen and their efforts to make us all more aware.

About the author

Debra Gaskill is an award-winning journalist with more than 20 years experience in newspapers in Ohio. She has an associate's degree in liberal arts from Thomas Nelson Community College in Hampton, Va., a bachelor's degree in English and journalism from Wittenberg University and a master of fine arts degree in creative writing from Antioch University.

She and her husband Greg, a retired Air Force lieutenant colonel, reside in Enon, where they raise llamas and alpacas on their farm. They have two adult children and two grandchildren.

She is the author of four other Jubilant Falls novels, The Major's Wife, Barn Burner, Lethal Little Lies and Murder on the Lunatic Fringe.

Connect with Debra on her website at www.debragaskillnovels.com or on her blog, http://debragaskill.wordpress.com. You can also connect with her on Twitter at @Debra Gaskill.

If you liked *Death of a High Maintenance Blonde*, please leave a review on Amazon.com or the website where you purchased the book. Your support is greatly appreciated!

Made in the USA
Charleston, SC
20 October 2015